Twisted
TEMPTATIONS

Annie Jocoby

VINCI
BOOKS

By Annie Jocoby

Temptations

Dangerous Temptations
Twisted Temptations
Dark Temptations
Wicked Temptations

Vinci Books

vinci-books.com

Published by Vinci Books Ltd in 2026

1

The publisher and the author have made every effort to obtain permissions
for any third party material used in this book and to comply with copyright
law. Any queries in this respect should be brought to the attention of the
publisher and any omissions will be corrected in future editions.
A CIP catalogue record for this book is available from the British Library.
Paperback ISBN: 9781036703127
The EU GPSR authorised representative is Logos Europe, 9 rue Nicolas
Poussion, 17000 La Rochelle, France contact@logoseurope.eu

Chapter One

I rested comfortably in the hospital bed, with Slade lying next to me. I could hear his heart beating as I lay against his chest. His skin felt incredibly warm, and I opened up the buttons of his shirt and put my hand on his incredibly hard pec. Even though I was exhausted from my ordeal, and still felt incredibly weak, I also found myself feeling very turned-on. I was safe, Slade was there with me, and his smell of clean aftershave and man was making me tingle. It didn't help that he kept bringing my face to his and would give me light, feathery kisses that would deepen before he would abruptly stop, telling me that I needed my rest and we couldn't possibly make love in that hospital bed.

I knew that he was right about that. Making love in a hospital bed wasn't a good idea, considering how often the nurses would come in to monitor my blood pressure and check on me. Even though I had a private room, there was no way to put out a "Do Not Disturb" sign, so Slade and I weren't truly alone.

Nonetheless, I was starting to crave him again. Now that

I knew that he was not guilty of Jordan's murder, I felt that I could truly open up to him. And, the fact that he came to save me meant a lot to me as well. I was worried, of course, about what kind of deal he had to make with Charlotte to get me out of that hell-hole, but that was another matter for another day.

At some point, of course, Luke and Dalilah came to see me with their new daughter, Olivia. They came in while Slade and I were cuddling on the hospital bed, and they both looked surprised to see Slade, to say the very least.

Dalilah had a bouquet of flowers in her hand, and Luke was carrying little Olivia in a swaddling cloth. The baby was only a few days old, but I could already see both of them in her beautiful little face.

"We have to stop meeting like this," Luke said, addressing me, but looking right at Slade.

"I know."

"Do you mind telling me what happened?"

I took a deep breath. "I seem to have run afoul of some mobsters. I'm defending one of them, and, well, let's just say that my defense of one of the mobsters didn't sit to well with the person that I was trying to bring down."

Luke immediately looked worried. "Serena, you're not in trouble are you?"

Just then, Dalilah put the flowers on a table, and she approached Slade, her hand out-stretched. "I'm Dalilah, Serena's future sister-in-law, and this is my fiance, Luke, who is Serena's brother."

Slade gave Luke and Dalilah both his free hand, while his other arm was tightly wrapped around me. "Slade Bridgewell."

Dalilah raised an eyebrow at me, and it didn't take an empath to figure out what she was thinking. *You lied to me when you said that you didn't have a man in your life.* She didn't looked pissed, though, merely amused.

Slade stroked my hair while I talked with Luke and Dalilah. "Let me see that little baby," I said. "Bring her here."

At that, Luke handed me the swaddled infant, who was fast asleep, but making faces as newborns do. "Who do you think that she looks like?" Luke asked me.

"Hmmm," I said, looking at the child's perfect rosebud lips and tiny little nose. She had a tuft of hair on her head already, dark hair, which meant that she took after Luke in that regard, as Dalilah was a deep ginger. "I see both of you, to be perfectly honest. It's hard to tell at this point, although she is a beautiful child."

Slade was mesmerized with the little girl, and he reached over to touch her nose. She didn't stir, but continued to sleep soundly. Just like my two dogs, I thought – this little baby was like all tiny infants, and would probably sleep through an earthquake. Not that there were any earthquakes in San Diego, of course.

Which reminded me, of course, about Bella and Gigi. "My dogs. Oh, crap. They're still at the day care. Not that they mind it, but I can't believe that I forgot all about them."

Slade kind of nudged me. "That's to be expected, Serena. You survived being kidnapped and thrown into a hole and left for dead. Your survival instinct kicked in, so little things like your dogs still being at the day care are probably the last thing on your mind." Then he kissed my forehead lightly. "But, don't worry, when you were sleeping, I called the day care place and made sure that they're okay there. They moved them into the doggie hotel, and the attendant said that they're having a ball playing with the other puppies. So, don't worry. They're safe and sound and will be waiting for you when you get out of here."

I let out a sigh of relief, and I gripped his hand tighter. "Thanks for doing that, Slade. That's wonderful that you know my needs without my even saying a word."

"Well, I know how much those dogs meant to you."

"Wait, so you have dogs?" Dalilah asked. "What kind?"

"French bulldogs. They've always been my favorite. I got two litter mates from the rescue agency. They're names are Bella and Gigi. I didn't pick out the names, but they fit."

Dalilah giggled. "I can't wait to meet them."

"How long will you guys be in town?"

Dalilah shrugged. "Luke has to be back in a couple of weeks, because he's starting a new painting that's been commissioned by one of the big hotels. Of course, he can get started here. We've talked about it, and we'd really like to stay awhile, to make sure that you're doing okay. It seems that you have a lot on your plate."

"Well, that's an understatement, of course. I've got a ton of stuff to do, and I take the bar this weekend in Sacramento." I didn't mention, of course, that Slade's case was my top priority. I didn't quite know how to tell them about Slade and who he was, although I had the feeling that Luke and Dalilah already knew. They paid attention to the news the same as anyone else, and I could see in their eyes that they were regarding him just a bit warily.

Slade seemed to sense that I was wanting to talk to my brother and future sister-in-law alone, because he offered to go to the vending machine and get me something to drink. "What would you like?" he asked me.

"Well, you know that I don't drink a lot of pop, so if they have some kind of tea just bring me that. Otherwise, a bottled water would be great."

He pointed at Luke and Dalilah, both of whom said the same thing as me. Tea if they have it, water if they didn't. "Thanks," they said in unison.

At that, Slade got off the bed and disappeared from the room.

I took a deep breath as Dalilah took my hand. "Oh, my god, that's Slade from the news casts. Everyone thinks that he brutally beat his business partner to death. I hate to ask this, but what are you doing with him?"

She seemed very worried, and I loved her for that. I saw in Luke's face that he, too, was worried. "Slade is actually a client of the firm's. I'm on his legal team for his case. I can't really tell you much more than that, though. I will tell you definitively that he didn't do it."

"How do you know that he didn't do it?" Dalilah asked. "I've seen the news, and it looks very bad for him. All the pundits think that he did it."

"Of course they do. They do because they're lazy and so are the police. I remember, years ago, that there was a murder case that involved a woman that was sleeping with a congressman. Chandra Levy was the girl's name. She was found dead in the woods. The congressman's name was Gary Condit. The pundits made this Gary Condit look guilty as hell, for a variety of reasons. Ruined his career and his life. Turns out his only crime was sleeping around on his wife. Some random person actually killed that poor girl, but you would never know it by watching the news that summer. That whole thing happened because of a lazy press and lazy police-work and tunnel vision."

Now that I knew that Slade was innocent, and I knew who did it, I was prepared to make a full-throated defense for him, no matter who asked me about it. "Okay," she said. "I just don't want you to get involved with..."

"A murderer?" I finished her thought for her. "Don't worry, I'm not." Of course, I *was* involved with him before, even though I didn't know for sure if he was a murderer or not, so I don't know what that said about me.

"Yes." Dalilah was still looking worried. "How do you know that he didn't do it?"

I sighed, looking at Luke, who now had little Olivia and was also looking at me with the same worried look on his face as Dalilah's. Would Dalilah understand the spiritual message from Jordan? I knew that Luke was going to call bullshit on the whole thing, so I was prepared for that. But Dalilah had the same abilities as me, even if she had a hard time acknowledging them.

I took a deep breath. "Jordan told me that Slade is totally innocent."

"Jordan. The victim?" Luke was incredulous. "What's that supposed to mean?"

"Now, Luke, you've always known that I can sense things. Talk to spirits."

"I've known nothing of the kind. You've always said things like that, but…"

"But what? I don't know how it is that you still don't believe me. I expect this from dad, Amy, Chris and Mark but not you. You're engaged to somebody who has the same abilities as me, after all, so you better brace yourself."

Dalilah was quiet, and pale, getting paler by the second. "She's right," she said to Luke. "I do know things. I've covered it up all my life, but somehow, when everything started to calm down between you and me and the whole Nottingham situation, I've started to…see things. I can't explain it, though."

"Oh my god," Luke said. "Okay, Serena, so you're involved with a guy. The whole world thinks that he brutally beat his business partner to death. And you're okay with being involved with him because of some hocus-pocus message that you hallucinated?"

I crossed my arms. *Thank god I didn't tell him that I saw Jordan when I was in that hole, after not having eaten or drank anything for days. He would really think that it was all a hallucination.* "You can believe what you want, Luke. Listen, I don't need the lecture from my baby brother. You haven't exactly been the paragon of great decision-making."

"I just don't want to see you end up hurt or dead, that's all. Just be careful."

I took his hand and squeezed it. "I am careful. He didn't do it." My heart quickened as I braced for the next question. Because I had no idea how I was going to bring Malcolm down. No clue whatsoever. I was going to have to find that video that was missing, somehow, someway. That was the only thing that I could think of that would show definitively who killed Jordan.

At that, Slade came back into the room. I hated to think that he might have heard what I was saying to Luke and Dalilah. I didn't want him to know that they were so suspicious of him, although I was quite sure that he was used to the suspicions. "Here," he said, handing me a bottle of water. He then handed Luke and Dalilah their bottles of water as well. "I looked for some iced tea, but they weren't selling that at that particular machine. I can keep looking for you if you like."

"No, this is fine," I said, opening up the bottle of water and taking a sip. "Thanks for this."

"You're welcome," he said with a smile.

Olivia woke up, and Luke handed the little girl to Dalilah. "Well, I think that I have to feed and change this little one," she said. "We better go. We'll be back to see you tomorrow, though, unless you're home."

"I should be home tomorrow. The doctor needs to come and check on me, though, but I would imagine that I can go on home. There's nothing really wrong with me, after all. I feel great, too."

At that, they both kissed me on the cheek and left. Slade climbed back onto the bed with me. "They seem nice," he said. "I'm sure that they warned you away from me, though."

"They did. But I think that I put them in their place."

Slade was quiet for a moment, just stroking my hair. "Do you now believe for sure that I didn't do it?"

"I do."

"What changed your mind?"

It was my turn to be quiet. I didn't know what to tell him. Like Luke, Slade didn't believe in my powers. He was going to scoff, I knew. But maybe he wouldn't. Maybe, since I now believed him for sure, he would be grateful for Jordan's message.

But probably not.

"I don't know, I just had an epiphany."

"An epiphany. Well, Serena, I don't know what brought the epiphany on, but I'm glad that you finally believe me. Now we can move forward with our relationship and not have that hanging over our heads."

He interlaced his fingers with mine and kissed me on my cheek, then on my lips. "I can't wait to get you alone. I've thought of little else since I found you, I'm ashamed to say."

I felt the tingles when he said that, as I thought of his lips exploring every inch of my body. I examined his beautiful hand, that was gripping mine. And, just like that, I thought of something.

"You're left-handed," I said. "At least you eat with your left hand."

"Yes, I'm left-handed. Why do you ask?"

I shook my head. The investigators didn't indicate if the killer was left or right-handed, and I had no idea if they could tell something like that from the crime scene. What I did know was that Malcolm was not a lefty. He was right-handed, like most of the world.

I knew that I was going to have to speak with the investigators on this case. It was something that so fundamental, I was surprised that I didn't think about it. Surprised and a little ashamed that something so simple escaped me. I realized that I was relying on Malcolm's analysis of the case, and not being proactive enough. I trusted that Malcolm was on the up-and-up, and, now that I knew that he wasn't, I was going to have to do the investigation that he no doubt was neglecting to do.

"I need to speak with the investigator for the police on your case." My heart started to pound. "I need to see if they were able to tell if the killer was left or right-handed."

Slade was quiet. A little too quiet. "That's a good idea." That was all that he said, though.

I looked at him. "Slade, what is going on? You've done very little to help with your own defense. In fact, you've thwarted me when I tried to go down a path towards finding out who really did this. Now, I'm telling you that I need to speak with the investigator about whether or not the killer is left-handed, and you don't exactly seem enthused."

He sighed. "Sometimes I wish that you weren't involved in this mess. I'm glad that you are in that, if you weren't, I never would have met you. But, Serena, you're mixed up with some dangerous people because of me. You were kidnapped because of me. I wish that you could just live your life without all this danger hanging over your head all the time. If something happened to you because of something I did, I honestly don't think that I could forgive myself."

"I am involved in this mess, and you should be too." I shook my head, trying to shake off the feeling that Malcolm wasn't the only person who was trying to throw his case.

It seemed like Slade himself was throwing it as well.

Chapter Two

"Slade," Charlotte was saying to me. She was sitting by the side of the pool, and I was in the water, lounging on an air mattress. "Where are we going tonight?"

I put my head on the pillow of the mattress, and my hands went into the water. I floated lazily to the side of the pool and shoved off the wall again. "I don't know. I have to study, so maybe we need to take a rain check."

I might have only been 18, but I was already in college, having been admitted to UCLA when I was just 16. Charlotte had a hard time trying to understand that, of course. She was my age, but had just graduated high school, as most people my age had done. She didn't have the kinds of pressures that I did. I put these pressures on myself, because I wanted, more than anything, to make something of myself. If anybody had asked me why, I probably couldn't answer them. It was embarrassing for me to admit the truth – I needed to take care of my mother. Not Helen, of course. She didn't need anyone's help. Well, maybe the help of a good shrink, not to mention rehab. But monetarily? She didn't need a thing.

My mother, on the other hand, was a completely different story. She was a convicted felon. Nobody would hire her. Not that she was well-off even before she killed my father. She wasn't, because she was a woman of few skills aside from raising a family. Her felony black mark therefore was just one thing that kept her from making a living. As it was, she was working for a fleabag motel as a maid, making precious little.

I knew that I was going to have to get out of school soon and get a job that paid well enough that I could buy her a house and make sure that she had food on the table every evening. So, when I was accepted to UCLA at the age of 16, I jumped at the chance to go. Helen and Scott were paying for everything, of course, so I knew that I didn't have to worry about financial aid and scholarships and all of that.

"Another rain check?" Charlotte said. "You're getting very boring, I hope that you know that."

"Well, you might think that I'm boring, but I see myself as driven. I'm driven to get out of school as soon as I can. You know that I'm going to soon be studying for my PhD as soon as I get out of UCLA, too, so you might as well get used to my not paying as much attention to you as you might like."

She rolled her eyes. "Listen, I'm busy too. When I'm not in school, I'm at a photo shoot, yet I still try to put you first."

I didn't roll my eyes back at her, yet I wanted to. I simply didn't have time for her bullshit. I had a path in life, and I was determined to follow it as quickly as I possibly could. The sooner I could get out of school and start making some serious money, the sooner I, and my mother, could start to live the way that we wanted to.

She took a sip of her drink and looked at me. "I know that you want to take care of your mother, but why can't you just get the money from Helen and Scott to help her live?"

"You know why." The short answer to that was that Helen and Scott didn't even know that I was still in contact with my mother. They would have blown a gasket if they knew. Helen made it clear, all those years that my mother was in prison, that I was to cut her out of my life. She refused to take me to see my mother in prison, and, when my mother was released, she lectured me about how I was never to see her again.

That's how much bullshit Helen brought to me. She couldn't control me now, of course, as I was of age. But, even when I wasn't of age, I still managed to sneak out at least once a week and see my mom. I would tell her that I was going out with the guys, and she didn't bat an eye. More often than not, I used my allowance to buy her food and I would take it over to her where she lived, which was in Watts. When I turned 16 and started working nights at a convenience store, I used that money to help support her. It was always difficult, though, because she was working, but making minimum wage, so I worried about her constantly.

I knew how much she was suffering. I was suffering right along with her. My father was a bastard, an absolute drunk bastard. He beat her constantly, and she took it. She tried to leave several times, with me in tow, but found that the battered women shelters refused to take animals. That was a deal-breaker for her, because we had a Sheltie, and my mom knew that the dog would be in grave danger if we just left her there at the home. She didn't have the heart to take the dog, Tara, to the animal shelter. All the no-kills were full, so my mother knew that poor Tara probably wouldn't find a home. She had a soft-spot for animals, which was where I got it, I guess.

So, she returned, and took the abuse. She always kept me out of it, though. She protected me, and told me to lock myself in my room whenever they would have a fight. It wasn't until he turned on me and beat me so badly that I went to the hospital, that my mother decided to finally take action. The night that I got back from the hospital, she shot him in his sleep. "You can do what you want to me, but I've always warned you never to touch Slade," she said with gritted teeth to the corpse. "You didn't listen to me."

The bottom line was that she killed my father to protect me. I would never forget that. I couldn't. When she got out of prison, I knew that I had to keep seeing her and doing what I could to protect her and make sure she had what she needed. I even tried to hire a lawyer to sever my adoptive parents' rights to me, so that I could return to my mother, but no lawyer would take that case. They all said that I was going to need permission from Helen and Scott, because there wasn't a reason to sever their parental rights. That was an impossibility, considering how controlling Helen was, so I never did return to my mother's home.

"Okay, then," Charlotte said. "I guess I'm just going to have to find another boy. Somebody who has some time for me."

I shrugged my shoulders. "If that's what you feel you need to do."

She made a face, but I knew that she was only bluffing.

They always said that the person who has the most power in any relationship is the one who cares the least. That certainly was true in my relationship with Charlotte. I couldn't care less about her, and I pretty much had her wrapped around my finger. Not that I intended it to be that way, but that's how it was. She had been hanging out with me for two years, begging for the scraps that I would give her. I didn't want to be cruel to her, because I did like her well enough, but my life was such that I simply didn't have the time to give to her. If she wanted to hang around and take my scraps, that was her problem, I reasoned.

"I don't know why you don't see what you have with me. I don't want to sound like a conceited bitch, but I know that I'm going to when I tell you that everybody considers me to be a hot girl. Everyone. Everywhere I go, I turn heads and men are constantly asking me out. I turn them down for you, and you don't even care."

I knew that Charlotte was a "hot girl." She didn't have to bring that to my attention, that was for sure. It was plain that she was truly stunning. Long legs, taut stomach, large natural breasts, big blue eyes and beautiful dark hair. She was an in-demand model, and had been since she was 15 years old. She was already offered a slew of cosmetic contracts, and, now that she was graduated from high school, she was able to take her pick. There was even talk of her being the "face" of Lancome. Victoria's Secret was going to feature her in their next big fashion show in New York. Charlotte was going places, that was for sure, and any other guy my age would be jumping at the chance to be with her.

Suffice to say that I wasn't any other guy my age.

Oh, well.

"Charlotte, I've told you before. You're free to do what you want. You're young, you're gorgeous, and you're soon going to be a superstar. Don't let me stand in your way. If you want to hang around, great. If you don't, well, I don't blame you. But I'm not going to change my study schedule to accommodate you. You know this, so you can act accordingly."

She narrowed her eyes, but said nothing. "Okay, then, I guess I'll go and see that new movie with Astor." Astor was her closest girlfriend. She was, like Charlotte, wealthy and completely smoking.

"Go for it."

I got home that night, which was the palace where Helen and Scott lived, and I went to my room to study. I got a phone call about midnight. As I recognized my mother's number, I immediately picked up. It wasn't like her to call me in the middle of the night like that, so I figured that there must have been something wrong.

"Mom, what's going on?"

All I heard was heavy breathing. And then I heard screaming.

That was all that I needed to hear. I raced out of the bedroom, and ran down the steps to my car. I was more than stunned to see Charlotte, who was drunkenly standing outside the house. She had a handful of rocks in her hand, like she was going to use them to tap on my window, which is what she did a lot. Whenever I didn't pick up the phone, she would appear outside my window and throw rocks at it until I would open the window to tell her to quit. Then she would inevitably shout something at me, usually about how much she was in love with me, and I would, just as inevitably, shut the window and ignore her for the rest of the night.

"What are you doing here?" I asked her, although I already knew.

"Was in the neighborhood," she slurred.

I then thought of bringing her to my mother's house. Something told me that, whatever was happening over there, it would be a good thing to have backup. Even if that backup was 115 lbs on a good day, and three sheets to the wind. "Get in the car."

"Oh, joy, we're going for a ride."

"Yes, we're going for a ride."

At that, she got in the car, and we took off. "Where are we going?"

"To my mother's house."

"In Watts?" At that, she buckled her seat belt and locked the door. "You're going to get us jacked, you know that, don't you?"

I knew that she was probably right. I was driving the Audi, which was given to me by Helen and Scott on my 16th birthday. I usually drove my beater 17-year-old Corolla, which I bought with my own money before the Audi gift, when I went to see my mother, but I couldn't take the chance that it would break down before I got to her. She was clearly in trouble, and this was confirmed when I tried to call her back in the car, and the phone went straight to voice mail.

"What is going on?"

"I don't know. I just know that she called me just now and didn't say anything, but started to scream. That's all that I know."

I felt like puking. I saw a red light ahead, and I gunned the car through it. I prayed that there wasn't a cop that was at the intersection with his lights off. I had been caught, more than once, blowing through a red light while there was a cop waiting. I somehow knew that every minute counted, and the ride from Helen and Scott's house in Brentwood down to Watts was going to take too long as it was.

I might have felt like puking, but so did Charlotte. I looked over at her, and her face was green. "You have to slow down. I've had a lot to drink tonight, and I'm about to hurl."

"I'm sorry, Charlotte," I said, and I was truly sorry for driving so fast that she felt like throwing up. I was dragging her along on this, after all, and she had no idea what she was getting into. Not that I exactly knew what I was getting into, but I knew that, whatever it was, it wasn't good. And Charlotte was going to have to witness it.

I started to regret having her come along, but that was neither here nor there. She was along, and that was that. It was a spur of the moment decision, and hopefully one that I wouldn't rue later.

The neighborhoods started to get sketchier and sketchier, until I finally came to a stop outside my mom's apartment. Charlotte got out of the car, stumbled really, and made a face. "If I wanted to throw up in the car, I really want to throw up now." She gingerly stepped over the broken bottles, trash and condoms that were littering the sidewalk. "Really, Slade, these people just don't seem to care about how their streets look, do they?"

I sighed. She was absolutely right, but she had to understand that, when you didn't have the basics, such as safety, enough food and a sound shelter, it was very difficult to care about anything else. Maslow's hierarchy of needs demonstrated this – you have to have your basic needs met before you can desire higher needs, such as having a clean living environment. If the people living around here didn't care about the trash outside their homes, there was a good reason for it.

She gripped my hand, and leaned into me. "I never thought I would be around here after dark. Oh, what am I saying? I never thought that I would be around here, period."

"Charlotte, again, I'm sorry for bringing you here. But my mom is in trouble. I'm almost positive of it."

She gripped my arm, having let go of my hand. She looked around her, as if she was afraid that somebody would just jump out of the shadows to attack her.

We walked into the front door of mom's building, and up the creaky stairs that always smelled like urine and curry. At the moment, only the urine smell remained. I doubted that anyone was cooking at this time of the night. I tried not to breathe in too heavily, and Charlotte was evidently doing the same. But she wasn't able to stand the smell, and the puke that was threatening in the car finally was released. She heaved in the corner, and I rubbed her back and held her hair while she did it. After she was done, I made a mental note that I would have to clean it up after we saw my mother. There was no need to add to the disgusting stench of the stairway.

"This is just so gross," she said to me, as we made our way all the way up the steps to the top floor, which was where my mother lived. "Why do we have to do this again?"

"Because," I said to her. "She's in trouble. I'm now sorry for dragging you along."

"Let's just get this over with." She gingerly stepped along the creaky wooden floor, as if she was afraid that she would be stepping on bodily functions. Not that I blamed her. I was afraid of the same thing, usually. Not at that moment, though. I was simply afraid that I was going to walk into my mother's home and see that she was dead.

I got to her door and opened it. "Mom?" I called out.

That's when I saw her. And him. She was standing over a lifeless body of a man who I didn't recognize. She was shaking, from head to toe, and didn't even appear to recognize me when she was looking right at me. She had a gun in her hand, and she kneeled down to the man, her hand on his wrist. She shook her head rapidly, and then lay down on top of the dead guy.

"Mom," I said to her, approaching her gently and slowly. "Who is that?"

I apparently startled her, because she popped up onto her feet and she pointed the gun right at me. I put my hands up, realizing that she was in some kind of altered state and there was a danger that she would shoot me. Charlotte, for her part, was standing right next to me, but she hid behind me when my mom pointed the gun at us.

"Margot, what did you do?" Charlotte asked her. "What happened?"

Mom started crying as she put down the gun, and she came over to me and threw her arms around me. She sobbed and I wrapped my arms around her. "Shhhhh," I said to her gently. "Mom, you have to calm down so we can help you. Let us help you."

She just shook her head and continued to sob loudly. Charlotte was sobered up by the whole thing and she went over to the dead body and picked up his wrist. I guessed that she wanted to be really, really sure that the guy was dead. I could tell that he was though, just by looking at him. He was perfectly still, his mouth wide open, as were his eyes. His face was a terrified mask.

After about an hour, my mom was finally cried out, and she seemed to be ready to talk. I made her some hot tea and sat down next to her at the tiny kitchen table. "Okay, mom, you need to talk," I said to her. "Who is that guy in the living room, and why is he dead?"

"He, he, he," she began, and then shook her head. "Oh, my god, I'm so ashamed."

"Mom, it's okay," I said. "But you need to talk to me. I need to know what happened, and I need to know how I can help you."

She took a deep breath. "His name is Hugh. I think that his last name is Robbins. Hugh Robbins."

"Okay. Go on." I felt surprisingly calm, considering the circumstances at hand.

"He's a prison guard. He was one of my prison guards." She had a handkerchief in her hand and she was twisting it around and around and around. "He wanted to go out, so we went out." She shrugged her shoulders. "I get lonely too, you know."

I nodded my head. "I know. Okay, so the two of you went out."

"Yeah. We went dancing and we had a very nice time. He showed me to the door and I thought that was the end of it, although I did want to see him again sometime."

"Okay. Sounds fine so far." It sounded fine, but it very clearly wasn't fine. Something happened, and I was getting impatient to find out what that something was. "So, what happened?"

"Well, I went inside my apartment and I was planning to turn in, so I took a shower and everything. Brushed my teeth, washed my face, you know the routine. When I came out of the bathroom, he was standing there in my living room. Hugh. Was right there," she said, pointing to the couch. "He was there, just kinda waiting for me. He had this look on his face." She shuddered as if she was remembering the look on this Hugh's face. "I asked him why he was there and he said that he forgot something."

I nodded my head. I knew where this was going, and it wasn't pretty. "Okay. So, he told you that he forgot something. What was this something that he forgot?"

She shook her head. "He came over to me and put his hands on me. I was scared. I really don't know him that well, Slade. He was a strange man in my house and I got scared. I was so scared that I ran into the bedroom and I got my piece."

She started to cry again and I held her head against my chest. "Mom, tell me what happened. Why did you shoot this man?"

"I shot him because I was scared. I don't know why, but when I saw him standing there in my living room like that, I started to think about all the prison guards who tried stuff with me and some of the other girls in prison." She looked ashamed as she cast her eyes down to the ground. "I was raped in prison by a guard. It wasn't Hugh, it was a different guard, but, I don't know, Slade, I started to think of that other guard when I looked at Hugh. And, well, he started toward me, and I panicked."

I looked over at Charlotte, who was white as a ghost. She finally spoke up. "Okay, Mrs. Facinelli, so it's self-defense. You have a right to protect yourself in your own home."

I shook my head. Charlotte was right, but very naïve. My mother was out on parole. She killed my father in cold blood. There was no way she was going to get the benefit of the doubt, and the fact that she killed a prison guard was going to make it that much worse. "No, Charlotte, we can't call the police about this. Mom will be back in prison, and she probably won't be so lucky this time." I shuddered as my mom started to sob again. "She won't be so lucky, and she might even end up on death row. We can't take that chance."

"So, what are we going to do?" Charlotte asked me. It was as if the entire weight of what had happened had settled on her shoulders, and she was finally starting to panic as well. "If we don't call the police, what are we going to do?"

I turned to my mother. "Mom, what do you know about this Hugh? Did you guys talk about your lives over dinner or whatever?"

"Yes. Why?"

"Does he have any children, any ex-wives, anybody at all who would miss him?" I didn't look over at Charlotte, because I knew that she was burning a hole in me with her eyes. I was quite sure she was disbelieving about all of this.

"No children, and he said that he's never been married." She looked up at the ceiling. "I don't know, though, but I think that he might be an only child. I do remember him saying that his parents were dead. He didn't mention siblings."

"Ah, okay, this is good. This is good." Of course, he was a prison guard, so, once he went missing, his disappearance would be noticed by his job. But, if he didn't have loved ones who would be tirelessly searching for him for years, it was a good thing, to say the very least.

My mind started to turn. "Alright," I finally said. "We got to do this, and we have to do it quickly. The sun's going to be coming up in a matter of hours, and, well, if we delay this, you're literally going to have a mess on your hands in this heat."

Charlotte was standing there, shaking her head. "No. I don't want any part of this."

"Okay, then," I said, giving my keys to her. "Take off. Take the Audi home. Mom will drive me home when this gets taken care of."

"I can't believe what you're about to do."

"Believe it. Because it's happening." I didn't even have the time to think about it. "Okay, mom, it's 2 AM. We have about 3 hours to get this show on the road."

Mom was nodding her head, but she wasn't shaking anymore. "Slade, I don't know about this."

"Mom, I do. I do. It's either we get rid of this body, or you're going down for murder again. You have a prior. I personally have no desire to see you behind bars again. And I really don't want to see you on death row. You were just starting to get your life back on track. Or trying to, anyhow. Mom, we need to do this. Now, you get his head and…"

"We can't just take him out of the house like this."

"I know. Give me the sheet off your bed."

At that, she went into her bedroom and brought out a sheet. Charlotte was still standing in the living room, seemingly in shock. "Are you in or out?" I asked her.

"Out. I'll, I'll, I'll see you later." At that, she went out the door.

Mom and I wrapped the body in a sheet and I lifted him over my shoulder. He was dead weight, of course, so he was incredibly heavy. I was hyped up with adrenaline at that time, and I had spent several years lifting weights, so I was able to carry him with relative ease down to my mom's van, which was parked on the street. I threw him in the back and mom and I got into the front.

I then drove off.

"Where are we going?"

"I have a boat in the slip on the Port," I said. "We'll just have to get far out to sea and hope to god that this guy becomes fish food."

"Don't we need cement or something? We need to weigh him down, don't we?"

"You're right." I looked out the window and noticed a crumbling brick wall. "Perfect. Listen, go up and get Tara's leash and I'll get some of these bricks." I got out of the car, and loaded the back of the van up with bricks while my mother went upstairs to get Tara's leash. I didn't see Tara when I went into the apartment, but I knew that she was probably kenneled, so I wasn't too alarmed.

Mom came back out with the dog leash and got in the front seat. "I hope you know what you're doing."

"I do. I think." Truth be told, I was more on autopilot than anything. All that I knew was that I wasn't going to allow my mother to be on trial for another homicide. Yes, it was seemingly self-defense, although it might not have even be that. Would a reasonable person in my mother's shoes feel that her life had been threatened? That was the test for self-defense, and, from what my mother told me, this guy merely approached her when she shot him dead. He was in her apartment, though, uninvited. Mom might have won this case.

She might have won this case, but I didn't want to take that chance. I knew, therefore, that she and I were doing the right thing.

We drove to the Port where there were rows of boats lined up in their slips. We got to mine and I carried the dead guy on my shoulders again. I looked around and was relieved not to see anyone. It seemed as if the stars were aligned for us, considering the fact that we hadn't run into a single person. It was late, or early, depending upon how you looked at it, but I knew that people often lived on their boat. I was deathly afraid of running into somebody, but nobody was awake at this hour.

I placed the dead guy on the deck of the boat and turned to my mother. "Okay, I'm going to drive this thing. You go on down below. If something happens, I want you to hide."

"Hide? Where?"

"Below the bed, there's a drawer. There's clothes in there, but you can fit. The drawer will shut by itself. You need to get in there and hide if you hear people up here talking to me."

"No. I won't let you get in trouble because of me."

"Mom. Listen. If anybody is going to get into trouble because of this, it should be me, not you. I'm 18 and my record is clean. My adoptive parents have a lot of money, so they're going to be able to hire the best attorney for me if it's needed. But you're a different story. You have no money to hire a good attorney. Your record isn't clean. No, mom. If I need to take the blame for this, I will, but I will not let you be involved."

She started to cry again. "I don't deserve this. I don't deserve you."

"Okay," I said, starting up the boat. "I know that you feel that you don't deserve me, but mom, I love you and I'll do anything to make sure that you're safe. Now, go on downstairs and get in that drawer if you hear voices up here. Please."

She went below and I got the boat running.

I drove out to the sea and when I got about three miles

off shore, I decided that the water was deep enough to where this Hugh would sink to the bottom.

Then, I chained bricks onto his entire body before pushing him over the side of the boat. I watched him sink before heading back to my slip.

It was only then, after I felt a sense of relief in getting rid of the body, that I allowed myself to feel. I could hear my heart beating and it was pounding out of my chest. My hand, which was gripping the steering wheel, was shaking. The boat was swaying in the water, I was shaking so hard. My mind also replayed what had just happened.

I just covered up a homicide. That truth hit me like a blast of cold air. The outside atmosphere was cool and there was a heavy fog. That was how I felt inside – foggy and cold. What was going to happen when this man was reported missing? I never even bothered to ask my mom if anyone knew that she was going on a date with him that evening. If somebody did know that she was seeing him, then the entire thing was going to cave in on both of us.

Although I don't remember the trip, the boat was now coming into the harbor, so I went down below to find my mother. She was sitting on the bed, a blanket wrapped around her, just staring at the wall. "Mom," I said to her. "Are you okay?"

She shook her head. "I put you in danger. I never should have called you. I just should have called the police. They would have believed me about how it happened. Wouldn't they?"

"We couldn't take that chance, mom," I said. "I admit, this plan wasn't well thought-out at all. I'm embarrassed to admit that I never even asked you if somebody knew that you and he were going out last evening."

She shook her head and wrapped the blanket around

her tighter. "No. Nobody knew that we were going out. He did tell me that – he told me that he was embarrassed to be going out with me, because the other guys he worked with look down on us prisoners. I was offended when he told me that he was embarrassed to be out with me. I now have to say thank god he didn't tell anyone, huh?"

I breathed a sigh of relief. There was a chance, just a slight chance, that nobody would ever point the finger at either of us.

Then it hit me, like another blast of cold air.

Charlotte knew what we did.

Chapter Three

Serena - Present Day

I ended up staying in the hospital for three more days. I guess that I was in worse shape than I had thought. Luke and Dalilah stayed with me, for the most part, while I was in the hospital, and so did Slade. I think that, by the end of my stay, the three of them had become friends. Much to my relief, because I really did care about whether or not those two approved of Slade.

At the end of the three days, I felt strong. I was anxious to get out of that bed and get on with it. Now that I knew, for sure, that Malcolm was going to try to throw Slade's case so that the suspicion wasn't on him, it was time for me to take the bull by the horns. I needed to speak with the investigator in Slade's case and find out more information about the killer. If the killer was right-handed, then, hopefully, that would take suspicion off of Slade.

So, when the hospital let me out, I knew that I was going to have to throw myself into the case. I was going to not only clear Slade, but also find a way to take Malcolm down. It wasn't going to be easy, because I had to do all of this while not attracting his attention. He couldn't know what I was doing, of course. If he even so much as sniffed that I was onto him, that would be all she wrote. I'd be off the case and probably would end up losing my job.

Proving that Malcolm did it was going to be a delicate operation. To say the very least.

When I got out of the hospital, Slade took me right to my home. "Bella and Gigi are waiting for you there," he said. "I got them out of the pooch hotel this morning."

I covered his hand with mine as I sat in the front seat of his hybrid Porsche. "You think of everything." I swallowed hard. I had to talk to Slade about this whole vision that I had with Jordan and I was going to have to get his reaction. He and I were going to have to put our heads together to figure out ways to bring down Malcolm and exonerate him. Yet, I could sense that there was something that he wasn't telling me. Something that was going to complicate my mission to clear his name.

What was it?

He turned and smiled at me and gripped my hand. "I really like your brother and sister-in-law," he said. "And their little daughter is beautiful."

"They like you, too." And they did by then. Slade had charmed them as he charmed everyone else around him.

I took a deep breath. I started to talk to him but I opened my mouth and nothing at all came out. I felt as if my words couldn't form. I was like a stroke patient who simply couldn't speak.

Why couldn't I speak?

We pulled up to my home and I unlocked the door. I could hear the little dogs barking excitedly inside their kennel and I raced to the kennel to let them out. Their little bodies squirmed in absolute delight. I picked each one up, and both dogs covered my face with kisses. I inhaled their puppy scent knowing that it was only a matter of time until they lost that special scent that I loved so much.

"Thank you so much," I said to Slade. "For bringing my babies home."

Slade smiled and walked over to me. "I know how much these dogs mean to you, so of course I was going to bring them home to you."

After I greeted them, I put them outside so that they could do their business. I watched them for a little while, as they sniffed around the flower beds and chased each other through the little yard. I had to admit, they brought me nothing but delight. Everything else in my life was in flux, but the love of these two dogs was a constant for me.

Slade came up behind me and put his hands on my shoulders. He massaged them lightly, and I reared back my head. It felt so good having his hands on me. They trailed my skin, leaving the little tingles and heat in their wake. He snaked his arms around my waist and one of his hands made its way up to my breast and cupped it lightly.

I sighed, feeling lost in his touch, yet, I was preoccupied. I had to bring up what I knew about Malcolm and I had no clue how he was going to react. He had been so weird about this whole case. It seemed that he not only had no interest in helping with his own defense, but had actively stood in my way when I tried to go down different paths to help him. He told me it was because he was concerned about my welfare and I had no doubt that this was true. But there was something else, and, now that I knew that Charlotte and Malcolm did this murder, I was suspicious again about Slade. It all seemed too convenient – Charlotte was the mastermind and Malcolm was the tool. Charlotte was Slade's ex-girlfriend. Malcolm was now his attorney.

I was clearly missing something in this picture. But what was it?

He started to kiss the back of my neck while his hand was gently exploring underneath my shirt. I couldn't help but lose my breath as I reveled in his touch. "I'm so happy that you're home. I've thought of little else but this for the past few days. Getting you alone has been paramount on my mind."

I smiled and bowed my head. I tried to get the distracting thoughts out of my head, but it was difficult. I had to talk to him.

I decided not to bring up the subject of Malcolm and Charlotte right away, but, at the same time, I wanted to put off having sex with him. I didn't feel that I was in the right frame of mind at that moment, and I didn't know how to turn off my brain about all that had happened and all that I had found out.

"How is your mother?"

He sighed and I felt his head on my back. "It doesn't look good. I want you to meet her, Serena. I don't know how much time she has left, but it's important to me that you get to know her. She's been such an important part of my life for so long that it's difficult to imagine a time when she won't be here. I guess I have to accept that, though."

I turned around and put my head on his chest. "I'm so sorry to hear that, Slade. You've already gone through so much. It doesn't seem fair. She's just too young."

He put his hand in my hair and I could hear his heart

pounding. His skin felt warm, which was comforting to me. "Well, never fear. My mother's church back in Brooklyn is praying for her."

I looked at him. "You're an atheist. Why are you comforted by people praying for your mother?"

"I'm not. I think that it's bullshit. And it is, if you think about it. If you assume that God has saved X, Y or Z, then you're saying that God plays favorites. Because for every person whose cancer was cured by the power of prayer, there are millions who die. Frankly, it's offensive to believe that God cured this person, but lets all these others suffer and die." He shrugged. "But my mother believes in it and she thinks that her parish will help her recover. Maybe there's a placebo effect in all of that. I certainly don't want her to give up hope, so I need to encourage her any way I can. I humor her when she gets these cards and letters from the people back home who are praying for her."

I smiled. "I know that you're a cynic, and believe me, I can relate. I've always asked those questions myself. Why there is so much suffering in this world, and how God can just turn a blind eye to the people who need Him? I don't believe that God gets involved with our individual lives, so I don't necessarily believe that he can save somebody either. But I will never go so far as to say that God doesn't exist. I think that he's 'laissez faire', in that he doesn't intervene in our lives, but I do believe that he's out there."

He held me closer and brought my face up to his. He kissed me full on the lips and I felt him devour me. I lost my breath and felt my body heat up. "I'd love to talk more about this, but Serena, I need to get you alone. Now."

In spite of my misgivings, I nodded my head and let him lead me, by the hand, to my bedroom. As I lay down on the bed, I realized that it wasn't my bed anymore.

Rather, it felt like his bed. "Did you buy me a new bed?" I asked him. "This bed feels like your Vividus."

He smiled. "You might not have allowed me to buy you an entire house, but I hope that you can accept this gift."

I had to laugh. This was a $70,000 mattress and worth every penny. My old mattress was a Sealy and wasn't exactly cheap, but it was nothing like this. I felt like I was sleeping on air. "I accept this gift, Mr. Bridgewell. Now, I hope you don't mind fucking my brains out on it."

It was his turn to laugh. "Oh, I will. And I can't wait." He raised one of my legs and stroked it gently. He squeezed my foot playfully while his other hand was slowly tickling my upper thigh. His finger found my clit, and he rubbed it lightly between his thumb and forefinger. I groaned as I felt his other fingers explore inside of me. I felt like I was soaking, waiting for his enormous cock to enter me.

Still, he teased me. He kissed my thigh while his free hand was stroking my calf and his other hand was still exploring inside of me. I groaned as I felt his hand go from clit to my ass and back again. His face was still buried in my thigh, as his lips and tongue were languidly making their marks on my skin. He made his way to my clit and I felt his lips and tongue on that part of me. I sighed, loving the feeling of him gently lapping at my lady parts. He did such an amazing job with this. It was exactly how I liked it – gentle, but not too gentle. There was passion in the way that he did this, as there was passion in everything that he did.

"Oh, Slade," I groaned. "You're driving me crazy. Please. I need to have you inside of me."

"I will get there. You just have to be patient. It's been a few days since we've been alone like this, and I want to savor it. I want to savor you."

My breathing started coming faster and faster and there

was no doubt about it. He was driving me wild. My skin was prickling and goosebumps had traveled throughout my body. I felt like my nether parts were on fire while he remained between my legs, his tongue and lips becoming more insistent with each passing moment.

He finally made his way up my stomach and breasts, and his tongue was lightly kissing, sucking and biting my nipples. At first he nibbled on my right nipple, as he always did. He soon was biting harder and harder, and I groaned. There was a slight ripple of pain as he bit down on my nipple, and it created a sensation like I used to get when I would experiment with nipple clamps.

I firmly held his head on my breast because I desperately wanted him to keep biting me like that. I wanted him to brand me, to mark up my breasts so that everyone would know that I belonged to him.

After a few minutes, he stopped biting me and he flipped me on my stomach. My bare back was exposed to him. He put something over my eyes and tied it behind my head. "Serena," he said. "What is your safe word?"

My entire body felt like it was on fire when he asked me that. I couldn't believe how excited I was. "Orange," I said. "My safe word is orange."

He chuckled. "Orange like the fruit or orange like the color?"

"Both. I like the fruit, but I also like the color. It's warm and the color of spice."

"Orange it is," he said.

And then I felt it. It was the drip, drip, drip of candle wax on my back. It felt so familiar and so right. I groaned a little, as the hot wax burned my skin. "Serena, I love you, but you can't disobey me the way that you have. You have to listen to me."

He immobilized my hands by putting cuffs on them. He secured my hands around the bars of the headboard, and I suddenly knew the real reason why he bought me a new bed. He wanted me to have a top-of-the-line bed, of course, but I now knew that he wanted a headboard that could be used for little games such as this one.

Then he also immobilized my feet by securing them, with handcuffs, to the posts at the foot of the bed. He wasn't gentle in doing this, either. He took one foot, and then the other, spreading my legs wide. He spread them so wide that I started to feel a bit uncomfortable, but that feeling of being uncomfortable was welcome to me, too.

I was feeling like I was finally coming home.

I was helpless, completely helpless, at that point. I couldn't see anything, I was on my stomach, and I was completely bound to the bed. I had no idea what he was going to do, either. That piqued my curiosity and I felt my body stand at attention. I couldn't stop my breathing from coming faster and faster. This was the best part, really – the anticipation on what was about to happen.

He started with a massage. He was sitting on the small of my back, and he rubbed his hands together. When he touched me, I felt the warm oil on my skin. He rubbed the oil on my back, his strong hands kneading my muscles. That hurt as well, because I was that tight. I could feel that my muscles were being loosened with every touch.

He got to the muscles on my shoulders and he whispered in my ear. "I need to punish you for what you did. Do you know what you did and why it displeased me?"

I could feel his demeanor shifting from the loving, caring man I had come to know into the powerful, controlling stance of a dominant. Although I had sensed that Slade had an inner dominant side, we hadn't really discussed it in detail. He didn't really know for sure that I would be willing, but I was intoxicated by the possibility of introducing this type of play into our relationship. I felt I could trust him to inflict just the right amount of pain to incite my arousal and give me the reprimand I craved. I decided to just follow his lead, so I answered his question. "Yes Slade. I do know that I displeased you."

"And what is it that you think you did Serena? Do you agree that it warrants a punishment?"

"I went against your orders," I told him. "I went to the prosecutor on behalf of Santino to try and get a lead on your case to help exonerate you. I was just trying to help keep you out of prison, trying to keep you here with me."

Tears started to leak from my eyes as the magnitude of what had happened in the wake of my actions hit me hard. "I'm so sorry Slade. I never wanted anything bad to happen. I was just trying to help. I never realized how quickly things would spin out of control. I should have listened to you."

"You put your life in danger and that can never happen again. I need to remind you that I am in charge of this case and you will obey all of my orders, no matter what your feelings may be about them. No matter if you understand my reasoning, or not."

When he said that, I felt my heart start to pound. I squeezed my eyes shut, which was a reflex, really, because they were still covered by the blindfold. What was going to come next? I had no clue, but I was excited to find out.

I could hear Slade pacing around the room. His breathing was very heavy. I sensed he had some unease about punishing me. This was definitely not an area we had discussed or entered into before, so he was being very careful. He did not know what my limits were, what I enjoyed, or what I would consider punishment. He needed to be careful to inflict a punishment that would leave a lasting mark on my psyche and not bring me to a state of utter arousal. This was a tricky area. He was going to have to recall everything he had learned about me before deciding on the right way to attack this dilemma. He would also be limited to the items available to him in my room.

He continued to be silent; this alone was starting to attack my psyche. The silence was entering my mind, swirling all of my thoughts about everything that had happened in the past few days. Leaving me alone to think about my actions and what was to come next was a lethal combination. I was convincing myself that I was wrong, that disobeying Slade was now forbidden, that I deserved to be punished. I had gone against his orders and this had caused some dangerous consequences. The dangers that lurked in the future were unknown so I needed to be more cautious.

The thoughts of what Slade would do next were causing an arousal between my legs to pulse. Liquid started to drip from my ready opening. My legs were still tethered to the bed so I was unable to help relieve my desire by clenching and rubbing my thighs together. I made some small circling motions with my hips to try and create some friction between the mattress and my clit. My nipples were starting to harden just from the thoughts in my head. I started rubbing my chest on the bed as well trying to heighten the beginnings of the arousal I was feeling.

And then I felt it - the thwack of his belt on my bare buttocks. I cried out in pain and ecstasy. This was exactly how I remembered it feeling. The sweet sting, the adrenaline coursing through my veins, the feeling of absolution for my sins. Slade was right – I had disobeyed him, and I paid the price. I almost paid the ultimate price. I deserved to be punished.

"No moving, Serena! Lay completely still. You will not receive the release you crave until I say so. You must learn your lesson here and until I am satisfied that you understand who is in charge here and have learned to obey my orders, you will be denied the sweet pleasure of release that you desire."

Of course, he had to know that I was going to go back to what I was doing, even if he didn't want me to. I had to, so that the truth would come out.

I had a feeling there would be more encounters like this one in the future, as I was going to continually disobey him until he had been absolved of this crime.

I was looking forward to them.

He punished me with his belt several more times, and each time was more savage than the last. I felt it like a crescendo. Like the adagio part of a powerful symphonic piece. That's what was going through my head – a classical symphony that was going faster and faster. The cymbals were clashing, the drums were beating, and the winds were playing like mad. Beethoven's *Ode to Joy* seemed appropriate in this context. I found myself humming some of the bars of this masterpiece as Slade hit my buttocks again and again. I started to breathe in through my nose and out through my mouth, as the sweet, sweet pain flooded my entire body.

Then, without warning at all, I heard the tell tale rip of foil and within seconds I felt something completely different. His huge cock had plunged into me. He lifted me up off of the bed, which stretched out my legs even further. He put his hands around my throat and squeezed firmly but lightly. An inkling of fear edged into my subconscious brain. He didn't kill Jordan, but he told me that he was capable of anything. That anyone was capable of anything. Was he angry enough to keep on going? Would he keep his hands around my neck until he breathed the life out of me?

That little kernel of fear got my adrenaline going again, and I cried out in a powerful orgasm as he simultaneously drove his huge manhood inside of me, again and again, while squeezing my neck tighter and tighter. "Do it," I said. "Make me fear you. Make me submit to you, whatever your will is. Show me your anger and your rage. I disobeyed you, Slade. Show me how angry you are about that."

He pulled my hair so hard that my head snapped back. As my breathing got heavier and heavier, he kept my head static in his hand. He bent his mouth to my ear. "Oh Serena, what have you done to me? I can't continue to deny you the pleasure you seek even though I am not certain that you have learned your lesson yet." His voice was strained. I could tell he was also on the brink of explosion.

I felt his lips on mine – hungry, searching, passionate and angry. I felt like his lips and tongue were devouring my own. He quickly released my arms from where they were bound and did the same for my feet. Then he flipped me over on my back, and hovered over me. My eyes were still covered by the blindfold at that point, so I still had no idea what to expect from him. I was filled with a tingly sense of excitement, mixed in with my high adrenaline and a hint of dread. It was an intoxicating combination.

I put my arms around his back and tried to bring him down to meet me. He resisted. "I'm not quite done punishing you," he said to me. "You have no idea how scared I was for you. Charlotte is capable of anything, absolutely anything. You're safe now. You need to make sure you stay that way."

At that, he took off my blindfold. My eyes were still closed. "Look at me, Serena," he commanded.

I did. I almost drew a breath when I looked into those piercing green eyes. Those eyes that bore right through my skin and set my soul absolutely aflame. They were mesmerizing, yet, at that point, they also showed deep hurt and concern. I could read his thoughts without closing my eyes and concentrating on them. The emotions on his face said it all.

I just nodded my head, and wrapped my arms around him. He didn't even have to say anything. I already knew.

He seemed to understand that I knew what he was feeling, because he put his head down on my shoulder. He played with a lock of my hair, twisting it around his fingers again and again. "Nobody will ever touch you again. I can guarantee this."

I shook my head. I saw something in his eyes, something that I wasn't used to seeing. It was an emotion that I didn't quite understand, but it was powerful. I shuddered and I looked at my arm. It was covered in goose pimples.

"Slade," I began. I needed to know what was going on behind those beautiful eyes of his. "You're hiding something. Please tell me what it is."

He just shook his head. "Later. Right now, I need to ravish you some more." At that, he lifted up my legs and put them behind his back. He plunged his manhood into me, which was still sheathed from before, again and again. The way that he moved in and out of me was almost savage and primitive. He was just pure, raw emotion right at that moment, and he was making sure that all his aggressions were taken out on me.

I felt that I deserved it, yet didn't. I knew that I had defied him. I also knew that I was going to keep defying him. I hated to do that, because I didn't want that tension to be hanging over our heads all the time. I had no choice in the matter, though. It was either defy him or see him fry. I knew what choice I was going to make.

I felt myself coming, harder than I had ever come before, and he did the same. He rolled over next to me and wrapped his strong arms around me. I could feel his heart pounding against me and his skin felt like it was on fire. "What's on your mind?" he asked me. "I could tell earlier that you really wanted to talk to me about something."

I wasn't quite sure how to broach the subject of Malcolm. I somehow knew that particular conversation was going to be one that wasn't going to go well. "Nothing. Well..." I almost brought up Malcolm, but decided against it. "You told me that I was safe now. How do you know that? Charlotte seems to be just a tad unbalanced, to say the very least."

He was quiet. Too quiet. I lay there in the dark, his body wrapped around mine in the stillness, and I felt uncomfortable. There was so much that was unsaid and was just hanging in the air like a thick cloud. "I just know," he said. "Charlotte won't bother you anymore."

I turned around and looked at him. I put my hand in his thick hair and felt his cheek. "What are you hiding from me?"

"What are *you* hiding from *me*?" He turned the question back on me, and I felt mildly irritated.

"I asked you first. Tell me what you're hiding from me."

He cleared his throat and ran his finger gently around one of my nipples. To my surprise, his face seemed to flush, as if he was embarrassed. "I broke the Mexican standoff," he said.

"What is that supposed to mean? Slade, I have no idea

what she has on you, or what you have on her. So, you're telling me words, but I have no idea what they mean. You need to be specific here."

"I can't. I'm sorry."

I shook my head. I was just now starting to trust that he didn't kill Jordan, but there was still more. Always more with this guy. He seemed to be a bundle of secrets and I didn't like that one bit.

"How are we ever going to move forward if we can't talk about simple things with one another?"

He looked annoyed. "Why don't you tell me? You're hiding something just as much as you believe that I am."

I turned my back on him in the bed. I didn't know how to talk to him. I hated that I couldn't excitedly tell him what I found out about Malcolm, and I hated that I couldn't brainstorm with him about how to bring him down. Not to mention Charlotte.

Slade reached around into my night table and found a jar of body butter that I kept there. He started to rub the soothing cream over my pink buttocks. As he worked, he left little butterfly kisses on my marks. Marks that I didn't mind being there. Seeing them would remind me who had given them to me and why. They would also serve to remind me who I belonged to now. I could sense that, given the chance, we could become perfect together, each helping the other to heal and survive.

In a few minutes, I heard him breathing heavily in sleep.

But I was still wide awake.

Chapter Four

Slade - Ten Years Ago

All my stress hormones were starting to abate and I was left with the awful feeling that everything was totally screwed up. Charlotte knew what I did. She wasn't to be trusted with that information.

Worse than that, she knew what mom did.

Mom came up from below. "Is it safe to come up on deck?" she asked me tentatively.

"Yes. Mom, listen, you need to leave the city. I don't want you anywhere near this place anymore. If there is ever a question on what happened to Hugh, I'll answer them. I won't let this stick to you, mom, but you really need to get out of the city."

"I can't just leave. I'm on parole."

"I'll hire you an attorney, mom, to ask a judge to have your supervision moved. That shouldn't be a problem. You're only on parole for the next year, and you've been stellar. You've done everything that they've asked of you.

That judge will approve your request to move, I know that he will."

She got quiet and then started to cry again. "You're going to be in trouble for this, Slade, and I hate that. You had nothing to do with Hugh being killed. It was all me. Me and my goddamned impulsiveness. I was very scared, though."

"Of course you were. That guy shouldn't have come into your home uninvited."

"He shouldn't have, but I shouldn't have shot him either." She shook her head. "What are we going to do?"

"We do nothing. As long as nobody knew that you were out with him, we should be in the clear."

"What about your girlfriend?"

I felt my shoulders slump when my mom asked about Charlotte. What about Charlotte? Was she going to throw both of us under the bus?

"I'll handle her."

"How?"

"I just will." Charlotte was wrapped around my finger and she had been since we met. There was a part of me that knew that she wasn't going to go to the authorities about us. But that would mean that I was going to have to step lightly around her from then on.

I felt trapped. This might mean that I could never actually break her heart, because if I did, she was going to turn me in. Worse, she was going to turn mom in. She was the kind of person who would do that just for spite.

"Slade, I don't trust her. I never did trust her. You don't have anything to blackmail her with, do you?"

I thought about that one hard. Charlotte was always in trouble, but none of it ever mattered. She had racked up three DUIs, but her mobster father, who was the powerful head of a powerful mob syndicate, got her out of them every time. She had also been involved with petty theft, which was actually to be expected from her.

From the standpoint of blackmail, Charlotte seemed to be Teflon. Nothing had stuck to her, and nothing probably would.

I stood there, at the steering wheel of the boat, trying to think of something, anything, that I could use to blackmail her. I had to somehow get her into my back pocket.

That's when it hit me. "You know what? Charlotte had an affair with her own uncle. Michael Garancino. He's not much older than her – he was the youngest of nine kids. But they had an affair last year, right before I met her."

My mom was looking mystified when I spoke with her. "So? I killed a man and all you have on your girlfriend is that she had an affair with her own uncle?"

"You don't understand. Charlotte is in the public eye now. She's a very sought-after model and she's trying to break into Hollywood. Having an affair with an uncle is something that the rest of the world considers to be wrong. It could be something that would dog her in the tabloids and embarrass her. That would be why she swore me to secrecy. I wouldn't have known about it myself if I didn't see the two of them emerging from a hotel together."

Mom shook her head. "Are you sure that's all you have?"

"Well, she's stolen cars and has been caught shoplifting more than once. And she's had three DUIs. None of that is a big deal though. It's to be expected with young stars. But an affair with an uncle…" I shook my head. "Edgar Allen Poe never did live down his affair with his young cousin. Say what you want but people still find affairs with one's blood relatives to be…icky."

Mom was shaking her head. "I wish you had more but if that's what you got, that's what you got. Go to her and tell her that you'll reveal her affair with her uncle to the press if she dares breath a word about what happened with Hugh."

"I will." I steered the boat into the slip and mom and I got out. It was 7 AM. We had time to get mom back to her apartment in Watts and for me to get home without Helen and Scott knowing that I was gone. It was a Sunday morning and I knew that they habitually slept in on Sundays. I prayed that this would be the case again. The less interrogation I got from people, the better.

I got mom home and slipped into my own home by 8 AM. I crept up to my bedroom feeling relieved that there wasn't anybody stirring. My adoptive sister, Alice, was away at college, so it was only Helen, Scott, and me in the home.

I got into bed and the panic started to wash over me. What did I do? What did mom do? Was this entire thing going to blow up in my face? In our face?

I called Charlotte, who picked up on the first ring. "Yeah?" she said to me.

"How are you feeling?"

"Better than you, I would imagine, but still not great. I have to cut back my drinking."

Good luck with that. "Listen, I need to talk to you about last night."

"You mean this morning? With your mother?"

"Yes. This morning with my mother. I need to talk to you about that."

She was quiet for a little while. "What about it?" she finally inquired.

"This is our secret, right?"

More silence on the line. She finally spoke after a full minute of silence. "Listen, Slade, I don't want to get into trouble for covering something like that up. What if somebody was watching us the whole time from behind a bush or something?"

"There are no bushes around there." That much was true. Mom's neighborhood was not exactly known for its green space.

"Okay, then hiding behind a car. What if somebody saw everything and turned you in? And they'll tell the police about me being there too. I can't take that chance."

I drew a breath. "You will take that chance, because if you don't, I'm going to tell the world about your affair with Michael. You know that he won't deny it if somebody asks."

"Oh, this is how you're going to play it?"

"This is how I'm going to play it."

"Slade, I was 16 at the time."

"And Michael was 20. How is that going to look to the press?"

More silence. I knew that she thought she felt defeated. "I wasn't of age. Michael won't say a word if somebody asks."

"Maybe he won't confirm it, but it will still be out there. It will be embarrassing for you, to say the very least."

"I'll just deny it, and so will Michael, and that will be that."

Gut check time. I was going to take a calculated risk and hope and pray that it worked out. "You don't think that those medical records will be used against you? In the right hands, with the right unethical reporter, your abortion records will become public. I'm quite sure that Michael was involved with that. His name was on the consent form, after all."

All of that was bullshit. I had no idea if that was true, although I had heard rumors that it was. I was bluffing and I held my breath waiting for her reaction to my Hail Mary.

There was a long silence, and then, when Charlotte started talking, her voice was tiny. "How did you know about that?"

I let out a long sigh of relief, although I hoped that it wasn't audible. "I have my ways."

"Those records are private."

"And unethical reporters have a way of making them public."

More silence. "Okay," she finally said. "You got me. I won't say a word."

"Thank you."

We got off the phone and I stared at the ceiling. Everything was up in the air. Charlotte was right - there might have been somebody hiding who saw it all. I doubted it though. It was at an odd time in the morning – too late for most people to be up, even if they were partying, and too early for others to be awake, especially on a Sunday. That should work in our favor.

In the days and the weeks to come though, I was going to be vigilant. Hugh was going to be missed at work. I braced myself for seeing his disappearance in the paper. There was also the chance that he was going to show up on shore. I tried to make sure that I was far enough out at sea and that he was weighted down, but would that be enough? He was liable to wash up on shore somewhere, and then the murder investigation would begin in earnest.

Please, please, please let it be that Hugh told nobody he was going out with mom. People saw them out, of course, so if mom ever became a suspect, it would be easy to place her with Hugh on the night of his death. If she never became a suspect though, it would be difficult to place her. I would imagine that Hugh used his credit card where he and my mom went, which would mean that the investigators would start at those places to ask about him. I imagined that the waiter would say that Hugh was out with an attractive woman in her early thirties, but that woman could be anyone.

Mom would be caught up in this if she ever came under suspicion. If her name never came up though, she should be in the clear.

One thing was for sure, I was going to have to spend the rest of my life looking over my shoulder.

Chapter Five

Serena - Present Day

First thing Monday, I decided that I was going to have to get a copy of Jordan's autopsy and find out if the killer was left or right-handed. That would be a start in proving that Slade didn't do it. I felt ashamed that I hadn't even looked at this report yet. It was important, but I was so preoccupied with other aspects of the case, not to mention preoccupied with Slade himself, that I just hadn't looked at this fundamental document.

Then again, Malcolm wasn't forthcoming with that or anything else. He had shut me out of the case for the most part, except when he encouraged my relationship with Slade. Now that I knew his game, I was going to have to counteract it as best that I could. If Malcolm was going to withhold this file, the information in it, and the witnesses who were being called in, then I was going to have to either be more demanding in seeing it or I was going to have to look at the file without his knowledge.

I went to his office. I found that just the sight of his face made me want to throw up. He was prepared to let an innocent man fry for what he did. Not to mention the fact that the man was pathetic, really. He killed this man to impress Charlotte. I doubted that Charlotte still wanted anything to do with him. What did he really gain for doing that for her?

Nothing. He gained nothing.

The man was just evil. Maybe he killed Jordan just because it was fun for him and Charlotte was just the catalyst. He didn't even necessarily look evil though. He was a handsome guy with copper curly locks and blue eyes. He stayed fit. He simply looked like an overstressed attorney and father of three, which was what he was.

I remember it being said that evil could take any form, and I believed that. Yes, Malcolm didn't look like a cold-blooded killer. That was because there wasn't a certain way that killers looked. Killers could be handsome and charming, like Malcolm and Ted Bundy. They didn't have to necessarily look the part of the loner misfit.

If we could only identify them more readily, life would be so many easier. We could all avoid these people.

He was sitting at his desk, reading legal research, his finger calmly on his temple. Just as if he didn't have a care in the world.

I cleared my throat and he looked up. "Serena. Just the woman I wanted to see. You missed about a week of work with no word. What's going on?"

I didn't know if Malcolm genuinely didn't know what had happened to me or if he was bluffing. Surely Charlotte would have told him about my kidnapping and false imprisonment.

Then again, maybe she didn't tell him anything. After all, Slade was able to save me, somehow, someway. There was something that I was clearly missing, and perhaps Malcolm wasn't in on everything that woman did.

I decided to give him the benefit of the doubt. Nevertheless, I had to lie. I couldn't necessarily tell him that I was kidnapped by Charlotte. It might make him suspicious that I knew about him and what he did. "I was in a car accident," I told him. I studied his face to see if there was any hint of him not believing me, and I closed my eyes and tuned into his vibrations. I felt no sense of anxiety coming from him.

I guessed that my initial hunch might have been correct after all. Malcolm didn't seem to know about my kidnapping. Which was interesting, to say the very least.

"You're okay, though?" he asked me. He seemed genuinely interested, and I closed my eyes again. I couldn't believe how sucked in I still was with this man. He was making me question whether or not the spiritual message was even accurate. Did I really see Jordan when I was at my lowest point, or was he nothing but an hallucination?

"I'm fine. I wasn't fine, of course, because I was in the hospital. But that was only because I spent three days in my car before somebody found me, so I was severely dehydrated."

"Why did you stay in your car? Why didn't you try to find help? You weren't incapacitated, were you?"

"No. I've just always heard that you should never leave your car if you get stranded."

I was making this story up on the fly, so I hoped that Malcolm didn't ask me specifics. I would just tell him that I was in the desert when my car went off the road and was disabled, and nobody was around. That should satisfy him, and it certainly did sound like a plausible story.

But Malcolm apparently didn't care that much. "Send me your hospital records, and I'll make sure that your leave is paid. But Serena, if you're ever in the hospital, and you're not incapacitated, you have to call me and let me know. I was a few hours away from calling the police to try to find you. It's not like you just to leave like that."

"I know, and I'm sorry." I wrung my hands as I stood there. I was going to have to ask him questions about Slade's case, and I didn't know how he was going to answer me. After all, he wasn't in it to win it at all. He was in it to make sure that Slade went down for what he did.

"Can I do anything else for you?"

"Yes. I need to see the Slade Bridgewell file. I need to read it from top to bottom. It's something that I was going to do anyhow, and I really need to see if there's anything that we aren't seeing so far."

"Here," he said, giving me three file boxes. "This is the discovery we've gotten from the prosecutors and from the investigators on the case. Have at it, but make sure that this isn't the only thing that you're working on. And don't forget about the Bar this weekend."

"Thanks," I said to him. "Don't worry; I'll get my other projects done."

I took the file boxes to my office and sighed as I realized how much I was going to have to sift through. Fortunately, the police report for the incident was right on top.

I scanned through the report but found that it only was a perfunctory description of the incident. It talked about Slade contacting the police after having found Jordan, and about the state of Jordan's body.

I read the report three times, trying to see what I had missed. Unfortunately, there wasn't anything on the report about the handedness of the killer. In fact, there wasn't anything in this police report that I didn't know.

The autopsy report wasn't much more illuminating. It

concluded that Jordan died from blunt force trauma inflicted by a baseball bat. Again, I didn't learn anything new from this.

The rest of the discovery detailed the drugs that Jordan was working on, interviews with his co-workers, and interviews with his family. There were also medical records for Jordan. Apparently he had sought treatment for his bipolar disorder on many occasions. He had been hospitalized three times for acute manic episodes and twice for suicide attempts related to the depressive end of the bipolar spectrum.

I tapped my pencil on my forehead as I looked through the file for something, anything that would indicate that Malcolm was involved. So far though, nothing was jumping out at me.

Something was nagging me. It had to do with the state of the video that showed the murder. There was part of it missing of course, but was there another copy of the video elsewhere?

Perhaps Slade would know the answer to that question.

Perhaps. But first, I was going to follow my initial inquiry on whether or not the killer was left-handed.

I went down the hall to Malcolm's office and rapped lightly on the door.

"I'm going to talk to the investigator on Slade's case," I told Malcolm. "I'll be back by the end of the day."

Malcolm furrowed his brow. "Why do you need to talk to the investigator? The report is in the file. And you're going to Los Angeles to talk to him? I don't think that's a good idea."

Of course it's not a good idea. Of course you're going to say that. You don't want me really finding out what happened here.

"There's something missing." I was going to have to step

lightly with this guy. The last thing that I wanted was for him to be suspicious that I was onto him.

"What's missing?"

"There are just some details missing. I don't have time to go through it right now – I already made an appointment with the lead investigator and I don't want to keep him waiting." That was actually a lie – I didn't make an appointment. I was going to go to the police station and hope that I could catch Trey Hanson, who was the person that I was going to have to speak with.

Malcolm furrowed his brow again but the phone was ringing. "I have to take this," he said to me. "Don't be long."

"I won't be."

At that, with a sigh of relief, I went to my car. I then headed down to the police station to try to find out the important answers I sought.

Chapter Six

I got to the police station and announced who I was. The police station was in Downtown Los Angeles, a beautiful modern structure with a wall of glass and sharp angles. I walked in and there were people bustling around. I was directed to a visitor's area and I went and gave the lady my name and who I was there to see. "Detective Hanson," I told her. "I need to see him. My name is Serena Roberts, and I'm one of the lead attorneys on the Slade Bridgewell case."

She nodded her head and called on the phone. She nodded to me while she talked to Detective Hanson's assistant, and then got off the phone. "He'll be right with you. In the meantime, can I interest you in some water?"

"Thank you," I said. The lady, whose name tag said *Mika Anoly*, brought me a glass of water as I took a seat in the open-air lobby.

In about five minutes' time, a tall man who was balding came out and extended his hand. "I'm Detective Hanson," he said. He seemed to be a very friendly sort, dressed in a blue button-down and dark blue pants. He also wore a bow-tie and suspenders. "You must be Serena Roberts."

I nodded and extended my own hand. "Very pleased to meet you."

He gestured to the end of the hall. "My office is down here. I have to admit that I'm surprised that you're the first person from Mr. Bridgewell's legal team to speak with me. I would have thought that I would have spoken with some-body by now."

I was tempted, sorely tempted, to tell this man the truth. That Malcolm, the lead attorney on the case, was the actual perpetrator so of course he didn't want to do too much independent investigation.

Then again, until I could prove something like that, I would be committing slander. I was going to have tread lightly, because this was a dangerous game I was playing. If I didn't play it just right, I was going to be the one who was going to pay, not Malcolm.

"Well, the discovery process is just getting going. The trial isn't for almost a year, so we've been engrossed in hear-ings, discovery and interviews. We haven't even started depositions on the case yet."

I followed Detective Hanson to his office, which had a beautiful view of the city. "Okay, come on in," he told me. "Have a seat."

I sat down and he also took a seat, behind his desk. He lifted a paper cup of coffee to his lips as he looked at me. "What can I do you for?"

"I reviewed the reports regarding Jordan's murder," I told him. "But I couldn't find out one fundamental aspect. What was the handedness of the killer?"

He furrowed his brow. "That wasn't in the report? I was sure that I wrote it in. But the killer was left-handed."

I felt my heart sinking as he said that. I shook my head and put my thumb and forefinger to the bridge of my nose. I fought back tears.

Unfortunately, Detective Hanson appeared to pick up on my distress. "Yes, left-handed. Is there anything wrong? You got white as a sheet all of a sudden."

It's not the end of the world. After all, Charlotte knew that Slade was a lefty. She would have told Malcolm to swing the baseball bat from the left side to mimic the way Slade would have done it. Charlotte would have been severely negligent if she would have allowed Malcolm to swing the bat right-handed.

Still, I was hoping that somehow, someway, Malcolm would have done just that − slipped up and used his actual swing. That certainly would have gone a long way towards proving that Slade had nothing to do with Jordan's murder.

Of course it's not going to be that easy. If only murder cases were that cut and dry.

"Is that the only thing that you wanted to ask me?" Detective Hanson inquired.

"Yes. That's the only thing that I noticed was missing from the file. I think that I have everything else I need, but I'll certainly call you if I think about anything else."

I left his office after saying goodbye, and got into my car. *Well, that was a fruitless trip.* Still, I was happy to have made this trip, because it gave me time to think. I always enjoyed a little drive whenever I was feeling out of sorts.

I drove back to San Diego by way of the Pacific Coast Highway. The vast ocean was on my right and I hit a few quaint towns on the way back. They were typical coastal small towns, with restaurants and boutique shops lining the streets. The houses around these towns weren't the stereotypical homes that people might associate with Southern California, but were vast colonial-style homes.

As I drove, I was fixated on so many things – what Slade was still hiding, why he was acting like he didn't really want to win his own case, and how was I going to bring down Malcolm? I wished that Jordan had given me more pertinent information when he contacted me in that hole. It certainly would have helped my situation right then.

At some point, I got out of the car. The ocean was beckoning to me, as if it had the answers to the questions that were going through my mind. Indeed, that was often the case. Being around the water calmed my mind, and cleared it of any extraneous information that was clouding my judgment.

I sat down on the sand, without even putting down a blanket or chair or anything. The sun was beating down and I had on a floppy hat to protect my face from the glare. I hugged my knees to my chest and closed my eyes. I listened to the waves that were crashing and the seagulls shrieking. I tried to become one with the universe, so that I could listen to what the collective consciousness was trying to tell me. The answer was right there, somewhere. The key that would unlock it all was so close I could taste it, as much as I could taste salt on my tongue.

I was starting to drift off into a place where I could access the answers that were inside of me when the phone started to ring. I answered it, although I was exasperated that it had to ring at such an inopportune time. "Malcolm," I said. "How are you?"

"Fine. Listen, you have to get back into the office ASAP."

"Why?" I didn't like the sound of Malcolm's voice.

"It's Slade. He wants to confess to the Jordan's murder and change his plea to guilty."

Chapter Seven

I blinked my eyes when Malcolm dropped that bomb on me. "What?" My breathing started to come faster and faster. "No. No. He can't."

"He can and he's going to."

"No. Let me call him."

"Don't call him. Listen, just stay calm. I'll try my best to talk him out of doing that, but Serena, maybe it's for the best. Let's face it; things aren't exactly looking good for him."

I had to bite my tongue when Malcolm said that bullshit to me. I wanted to tell him that I knew the truth. I also knew why Malcolm was so ready and willing to let Slade go down for Jordan's murder. It would take the heat off of Malcolm altogether. Once Slade pled guilty, all eyes would be off of Malcolm forever. He would have gotten away with it and Slade would be the one who would be punished.

I couldn't possibly let that happen.

"Okay. Listen, I'm driving, so…" Of course, I wasn't

driving - I was sitting on the beach. But I wanted off the phone with him ASAP, so I lied.

"Talk to you later."

At that, I immediately called Slade.

To my surprise, though, he didn't pick up. In fact, his phone didn't seem to be on, because it went straight to voice-mail.

I shook my head. I was going to go to his home and hope that I found him there. I needed to talk some sense into him. I had no clue why he was going to do this either; none whatsoever.

This whole thing presented another mystery for me to solve. Slade was protecting somebody, but who? Was he protecting Charlotte? Gianni? Malcolm? All of the above? Why would he be doing that?

I got off the highway and made my way back up to Del Mar. I was determined that I was going to talk to Slade.

I needed to find him and talk to him before he made a horrible mistake.

It could be the most devastating mistake of his life.

Chapter Eight

Slade - Ten Years Earlier

After Charlotte and I came to our "understanding," things were certainly tense, but bearable. I held my breath as I saw the news reports, night after night, about the missing prison guard. What soon became clear was that, thus far, there was no suspicion on either my mother or me about the disappearance. I kept expecting that the authorities would call her in at any moment – perhaps somebody from the bar where she and Hugh went recognized Hugh from the pictures shown and managed to perfectly describe my mother as being the woman with him that night. Maybe there was a picture that was inadvertently taken of the two of them together.

But no. The weeks went by and then the months, and at some point, the news of Hugh's disappearance was no longer splashed on the front page of the paper. It was no longer mentioned on the evening news. It seemed as if the trail on Hugh's disappearance had grown cold and the police no longer seemed interested in it. Hugh was just one more person who just disappeared out of thin air, never to be seen or heard from again.

After six months of nothing, I breathed a sigh of relief. My détente with Charlotte was holding, my mother seemed to be in the clear, as was I. I felt as if we were truly out of the woods.

Charlotte and I continued to see one another at the same level we were on before – which meant that we went out once every couple of weeks and had sex about once a month – and even though Charlotte clearly wanted more from me, I kept it as casual as possible. She tried to blackmail me once or twice – she would tell me that she would go to the police and tell them everything if I didn't give her the attention she was demanding – but I called her bluff every time, and every time, she proved to be a lot of hot air.

I knew better than to give into her blackmail. I had her right where I wanted her, and she knew it. She also thought that I had "proof" of her affair with Michael, because she erroneously thought that I had her abortion records. Thank god she never actually asked to see these records for herself though. If she did, she would have figured out that I had nothing at all to prove that she had been with Michael. That might have changed the dynamic, possibly. But, then again, Charlotte seemed loathe to doing anything that would permanently put a wedge between her and I. She always had it in her head that I was going to end up with her.

I walked the tightrope, afraid that I was going to fall off at any time. But, day after day, when there was no news and no shoe that dropped, I felt more and more relieved. My mother and I were finally in the clear.

My mother had also moved to New York City, at my

urging. She had family there, and I really needed her to get out of the state. I wanted her to be able to make a run for it if she had to, and being near a large international airport like La Guardia was going to possibly come in handy. Her parole officer didn't have a problem releasing her to another state, because mom had been a model parolee. So, her move was another thing that was good. I missed her, but I sent money to her whenever I could. I knew that she was in good hands too, because her sisters lived in Brooklyn, and one of her sisters, Tessa, took her in and let mom live with her.

That's how it was for years. As the years went by, the memory of that night with the prison guard receded more and more from my memory. Mom and I never talked about it. Ever. And, after a while, even Charlotte gave up her threats to blackmail me over it. She finally figured out that blackmailing me was getting her nowhere and she always thought that I would bring her down anyhow if she breathed a word. So, she didn't.

Our stalemate was therefore what defined what had happened that night with mom and the dead Hugh. I got my PhD, with honors, and went on to found my pharmaceutical company with seed money from some venture capitalists who were friends with Scott, money that I managed to save over the years, and money that Jordan had from a substantial inheritance. My company took off with the introduction of what was being hailed as the best antidepressant the market had ever seen, and things were rolling.

Life was good.

Until it wasn't.

And, just like that, everything changed.

Chapter Nine

Serena - Present Day

I got to Slade's house and rang the doorbell.

Nobody answered, so I used my key. Slade had just given me a key to his home, telling me that it was time to move our relationship to the next level. This showed how much he trusted me, he told me.

I opened the door and looked around. Nothing was out of place, except he had some magazines that were piling up on the coffee table. I furrowed my brow as I looked at the magazines that didn't seem to belong to him. There was a *People* magazine, a *Star* magazine, a *Redbook*, *Vogue* and *Elle*. Among those magazines were ones that seemed more like Slade – *Inc., Businessweek*, and *Forbes*.

Then I heard it. A female voice. "Slade, is that you?" the voice said from a bedroom up above. "Did you bring me my soup?"

I drew a breath, not wanting to go upstairs to find the origin of the voice. I wasn't going to jump to conclusions, but I certainly wasn't encouraged by any of this. It seemed that he had a woman living there with him, when he never told me that this was the case.

I looked around the rest of the house, the lower level, and, just when I was getting ready to leave, I turned around and saw a slight, but very beautiful woman. I narrowed my eyes at her because there was something that was just a tiny bit off.

She looked to be around her early forties, with dark hair and green eyes. Eyes that were similar to Slade's own.

And that's when it hit me – this was Margot. What was unusual about her, the thing that I was trying to put my finger on before, was her skin color. It was slightly yellow. She was obviously jaundiced from her disease, and my heart went out to her.

She raised an eyebrow, but said nothing.

I finally went over to her, extending my hand. "Hello. I'm Serena. You must be Margot."

"I am," she said, extending her own hand to me. And then she smiled broadly. "Oh, yes, Serena. You're the woman that my son is seeing. He's told me all about you. I thought that we were going to meet, and here we are! Of course, Slade didn't set this meeting up. Did he?"

"He didn't." I stood there, wanting to ask this beautiful woman so many questions about Slade. She knew him better than anyone, after all. But, I had no idea how I was going to ask him these questions.

"Well, have a seat. He went to the grocery store to get me some soup." Then she smiled. "Slade told you about my condition? It's been hard for me to get solid food down these days."

I nodded, taking a seat. Margot poured a glass of wine for me. "Slade tells me that you love this particular brand of cabernet," she told me. "I wish I could have a glass of wine, too, but I'm on these damned drugs, which don't mix well with alcohol."

As I drank my wine, I was confused. She referenced the drugs that didn't mix well with wine, but what about her cancer? It was difficult to bring that up to her though. I didn't know if it was a sore subject or any of my business.

"What did Slade tell you about me?"

She shrugged. "He just said that you and he were in a relationship with each other." Then she giggled. "I told him that I had never known him to be in a relationship with anyone, ever, so this is really something."

I smiled. "Yes, I guess Slade, uh, never really had time for anything serious."

"Yes. And he never met anyone who floats his boat quite like you do." She smiled when she said that. "Sorry for my goofy expressions. I learned them from my mother."

I nodded, feeling connected to her when she said that. I learned some goofy sayings from my own mother, even if I did learn that she didn't create them. "I understand, believe me."

She put her teacup to her lips and drank daintily. "This tea helps me feel better. The antivirals haven't quite kicked in, but I hope that they will soon."

"Antivirals? Is that how they're treating pancreatic cancer these days?" That was something new to me, although I knew that there was always some kind of cutting-edge treatment options that were emerging all the time.

She smiled. "No, but it turns out I don't have cancer. I got a second opinion and the lab results just came back today. I have an advanced case of Hepatitis C, but the doctor has told me that it's treatable with these antivirals.

I'm very hopeful. It will never be cured, but it can be treated. Kinda like HIV."

I felt a sense of relief when she told me this. Slade was going to be so happy. "That's wonderful news. I wonder how a mistake like that could happen?"

"I don't know. I think that it was a lab error with my doctor in New York. Slade wants me to sue for malpractice, but I really don't have the energy for all of that."

"I can certainly relate to that. Lawsuits are no fun, to say the very least." I personally hated trying malpractice claims. They were expensive to bring to trial and the juries were often skeptical of the plaintiff's claims. Like police officers, doctors were often given the benefit of the doubt. Margot was probably right in refusing to bring a lawsuit in this case.

"No, I guess that they're not." Then she patted my hand. "I'm really glad that I finally have gotten the chance to meet you. Now that I'm going to live for longer than a few months, I'm really looking forward to seeing my son happy in life. I had thought, when I got that other diagnosis, that I was going to die before I could get the chance to see him truly fulfilled. It's so wonderful that that's no longer the case."

"Me too."

Just then, Margot's phone started to ring. She picked it up and she said a few words, and then mentioned that I was there. "Serena's here," she said. "I'll tell her, unless you'd like to tell her yourself."

She handed the phone to me. "I guess that Slade is held up somewhere. But I'm sure he'll be back soon."

I shook my head. I knew what "held up" meant in this situation. "No," I said aloud. "I need to talk to him." At that, I put the phone to my ear. "Hello?"

I took the phone into the other room, so that Margot couldn't hear me speaking. "Slade, what's happening? I need to see you right now."

"Things have changed," he simply said. "I'll explain it all later."

"Not later, now. Now, Slade. Malcolm told me some very distressing news."

"I have my reasons for doing this. Now, I don't know if I'm going to be a free man for much longer. I know that I'm springing this on you, but things have changed. My mother isn't dying now."

"I know that she's not, but what on earth does that fact have to do with anything at all? I'm missing something here, Slade. Please tell me what it is."

"It's a long story. One that I'll probably never tell you. All that I can say is that I'll go to my death protecting the ladies that I love. That's all that you need to know."

He was sounding so weird and so cryptic. I had no idea what he was talking about. How was his falling on his sword in Jordan's murder going to do anything to protect anyone at all?

"Okay. Listen, I'm coming into the office. That's where you're heading, isn't it?"

"No. I'm heading to the police station in Los Angeles. I'm heading there, and I'm almost there right now. You can't stop me from what I'm about to do, so don't even try."

No. No. No. Slade was going to confess to Jordan's murder.

And I had no idea why.

Chapter Ten

Slade - Present Day

I got to the police station. I had made an appointment with the lead detective on the case, Detective Hanson. I didn't want to do this. God knew I didn't want to do this. I knew what it was going to mean – that I was going to spend the rest of my life in prison for a murder that I didn't commit. But, at the same time, the events that have recently happened forced my hand on this.

It was all so simple before...Charlotte and I had our détente, and the status quo was serving both of us well. Then Michael died. He was pumped full of lead by some-body in his own organization. That sent my agreement with Charlotte off-kilter. She was emboldened, knowing that if I ever exposed her affair with Michael, she would have an easier way out of it, seeing that he was dead and couldn't corroborate my story anymore.

"Okay," Charlotte said when both of us found out what

had happened to Michael. "You don't have anything on me anymore. I really don't care if you tell the world that I had an affair with Michael. I'll just deny it, and now that he's dead, he won't be around to confirm your story." She crossed her arms. "And I'm finally calling your bluff about my abortion records. I don't think that you have them."

"What are you saying?"

"I'm saying that you're vulnerable again, so you better kiss my ass better than you've been doing. I'm tired of reading in the papers and tabloids about you and some piece of ass of the week. From now on, when I say 'jump', you're going to say 'how high?'"

I simply shook my head. "No. That's not how it's going to work. Listen Charlotte, we had an agreement, and that's that. I won't have you controlling my life."

She raised an eyebrow. "Oh? Listen Slade, it's not you that you're defending here. It's your mother. She's the one who is going to be in a lot of trouble, big trouble, when I go to the authorities with my tip about the disappearance of Hugh all those years ago."

I bit my lip, angry that I had let her trap me into this situation. But, she was absolutely right. I was going to have to kiss her ass, and kiss it often, if I ever hoped to make sure that the ghost of Hugh never rose up to threaten either me or my mom.

And that's how it was, for a few weeks.

At least that's how it was until Charlotte decided to get her ultimate revenge on me.

The Hugh thing wasn't good enough for her – the one person who would be most damaged from the Hugh inci-dent becoming known would be my mother. I would be too, because I helped cover up the homicide, but mom would be the one who would spend the rest of her life in prison, if not on death row.

No, Charlotte wanted something more.

So she framed me for murder. And there wasn't a damned thing that I could do about it.

Chapter Eleven

Serena - Present Day

After I got off the phone with Slade, I was absolutely frantic. He said that he was close to the police station in Los Angeles and that I wasn't going to be able to stop him from confessing. I was totally confused about why he was confessing and what that had to do with his mother's misdiagnosis. The puzzle pieces were jumbled up and I couldn't make sense of them at all.

Nevertheless, my instincts kicked in and I called Detective Hanson.

Thank god, he picked up on the third ring. "Detective Hanson," he said, answering the phone.

"Detective Hanson, this is Serena Roberts. I just saw you about Slade Bridgewell."

"Yes. Hello."

"Hello. Listen, Mr. Bridgewell is on his way to see you. I understand that he might be telling you things about the Jordan Harris case, but I want you to know that I don't want you to talk to him until his attorney can be there. I hope that this is perfectly clear."

"I understand but he was going to waive his right to counsel. I have a waiver prepared for him."

Think Serena, think. I knew the law in this area backwards and forwards, so there was just some case law that I was going to have to pull out of my ass before I could convince this man not to talk to Slade when he comes in.

"He can't waive his right to counsel when he already has counsel on retainer. One of us has to be present when he gives his confession and that person is going to be me. I'll be there in about two hours. I know that he'll be there sooner than that but I need for you to tell him that you won't talk to him until I'm there."

I took a deep breath, not really knowing if what I was saying was correct. The nuances of the "right to counsel" were deep and esoteric, and I was going to have to pull up case law to find out if what I was saying was correct. Yes, a person in custody has the right to waive his right to counsel, but if that person is already being actively represented by counsel? I would think that this would be a different story.

I would think that would be the case. But I didn't really know for sure, and I didn't have time to pull up case law to find out. I just hoped that Detective Hanson believed me when I told him this.

"Okay," Detective Hanson finally said. I could tell that he was disappointed, and well he should be. He was about to reel in the huge fish and I was clearly thwarting it. "I'll detain him when he gets here, but I won't talk to him about the case until you're here as well."

"Good." I let out a sigh of relief. I then turned to Margot. "It's been a pleasure meeting you, a real pleasure.

Unfortunately, I have to run. Um, hopefully we'll have dinner or something when this is all over?"

"Yes, I would like that." She came over to me and gave me a tentative hug. "You're just as pretty as how Slade describes you. I think that he's found a keeper."

I smiled. She was a sweet woman and I found myself grateful that she wasn't dying after all. Slade had to have been ecstatic to find that out – I knew how much he cared for his mom.

Now, I just had to find out what the hell was going on. And I needed to find that out quickly.

I broke the speed barrier getting up to LA. I didn't take the leisurely route of the PCH – I took the highway the whole way. I even had a "secret weapon" that I only brought out when things were desperate – a blow-up doll to put in my passenger seat. I needed to be able to drive in the carpool lane as much as I possibly could because that lane wasn't usually crowded. I hated doing that because I knew how important the carpool lane was to the state of California – it was used as a carrot to encourage people to save on gasoline by pooling with their buddies to work, and I was simply abusing the privilege. Nonetheless, desperate times called for desperate measures and this would certainly qualify as a "desperate time."

I got stuck in traffic quagmires along the way and I usually was able to get around them by getting into the carpool lane. There were a few times, however, that I got stuck and I was really and truly stuck. When that happened, I would take the shoulder and get off at the nearest exit, and then immediately got right back on the highway. I had to do this several different times, and this little cheat shaved another good half hour off of my drive up to Los Angeles.

All I could think of, the entire time I was behind that wheel was Slade. Was the detective really going to hold him there, or did he get some legal advice that said that Slade didn't need his attorney there? I knew one thing – if there was a way for this detective to take Slade's "confession" without counsel being there, he would have. That would be the biggest fish that could possibly be landed. Ever.

I finally got close to the police station, only to find out that the media had evidently been tipped off on what was happening. There were throngs of reporters on the police headquarters steps, and, I as I stepped next to a man with a microphone, I could hear what he was telling his television audience. "We're outside of the Los Angeles police department where the reports are that Slade Bridgewell will be offering a confession to the murder of his business partner, Jordan Harris. Mr. Bridgewell is inside the police headquarters right now speaking with the detective on this case. We will bring you the entire story when Mr. Bridgewell emerges."

I bent my head, hoping that nobody would notice me. Unfortunately, somebody did. "Ms. Roberts," an eager blonde woman reporter said, thrusting a microphone in my face. "You're the attorney for Mr. Bridgewell. Do you care to comment on the story? I understand that Mr. Bridgewell is set to confess to the murder of Mr. Harris."

I shook my head. "No comment." I shoved other reporters aside as they all, one by one, tried to put a microphone in my face. They didn't touch me, of course, because I would have hauled off and hit anyone who put a hand on me. And then I would have marched into the police station to report whoever had the gall to touch me.

I was in no mood for any bullshit.

I finally got up the steps and entered the station. I gave my name to the receptionist, telling her that I needed to see the detective right away. "My client is back there, so I have to make sure that I get there before anything happens."

"Yes, ma'am," the woman said, and she called on the phone. "Go on back. He said that you know where his office is," she told me as she hung up the phone.

"Thanks," I told her, as I went back to Detective Hanson's office.

I got there, and I saw that Slade was sitting in a chair. He saw me, and the look in his eyes...I shuddered. He was angry, very angry, and there was no hiding it. I knew that there was going to be hell to pay for this, but, no matter. If I stopped him from telling the detective anything, then his anger will have been worth it.

"Detective Hanson," I said, extending my hand to him. He shook it. "Thanks for waiting for me." I looked over at Slade, who wasn't meeting my eyes. "And you did wait for me, didn't you?"

"Yes," he said, and I breathed a sigh of absolute relief. "I told you I would. Now, I suppose you would like a chance to have a word with your client, so if you would like to have some privacy, I can direct you to a room."

"This room doesn't have a two-way mirror, does it?"

"No. This room will be completely private."

"Okay."

At that, the detective led Slade and me to a small room with nothing in it but a table and four chairs. I took a seat and Slade sat across from me. The detective left the room, and Slade and I just sat there in silence staring at one another.

He narrowed his eyes. "You shouldn't have come."

"I know. But I did. I had to stop you."

"You can't stop me. I understand why you're here, but you don't really understand why I'm here. And you don't understand because I can't really tell you."

I drew a breath. "Please stop. Stop with the games, stop with the cryptic hints. Just tell me, straight and narrow, why you want to confess to a murder that you clearly didn't do."

"I can't. If I told you why, then you would have something on me. The fewer people who know what I did, the better. So, that means that only I, my mother, and Charlotte know. And that's how it's going to stay."

I felt like strangling him when he was talking to me like that. What the hell was he talking about? "I don't understand."

"I know that you don't understand. I do. But, believe me, I know what I'm doing, and I have to do it. I have to, and you can't stop me. You made a trip all the way up here for nothing, really. You've accomplished nothing."

I felt hot tears coming to my eyes. "No. I refuse to accept that you're going to do this. Not when I know…" I stopped short. Was I ready to tell him what I knew about Jordan's murder? That Malcolm did it? I just had to find out a way to prove that Malcolm did it.

"Not when you know what?"

I took a deep breath. "I know who did it."

Then I looked at his face, and I knew.

There was no mistaking his expression.

Slade knew who did it too.

Chapter Twelve

Slade - Approximately Two Weeks Earlier

I was in the hospital with my mother. I had to be by her side while she went through the battery of tests. It was important that I was there to try to help her battle this cancer the best that she could. My phone was turned off because I didn't want to be distracted by the press, which was constantly calling me, or by Serena. I was upset with her, because she was always going against my wishes, and she had no idea who she was messing with. No clue. She was going to end up dead, and I couldn't live with myself if that happened.

I finally brought myself to turn my phone on, and I decided to track Serena. I hated that I was so obsessed with what she was doing and where she was going, but I couldn't help it. I knew that it was only a matter of time before Charlotte got to her, and that was why I felt that I always had to know where she was.

To my dismay, her phone showed that she was in Los Angeles and that she had been there for the past three days.

I shook my head, feeling upset with myself for not being more diligent with Serena's whereabouts. "Mom, I have to go," I told her.

She looked hurt, but I knew that I had to get going. Now. Serena had been in Los Angeles for three days. God knew what was going to happen. God knew what had already happened. "Okay, Slade. But I'm supposed to get the new test results back any moment. I'm very scared. I hope that the original diagnosis was wrong, but what if it's not?"

I put my arm around her. "Mom, I know what you're going through. But there's somebody that I care for very much, and she's in trouble. I have to go to her and make sure she's okay. I'll be back as soon as I can, but it might not be for a few days."

We said our goodbyes and I hopped in my car. I drove like a bat out of hell to Charlotte's house.

I got to her house and I walked right in. "Charlotte," I said to her. "Serena's here. I need to see her. I need to get her out." I dispensed with the niceties, of course, because I just wanted to get to what I wanted. I had to negotiate for Serena's release, of course, and I didn't know exactly what Charlotte was going to extract from me.

"She is here. Yes, she is. She's resting comfortably."

"Okay then, I want to see her. I want to see her this very second."

"You can't." She raised an eyebrow and her goons moved closer to me. I had come to her house packing, of course, but even I was going to have problems getting what I wanted from Charlotte. This wasn't the movies where the hero kicks ass in all kinds of unrealistic ways. The reality of this situation was that I was one man and there were three goons in the room, all of whom were at least 6'4" and 225 lbs of muscle. Those were the stats for the smallest guy in this room. They were all packing too. If I was a crazy person, I would have tried to take the three goons on. But, I wasn't a crazy person, so I was going to try to negotiate my way out of this problem.

"Okay, what do you want?"

Charlotte crossed her arms. "As I see it, I finally have the upper hand with you. Maybe I have your attention? I hope so, for your sake."

"You certainly do have my attention." I tried not to lunge at her. She was holding Serena hostage and who knew what kind of shape Serena was going to be in once I finally got to her? Who knows if she would even be alive? I was going to have to find Charlotte's sweet spot, what would finally get her to set Serena free, and I had to find it soon.

Charlotte crossed her arms. "Okay, here is how I see things right now. Your mother is dying, so you're now willing to go to the authorities about Hugh. Is that right?"

"Yes. And, when I do, that takes your bargaining chip off of the table. All I would have to do would be give my copy of the videotape of the murder to the right person, and you and Malcolm will be going away for a long, long time."

Charlotte just smiled. "Well, then, I think that you know what I want. If you give it to me, then you'll get Serena out of that hole. If you don't, well, then, let me just tell you that she's been in the hole without food or water for almost three days. I don't think that she'll last much longer."

I took a deep breath. There wasn't much time to think, let alone make a decision such as this one. What I did know was that Serena was going to be safe. No matter what, that was the first thing on my mind. "So, if I agree to take the fall for Jordan's murder, you'll let Serena out? And you'll never bother her again?"

"Yes, that's what I'm saying. If you agree to confess to killing Jordan, and plead guilty to his murder, then I'll not only let Serena go free, you have my word that I won't touch a hair on her head. If you don't agree to do that, then I won't let her free, and she'll die in that hole. If you agree to that, and don't hold up your end of the bargain, then Serena will continue to be in danger." She smiled at me, an evil smile. "It's entirely your choice."

I hung my head. Charlotte was leaving me no choice, really. She said that I had a choice, but that was wrong. If I wanted to have Serena as a girlfriend, then I had to do this. I would be leaving her behind when I went to prison, and I doubted that she would stick with me. But that was okay – as long as she was safe, and she continued to be safe, my sacrifice would be worth it.

"Okay, I agree. Now, please, let me get her and take her home."

She rolled her eyes. "I don't think that you would have ever done something like this for me."

I didn't want to antagonize her, which I knew I would do if I would have agreed with her when she said that, so I bit my lip and said nothing. She was absolutely right, though – I never would have even thought about doing something like that to protect her. Never in a million years. Serena was special, and I was willing to do just about anything to ensure her safety.

"Okay, then, go and get her. Get her out of the hole, and I expect you to be pleading guilty to Jordan's murder within the month. If you don't, then I'll go to Plan B. You might bring me down, Slade, by giving that videotape to the right hands, but I'll bring you down as well. And Serena, too. You're not in a position to bargain, so don't even try."

At that, I followed one of the goons to a room. He opened the door, and there was Serena. Her skin was cold and clammy, and she was shaking all over. She looked at me, but it was as if she wasn't seeing me. I knew that I had gotten to her just in time.

She was safe. Now, I had to do what I had to do. I was going to spend the rest of my life in prison, but at least she was safe.

That was really all that mattered.

Chapter Thirteen

Serena - Present Day

"Goddammit. You know. You know who did it, and you've known all along. Am I right? Am I?"

"Serena. You don't understand."

"You're damned right I don't understand. Help me to understand, Slade. Why?" I was furious. "Why would you do this?"

He just shook his head. "It goes back to something that happened a long time ago. And now I have to take my lumps to protect my mother - and to protect you. Just know that this is the reason why I'm doing this. It's the only reason why. If I don't, then both you and my mom will be vulnerable, and quite frankly, I can't let that happen."

I rapidly shook my head feeling that I was going down the looking-glass. "What does this have to do with my safety or the safety of Margot?"

"If I told you, then you both would be in danger. Just leave it at that and let me do what I'm going to do. You really have no choice, Serena. You can go in with me to talk to the Detective, but I'm going to tell him what I need to tell him. Whether or not you're in the room is up to you, but it's not going to change the course of events."

I pounded my hand on the table in frustration. "Slade, I know that…"

"Shhhh. You're going to tell me that somebody that you know, somebody that you know well, did it. I can see it in your eyes that you know. I've seen that look in your eyes for awhile now. That's great that you know. I'm glad that you know. But life isn't always fair, and he won't get his comeuppance. I'm taking it for him."

I pointed at him. "This isn't over. Even if you confess, I'll get it thrown out. I'll get it thrown out, and I'll discredit it on the stand. Once I figure out exactly why you're doing this, I'll be able to discredit this whole interrogation."

Slade shook his head. "You don't get it, do you? Do you? Let me break it down for you – there isn't going to be a trial. I'm going to plead guilty. You know as well as I do that there will be no coming back from that. Once I plead guilty, the deed is done. You can't appeal. There will be nothing that you can do to stop me from going to prison. Nothing. So, just quit. Today I talk to the Detective and early this week, I'll be in court giving the judge my plea bargain."

"No. I won't let you. I won't -"

He took my hands and kissed them lightly. "Serena, the only reason why I was allowed bail is because my bond hearing attorney convinced the judge that there was a good amount of reasonable doubt that I did this murder. Once I confess, that reasonable doubt will be gone. I would imagine that I'll be remanded to the county jail immediately after I give this confession, and I would imagine that my bond will be revoked. So, this might be the last time, in a long time, that you and I can be alone like this."

I felt hot tears stream down my face. It wasn't supposed to be like this. I was going to be the hero who found a way to bring down Malcolm, and Slade was going to be eternally grateful to me. How did we get here? Why were we here?

"Slade, you need to talk to me. Tell me what's going on."

"No." He moved over next to me and took me in his arms. "I won't tell you what's going on. I'm sorry. But Serena, I need to feel your soft skin one last time." He buried his face in my shoulder and I put my hands behind his head.

I could feel my heart pounding, just like it always did whenever Slade touched me. But it wasn't pounding with desire. It was pounding with fear and utter helplessness. There had to be a way around this, but what was it?

"You're scared," he said. "Maybe we can use this to our advantage." He raised his eyebrows and brought me closer to him. "That Detective might come in here at any moment, too. We should probably make this quick, although I would love to give it to you slow. Hard and slow."

I tried to hold back the tears that were threatening, but, in spite of the situation that we were in, I found myself becoming more and more aroused by Slade's suggestions. I found myself involuntarily spreading my legs as I sat in my chair.

"Slade," I whispered, "we can't do this. Not here. That detective is going to come in at any moment. He has a key."

Slade just got up and checked and made sure that the door was locked. "So what? If he comes in, he comes in. I have to be inside of you, and I have to feel my skin against yours. You can't deny me, Serena. You can't deny me because I won't let you."

His will was so strong, and I tried to show that my will was just as strong. Yet, I couldn't. My netherparts were filling up with blood as he spoke to me, and I knew that it didn't matter that we were probably going to be caught. The only thing that mattered at that point was that Slade was possibly going to be going to jail in a matter of hours, and I would always regret not making love to him before he went away. I knew the drill, too – he wouldn't have a bond if he were thrown into jail, and he probably would never see the outside world again. That would devastate me beyond measure, and I didn't think that I would ever recover from losing him.

Slade put me up on the table and spread my legs. His strong hand stroked the top of my thigh, and his lips met mine desperately. I let out an audible breath as I gripped the side of the table. His hands went from my inner thighs to my clit and he tickled it lightly. I wasn't wearing hose, and my panties were light and thong-style. I soon felt his warm tongue lightly grazing my opening while his fingers played inside me. I groaned, feeling my ecstasy growing with each stroke of his talented mouth and fingers.

His strokes were long and slow and tender. That was just how I liked it, and he knew that. I soon felt myself burst so that I wanted to cry out , but I bit my hand instead. It was all that I could do to keep quiet, though. The last thing that I wanted was for that Detective to come in and see what we were doing.

His tongue traveled from my clit to my waist, as he casually unbuttoned my blouse, which he did slowly and deliberately. Despite the desperate situation, there was no hurry to what he was doing. It was almost as if he had all the time in the world. I was trying to capture that moment, trying to bottle it and keep it with me always. If I never saw Slade again in the outside world, I needed to always remember that moment forever.

My bra was next, as he casually unhooked it and licked and sucked on each of my nipples. I reared back my head, as I felt my breathing coming faster and faster. My heart was pounding, and every single one of the hairs on my body were standing to attention. He was still fully clothed, and I still had on my skirt and my high heels, but my blouse was off, as was my bra. His tongue was traveling from my clavicle to my neck, and he bit and sucked it lightly as his hands explored my waist and traveled down to my clit once more. He firmly put his thumb and forefinger on my clit and swirled, while he put another finger inside of me. Once again, I wanted to cry out. I was desperate to cry out. The fact that I couldn't make a sound, when every fiber of my being wanted to, was painful for me. It was so painful that it made me even more aroused, and I bit my tongue.

"Slade," I began, wanting to tell him that I was afraid that the Detective would come in at any moment.

He put his hand over my mouth. "Don't say it. I know what you're thinking, but don't say it. I'm not nearly done with you, so Detective Branson is just going to have to cool his heels. I want to make this last, because who knows if we'll ever get the chance to do this again?"

I nodded my head and said nothing. I was, as ever, a prisoner to his will. I couldn't ever deny Slade, and I really couldn't at that moment. He was too powerful, too strong, and I wanted him to completely control me. I bit my lower lip, not wanting to be punished later for giving him backtalk, yet hoping that I would get the chance for just such a punishment.

"I don't have a condom on me,"he whispered. "I want to take a chance."

I nodded my head, unable to say a word. I was on birth control pills, but I had forgotten to take one of them that month, so I was unsure whether not using a condom was a prudent idea or not. No matter, I wanted him so desperately at that point, I pushed the thought of an accidental pregnancy far out of my mind. "I want you to take a chance, too," I said, feeling that we were playing Russian Roulette, yet not caring one bit that we were.

He unbuckled his pants, springing his glorious and huge cock out with one move. I sighed as I saw it, knowing what was going to come next. He jerked my legs towards him, and spread them wide. His cock was getting ever closer to me, but it was teasing me, because he put the tip into my opening and immediately took it back out.

"Just a taste," he said. "Just a taste to whet your appetite for me. I'll be making you want to scream, but I don't want you to even know what is coming."

I didn't know what he was talking about, but I soon found out. He took off his belt and wrapped it around my eyes. He secured the belt tightly around my head, so tight that it hurt, and I knew that giving me pain was deliberate on his part.

If I doubted that causing me pain was deliberate, I had my suspicions soon confirmed to me when he said "how does that feel? Is it painful for you?"

I shook my head, and he tightened the belt even more. "How about now?"

I had to admit, my temples were throbbing because that belt was so tight, and I nodded my head. It felt exquisite to have that belt around my eyes, because it hurt, but, more than that, I had no idea what to expect from him. I couldn't see a thing, so I was completely at his mercy.

What came next was him taking off my belt that was around my skirt. My hands were around his neck, and he gently forced them off his neck and put them in front of me. He wrapped my belt around my wrists and secured them, and then leaned me back on the desk. He lay down on top of me and forced my hands above my head while he kissed my breasts and torso lightly.

Because I couldn't see a thing, my senses were heightened. The back of my mind was terrified of hearing the door opening, yet that fear only served to make what Slade was doing that much more powerful. My sense of smell was also heightened, and Slade's scent – musky, sweet, and spicy – filled my olfactory and added to the ecstasy that I was feeling. I was anticipating his cock plunging inside of me, and I was aching for it by then.

I bit my lip, and Slade's finger touched my mouth. "Serena, you need to know that I'm in love with you. I don't ever want to leave you. You need to remember that and remember this moment in the future. I need you to never forget what this feels like with me. I want you to touch yourself right now, so that when you touch yourself tomorrow or the next night or the next night after that, you will automatically think about how this felt with me right at this moment."

I tried not to think of the implications of what he was saying. This was possibly the last time we could be together, and he wanted me to always think of it whenever I was touching myself in my bed late at night. I knew that I would be, and, if the very worst thing happened, I knew that I could never bring myself to orgasm without thinking about this time with him.

He ran his fingers through my hair, tangling them and pulling the strands. That caused me to finally try to cry out, but he put his hand over my mouth again. "Quiet, Serena. You can't make a sound. If you do, there will be hell to pay the next time I make love to you like this."

I felt sorrowful knowing that there probably wouldn't be a next time, but I stifled my cry anyways. "Please give it to me, Slade," I pleaded. "I'm dying for it now."

"Are you? How much are you dying for it?"

I couldn't express how much I was desperate for his hard cock to be inside of me. There were no words at that point. "There are no words."

"Tell me."

"If you don't give it to me within the next few seconds, I think that I'm going to go completely crazy."

"Good. That's what I wanted to hear. I want you begging for it."

"Please."

"That's not good enough."

"Slade you have to give it to me right now."

He kissed me lightly, and then his kisses got more urgent, passionate and desperate. I could almost feel how much he wanted to be inside of me right at that moment, and that it took every ounce of his willpower to hold back on me. He stroked my cheek and kissed my forehead and brought me closer to him. "Okay, Serena, I'm going to give it you, slowly, so that you need to scream. But I won't let you scream." He apparently pulled a silk handkerchief out of the pocket of his jacket, and then he tied it around my mouth. My heart quickened, knowing that I was completely at his mercy and I was helpless to do anything at all.

As his enormous manhood entered me, I thought that I was going to pass out. I was so ready for this – my entire body was tingling and on fire, and my netherparts felt like they were so engorged with blood that they were painful. His cock eased that particular pain and replaced it with pure unadulterated ecstasy.

He stroked in an out languidly, but it was enough for me to feel that I wanted to explode. I couldn't do anything, though – I couldn't cry, I couldn't see, and I couldn't move. Somehow, though, the fact that I was helpless only served to heighten all my senses all the more, which made my pleasure sensors go on overload. As these sensors went into overdrive, I could feel the endorphins coursing throughout my entire body. I didn't have an outlet to get my emotions out, though, so these wonderful feelings had no place to go. My breathing started to get heavier and heavier, and, finally, I felt the orgasm that was threatening to release itself build inside of me and burst like it never had before.

Slade kissed me with his devouring lips, and I tried to put my bound wrists behind his head, but he took his hands and raised mine above my own head instead. "Tell me what you want," he whispered.

I want you. I want you to be with me forever. That means that I need you to not do what you're about to do. "You," I said weakly.

"You have me."

"Forever."

"I can't give that to you." His voice was regretful and sorrowful. He sighed as his mighty cock exploded inside of me. "I'm sorry Serena."

In spite of myself, I felt a hot tear soak the leather belt that was still wrapped around my eyes. He loosened the belt around my wrists and took off the blindfold and the gag. "I want forever with you too," he said softly. "But we can't always get what we want."

I looked him right in the eyes. I closed my own eyes and

felt the love, passion and regret that was roiling beneath his careful façade. To the outside world, it seemed as if Slade didn't really care that he was doing this. He didn't care that he was going to spend the rest of his life in prison for something that he didn't do, and that he would be leaving me in the process. When I felt his emotions, though, I knew better. He did care. He cared very much. I felt his despair in my bones, and I felt yet another tear come down my cheek.

He lowered his head. "I need to go now and speak with Detective Hanson."

"No," I said. "You can't do this."

"I have to do this. I have to. I'm sorry, but I have no choice."

I felt myself coming down, back to earth. Back to reality, which was that Slade and I were in a tiny room, and that Slade was about to do something that would inalterably change the rest of our lives. He was about to take himself away from me forever. He was about to commit himself to living in a tiny cell throughout the rest of his days. I couldn't stomach that. I couldn't fathom it. It was too horrible and too surreal.

He handed me my blouse, bra and panties without a word. I took them, but I tried to make him look me in the eye. He couldn't. His pained expression was facing the window, and, when I closed my eyes, I knew that he couldn't feel more depressed than he did right at that moment.

"Thank you for making these moments special," he said. "I'll never forget this."

"I need to go in there and speak with the detective with you, and I really need for you to change your mind." I felt tears coming to my eyes. "I can't lose you." My voice was small, pathetic, pleading. I felt like my soul was being ripped completely in two.

He held me, his strong fingers gently combing through my hair. "Serena, I don't want this. I don't want to lose you, either. I think that losing you would be even more devastating to me than doing time. But I wish that you could understand that it's either I do this, or I lose you for real."

"I don't understand, although I do think that this whole thing has something to do with Charlotte."

I knew when I looked at him and saw his expression after I said that the whole thing has to do with Charlotte, that I was right. It *did* have to do with Charlotte. But how? Why? What, exactly, was going on?

"It's complicated." Slade just stated the obvious.

"If Charlotte is blackmailing you, then we can fight this. We can."

He shook his head. "You're so naïve sometimes. It's strange – you're so worldly and sophisticated in some ways, and in others…well, I hope that I don't offend you when I say this, but there are ways that I can tell that you're the daughter of a fisherman. And that you're from a small town. You didn't grow up in a rough environment where people aren't always good or kind-hearted. You don't know how black some people can be. How soulless. How some people will absolutely rip you to pieces just because of who you are."

I bristled when he said those things. He didn't know what I had gone through. He knew about my mother being murdered, and that really should have been enough for him to realize that I wasn't as sheltered as he might have thought. He didn't know the other things that made me the way that I was. He has no idea, no clue, the depth of my pain. Yet, he was going to add to it.

I had no idea myself what was at stake here, but what I did know was that I was willing to sacrifice anything to make sure he stayed out of prison. He didn't belong there, and he was clearly about to confess to that murder because of something that was going on between Charlotte, him, and me. If my life was somehow on the line because of Charlotte, so be it. I wasn't going to let him die so that I should live.

Slade continued on. "I read a book when I was in high school. It was called *The President.* It was about a dictator in Central America who was unbelievably cruel. He put one of his political enemies into a prison where there was no light, no heat or air conditioning, so the box was sweltering in the heat and freezing in the cold. This dictator put this man in this prison for no good reason, really. This man was a good man. That's how Charlotte will treat you. You've done nothing to her, but she'll have you tortured and killed just the same. She won't even bat an eyelash about it. I simply can't let that happen."

"Slade, you're not making sense. What does any of this have to do with Charlotte or me?"

He sighed. "I guess that I have to trust you with my deepest, darkest secret. Maybe then you can understand why I'm doing this and why I have to go through with it."

I let out a breath. Slade was finally ready to open up.

Then maybe I could do the same.

Chapter Fourteen

Slade's eyes got slightly misty, which was something that I didn't expect to ever see from him, when he started telling me the story of how it was he got to where he was going to confess to a murder that he didn't commit. "It all started about ten years ago. Charlotte and I were dating from the time we were both around sixteen. I wasn't serious about her, but she clearly was about me. But I had other things on my mind – namely, getting my PhD at a young age so that I could make the kind of money that I needed to make to support myself and my mom. It was very important that I could take care of my mom, because she was a felon, so she couldn't get a decent job anywhere. She pretty much worked maid service jobs at sleazy motels, which didn't pay her enough to eat. So, I was very focused, laser focused, on getting ahead so that I could support her."

I smiled and played with his hair. "Well, you certainly did accomplish that."

"Yes, I did. And I have made sure that all my wealth is tied up in trusts and other entities so that a felony conviction won't do anything to my assets. Even if a wrongful death lawsuit is filed against me by Jordan's widow, most of my wealth won't be touched. But that's neither here nor there."

I was quiet, wanting him to keep telling me his story. He continued.

"Long story short, something happened. I still can't tell you what that something is, because it would clearly implicate somebody who I care very much about. I can never take the chance that you or anybody else knows about this. But suffice to say, Charlotte knows about this incident. And she and I had an understanding for a long time that Charlotte wouldn't say anything to anyone about this incident, because I had something on her as well. That's the best way to get somebody to keep a secret — you find something to blackmail them with. I'm not proud of doing that, of course, but with Charlotte, I needed an insurance policy. If it was just me whose ass was on the line, I probably wouldn't care as much. But it wasn't just my ass, it was…."

I knew who he was protecting. It was his mother. He didn't have to tell me that. What she did, I had no idea. But it was pretty clear that his mom was the only person in Slade's life who he would go to the bat for. And, apparently, me.

"Things were going fine until, well, Michael Garancino was killed. After that happened, Charlotte started making noises about going to the authorities about the incident."

I was holding my breath. The puzzle pieces were about to fit together and I was excited to know, yet dreading it all at the same time. *Okay, Michael has something to do with this.* I had to admit that I still felt completely in the dark, but I knew that Slade would clear up everything to the best of his ability.

"Okay. Well, here's where it all gets complicated. Charlotte decided that she really wanted me to pay for not being what she wanted, which was a husband. She has always wanted to marry me, and I haven't been interested in her romantically for quite awhile. So, she had Jordan killed and framed me. But I had the ace in the hole – I have the video portion where the killer attacked Jordan, and it clearly shows somebody who is not me. In fact, you can see this person's face on the video."

I blinked my eyes. This was HUGE. I started to feel excited when Slade was talking to me.

"Oh my god. I could kill you for not telling me about this videotape, but that's the best piece of news I have ever heard. You can clearly get out of the murder charge now, and the right person is going to go down for it."

I couldn't contain my joy when he told me about the videotape.

He breathed in. "No. I told Charlotte that I would take the blame for Jordan's murder, because she told me that if I didn't…" He shook his head. "Okay, let me just tell you that this whole sorry affair has to do with my mother. And me, but mainly her. Charlotte told me that if I didn't take the blame for Jordan's murder that she would turn in my mother. And, quite frankly, I couldn't see that happen. Charlotte had my balls in a jar, and she has for all these years because I was stupid and brought Charlotte along to see my mother when I knew that my mother was in trouble. Charlotte knows about what I did, but more importantly, she knows what my mother did."

My head was starting to hurt. I had heard of people who were selfless, but I had never heard of something quite like this. He was willing to go to prison to protect his mother? He was really an amazing guy.

"Anyhow, when my mother was diagnosed, I thought

that she didn't have much time left. At that time, I went to work another deal with Charlotte. I was going to confess to my role in the incident with my mother, which would take Charlotte's chip off the table. Then I would have been able to go take that videotape of Jordan's murder to the authorities and my name would be cleared."

Things were getting closer and I found myself breathing harder and harder as I waited for the end of the story.

He hung his head. "I play Charlotte's game well, but not well enough. If I could, I would have done everything differently. Mainly, I wouldn't tell her what I was going to do. I just would have done it. Anyhow, after I told Charlotte what I was going to do, she kidnapped you. When I finally got to you, I knew that it was a matter of time before you couldn't hang on any longer. People can't go for days and days without water and it was really hot that week, so I knew that you probably were near death in that hole."

Ah, finally it was all becoming clear. "You told Charlotte that you would confess to this murder if she let me go, didn't you?"

He nodded imperceptibly. "Yes. And, as it turns out, I wouldn't have been able to go to the authorities about the incident with my mother, because, as you probably know, she's not actually dying. She was misdiagnosed. So, her recovering put the kibosh on my ever telling the authorities what I did, so Charlotte has me by the balls in two different ways. If I don't confess to this murder, she'll have you killed. She told me this, and I'm not fucking with her. Plus, she'll possibly go to the authorities about what my mother did ten years ago."

I closed my eyes.

I suddenly knew exactly what to do.

"Slade, I love you for doing this to protect me, but you have to know that I can't allow you to do this."

His eyes flashed with anger. "You have to let me do this. I don't know what you have up your sleeve, but I'm warning you to back off. Back off, or else."

I opened my mouth to protest, but, just then, there was a knock on the door. "Hey, you two. I'm just about ready to pop off for lunch, so you, Mr. Bridgewell, not to put too fine a point on it, but you gotta shit or get off the pot here."

Slade started to leave, but I clutched his sleeve. I gripped him hard, because I refused to give up on this. "Slade, don't. Please don't."

He just jerked his arm away from me and followed Detective Branson to his office.

Chapter Fifteen

Slade - Present Day

I followed Detective Branson into his office. Serena was right behind me. There were tears in her eyes, and I felt awful. Truth be told, leaving her was killing me. It was killing me more than anything else. Yes, I was going to spend the rest of my life in prison. Because I was pleading guilty, the death penalty would be off the table. Malcolm assured me of this. So, that was the silver lining.

As I sat across from the detective, I looked over at Serena. She wasn't looking at me, but I could see in her eyes that she was a fighter. She wasn't going to let this whole thing go down peacefully. I tried to give her a warning look, but I couldn't catch her eye.

I loved her. I loved her from the first time I saw her. That was why I had to try to stop her from doing whatever she could to get me out of this. It was a battle of wills with her, always. That was part of why I was in love with her. She wasn't a shrinking violet, and she wasn't somebody who was going to be ordered around. She also had a very strong ethical compass, and she knew how unjust this all was.

I just hoped that she didn't have something up her sleeve. Knowing her though, she did. She was formulating a plan to make sure none of this happened the way that I needed it to.

"Okay, let's begin," Detective Hanson said. "Tell me in your own words what happened to Jordan Harris the night of May 10 of this year."

Serena gripped my hand and I was able to make eye contact with her. She looked haunted and pale. She seemed as if she had given up, but I knew better. "Mr. Bridgewell, I want to be on record here. I want to be on record that you are doing this against legal counsel," she said.

I nodded my head. "I understand. Well, Detective Hanson, on that night, Jordan and I had words. Jordan had been erratic all that week – he stayed up 24 hours a day and he seemed to be very much in the throes of a manic episode. I have some experience with that, so I know what signs to look for. He might have also been doing drugs during this period, as Jordan was known to have a problem with substance abuse."

Detective Hanson took a donut out of a cardboard box and poured himself a glass of milk while he listened to us. He offered both of us a donut but we both turned it down. I knew that I couldn't possibly think about eating at that point and I doubted that Serena could either.

"Okay, so you went to the lab that evening. Did you have the baseball bat with you?"

"No. We kept the baseball bat in the lab, just in case somebody broke in. We also keep a firearm in that lab, but the reason why we have a baseball bat is to protect us and our inventions without resorting to lethal force."

Detective Hanson was busy scribbling words down on a pad of paper and he looked up at me. "Go on. You got to the lab, there was already a baseball bat there, and you had words with Jordan. What kind of words?"

"Heated words. I was trying to talk some sense into him because the Board of Directors had been breathing down my neck to rein him in. They all knew how brilliant Jordan was, but they also knew that he was dangerous in many ways."

So far, I thought that Slade was speaking the truth. It had to have been so difficult to see his friend going through all of that.

"Can you be more specific about your words to him?"

Slade looked down at the desk and I closed my eyes and felt the guilt and the sadness pour out of him. "Um, I don't want to bring these memories up. You know how people get when they're really angry. They start to say things that they don't mean. Things that never should be said. I'm sure you've been there."

Detective Hanson nodded his head. "We've all been there."

Slade took a deep breath. "I told him that he was a waste of space and breath. That the world would be a better place if he weren't in it." He shook his head. "I was unbelievably angry. My patience with him and his issues had long since run out, and all that I could feel for him was contempt at that point. I'm not proud of how I spoke with him of course, but it is what it is."

Detective Hanson was looking at Slade with keen interest. "So, you told Jordan that he would be better off dead, and that the world would be as well?"

"Yes. That's what I told him. He gave it back to me as

good as he got though. Of course he did – he was high as a kite that evening. And…"

Slade looked at me with sorrow. I could tell that he was going to come out with something that he had previously lied about.

I wasn't disappointed. "Jordan was developing a testosterone pill. It would be something that athletes and body builders could take that would replace typical steroids. Jordan was perfecting it, and it was almost ready to come to market. He said that it would revolutionize the world, not just because it was good for athletic performance, but also because it would do amazing things for men who are going through andropause. The only problem with this pill was that Jordan tended to become belligerent when he took too much of it, and it makes him stronger than usual."

I looked at Slade and knew that he was telling me the truth. I had specifically asked him if Jordan was developing a testosterone pill that made Slade nervous for Jordan, and Slade had told me a definitive "no." Yet, he was now telling Detective Hanson that just such a pill was in the works.

Slade took a deep breath, and then told the lie about how Jordan was killed. "We had words, and Jordan started to charge me. I saw in his eyes that he was dangerous. You can see a look in a man's eyes, a look that tells you that he's outer limits and is capable of anything. So, I picked up the baseball bat when I saw him coming at me, and I swung at him."

"You swung the bat and you hit him, correct?" Detective Hanson asked.

"Correct."

Detective Hanson continued to jot down notes. "Okay. According to the report generated by one of the officers on the scene, Officer Petty, the victim had been bludgeoned with at least 10 blows. What happened after the first swing of the bat?"

Slade looked at the ceiling. This was horrible for him to have to talk about and I felt for him, and was angry with Charlotte at the same time. I felt tears coming to my eyes, but I vowed to do anything possible to keep him from actually entering the guilty plea on this case. Once he entered the plea of guilty, the case would end. There would be no appeals, and Slade would be stuck in prison for the rest of his life.

That wasn't going to happen.

Slade continued. "After that first swing, he didn't go down. It didn't even seem to affect him. It was like a bad fifties sci-fi movie, where there's a monster that's charging and no bullets seem to affect it. Jordan was like that, so I kept swinging and swinging and swinging until he was finally on the ground."

Detective Hanson was looking at something and I saw that it was the toxicology report for Jordan. "I'm listening. I was just looking at the tox report to see if Jordan had anything in his system that would create the superhuman strength. It does say that he had increased testosterone in his blood stream, along with cocaine and Oxycodone." He made a bridge with his hands as he listened to Slade. "These drugs in his system could have caused him to act the way that you said he acted. The cocaine and enhanced testosterone could certainly cause rage, and the Oxy would cause him to have a very high pain threshold."

Slade nodded imperceptibly. I saw on his face that he was suffering because of this. It was unavoidable. I knew that he was lying about killing Jordan, and that made me feel horrible. I reached over to pat his hand, but tried to do it discreetly. I didn't necessarily want Detective Hanson to know how I felt about Slade. Not that he would care, because it wasn't his business, but I still felt weird about it.

"So Jordan was in an altered state, and he was about to attack you when you got the baseball bat and starting to hit him. It certainly sounds like you have a case for self-defense." He looked at his notes again. "Why didn't you tell Officer Hyatt, your interrogation officer, the truth about Jordan?"

Slade looked over at me, and I looked away. I hated that he was doing this, and I wanted no part in it. None whatsoever. I wasn't going to give him encouragement, even subtle encouragement, with my eyes. He was on his own with this.

"I didn't tell Officer Hyatt the truth because I panicked. That's why I destroyed that part of the video as well. I panicked."

Detective Hanson narrowed his eyes when Slade started talking about the video. "Yes, that video. It says here in the file that a good portion of it was destroyed. There wasn't a backup of this video?"

Yes, there is a backup, and Slade has it. I crossed my arms and raised a single eyebrow at him. I wanted to see him squirm about this question.

To my dismay though, he didn't squirm. He answered it smoothly and clearly. "No. There was only that one video-tape, and I destroyed the parts that showed me killing Jordan. So, I destroyed evidence on top of everything else."

I wanted, more than anything, to convey to Detective Hanson the truth about all of this. But it wasn't going to do any good. No, the only thing that was left for me to do would be to prove, once and for all, that Malcolm did this murder. But I had to somehow find a way to prove this before Slade's court date. He was going to plead guilty, and thus far, he didn't have a court date to do it. Hopefully, that date wouldn't be too soon. If it were, then I wouldn't have the chance to find the proof that I was going to need to find.

"Okay. So, you killed Jordan in self-defense, and now you want to plead guilty to his murder. Why are you doing that? Why don't you want to take this to trial? The jury might acquit you once you tell your story. The toxicology screens show that Jordan was pumped full of drugs that night. I would think that you would want to take that chance with the jury, as opposed to pleading guilty and just shutting that door completely."

I looked over at Slade. *Yeah, Slade, what of that? Take the case to the jury and see what happens.* Even that was a better idea than what Slade was proposing. It certainly would buy me more time for getting together what I needed to gather to show that Malcolm was the guilty party in this murder, not Slade.

Slade looked over at me. "You raise a good point," is all that he said. I knew why he was hesitating – it was Charlotte. But Charlotte only wanted Slade to take the blame for this murder, so that the heat would be off of her and Malcolm. Then again, Charlotte wanted Slade to go down for the murder, because that was the whole point in framing him. If he didn't suffer the consequences for Charlotte's evil plot, then I doubted that she would be satisfied.

"Okay," Detective Hanson said. "It's lunchtime. So, if there is anything more that you would like to tell me, speak now or forever hold your peace. Or at least hold your peace until 2 PM, which is when I get back from lunch. Right now, I have a pastrami sandwich with my name on it, and I must attend to it."

I smiled. "You mustn't keep a pastrami sandwich waiting."

At that, we all got up and said our goodbyes. Slade and I made our way out of the building and to our individual cars, passing the crowds of reporters on our way out. Slade, in particular, had to push everyone off of him, as he told all of them that he had no comment to their reports that he was about to plead guilty.

"Well, I guess I was wrong," Slade said to me, when we finally made it to our cars. "I guess Detective Hanson wasn't going to pursue putting me in jail right this second. But the judge certainly will when I make my guilty plea."

I crossed my arms, and when he leaned in for a kiss, I turned my face. I wasn't having any of this. If Slade thought for one second that I would just roll over and let him ruin his life in this way, he certainly had another thing coming. "You were quite the actor in there Slade. Quite the liar." I narrowed my eyes. "If you think for one second that this is the end of it, you can think again."

Slade wrapped his strong arms around me. "I know you have something up your sleeve, but I'm here to tell you to stop. Just stop. You're digging into some very dangerous territory and dealing with some seriously unhinged people. And they're unhinged people who would stop at nothing to get what they want. Trust me, Serena. You need to back the hell off."

I looked into his eyes, and I knew. I knew that even if I put my own life on the line, I was going to save his. Charlotte could do what she wanted with me – she could put me back in that hell hole, starve me to death, whatever she wanted to do with me – but I was going to make sure that Slade didn't pay for what she did.

I cleared my throat. "Is there a date that you're going to go in to plea?"

"Next Wednesday, so you and I have a week and a half

to have some fun before…" He sliced his hand across his throat.

I pushed him away and kept him at arm's length. "We aren't going to be having fun. There's no way that I can do that when you're facing what you're facing." I glared at him. Truth be told, I wanted him to suffer, as he was making me suffer. I wanted him to feel the knife twisting into his gut, the tip slicing, the pain excruciating. I hated that he was so nonchalant about it all. How could he possibly be, when he was probably going to prison for life for something that he didn't even do?

He finally got a kiss planted on my lips, and even though I was feeling pissed at him, I soon felt myself melting into the kiss. He put his finger on my chin, and his entire mouth was devouring my own. His kisses always got me going, because he was an amazing kisser. His kisses were passionate, yet he knew when to slow down for maximum effect. I wrapped my arms around his neck, feeling like I was trying to breathe underwater. My head was swimming, and the peril that surrounded us was forgotten.

"Serena, are you expected back at the office?" he asked me, as his hands leisurely explored my backside. We were out on the street, in front of the police station, and the reporters were behind us, taking our picture and looking like they were ready to pounce. Nevertheless, Slade seemed way too calm. He even had a hard-on, as was evident when he leaned into me.

My back was against my own car, but that detail seemed lost on me. The whole world had faded away as Slade had begun to kiss me, so even the reporters seemed to be on a different planet than the one I currently occupied.

"I am," I whispered, my lips trying to find his again. He obliged, his tender mouth searching mine. His hands went from the small of my back down to the curves of my butt, and he gently stroked his hands up and down on that area. "But I can be persuaded to take a sick day."

"Hmmmm, I was going to suggest you taking another hour or so before going back to work, but having a whole day with you sounds great, too. I can just imagine all the ravishing I could do to you this entire day." He inhaled my hair. "You always smell so amazing."

I bowed my head, not wanting to part with him. "As do you."

"So," he said, lifting my chin up to him again as he planted another kiss on my lips. "Shall we meet at my place or yours? I would suggest your place, because I know that you want to see your dogs, although I'm sure that they're fine in their day care place. I'm fine either way."

"Let's go to my place. We can walk along the beach and build a fire in my fireplace." I suggested the fire in the fireplace not because the weather called for it, because it didn't, but because I found the fire romantic. I was born under the sign of fire, as I was a Leo, and it was something that always drew me in.

"Your place it is," he said.

The two of us then parted and got into our respective cars.

We would meet at my house, and I hoped that I could still find a way to talk him out of what he felt that he needed to do.

If I couldn't, I knew that there was always Plan B.

Chapter Sixteen

Slade - Present Day

As I drove my car down the Five freeway, I knew that I was completely looking forward to being with Serena that whole day. I also knew that we had to cherish every single second together, because if we didn't, then that would be a shame. Once I pled guilty to the murder of Jordan, I doubted that Serena and I would see one another again. Indeed, I would discourage it, because I didn't want her to waste her life on somebody who would never be able to give her what she needed and deserved – she needed and deserved somebody who could give her stability and comfort. Once I got to prison, I wouldn't be able to give her either of those things.

There was a part of me that felt guilty about keeping Serena until the last second. I really should have just let her go right then. But I didn't want to. I wanted to be with her as long as I could, and I was so grateful that Detective Branson didn't move to put me into jail when I just made my confession. Maybe it was because, with the story that I gave, I had grounds for a self-defense instruction to the jury. What he didn't know was that there was no way I would pursue self-defense, because it would completely negate the entire reason why I was making this confession.

I hated that Malcolm and Charlotte were going to get away with killing Jordan. But, at the same time, I knew that it was best. My mother and Serena were protected, and that was really all that mattered at that moment.

Charlotte called while I was in the car, and I turned on the blue tooth to talk to her. "Yeah," I said to her when I saw that she was calling. "What do you want?"

"Just making sure you're keeping up your end of the bargain."

"I am. I just saw the detective, and I have my guilty plea teed up for a week from Wednesday. So, yes, the wheels are in motion for me to plead guilty for the bullshit you and your crony did."

"Good." She paused. "I'm doing this for your own good, and for the good of your mother and Serena."

"Whatever. Listen, I'm going to get some assurances that you'll never double-cross me and go ahead and talk about my mother or hurt Serena. Don't forget that I have the entire videotape on my hard-drive and in various vaults around the nation. There's no way that you could possibly confiscate all the copies I have of that videotape, so if anything ever happens with either Serena or my mother, these videos will conveniently make their way to your nearest police department for authentication."

"Don't worry, Slade, I have no intention of double-crossing you. I just want to make you suffer for all those years that you made me suffer through your indifference towards me. I loved you, Slade. I still love you. Why you ever thought that you could treat me as callously as you have, I will never know."

If I ever believed in an entity that was beyond my comprehension, which I didn't, but if I ever decided to, I would have believed that I was being paid, karmically, for the way that I used Charlotte when I was younger. The only reason why she was ever able to blackmail me was because she was outside my house when I went to see my mom that fateful night. The only reason why she was outside my house was because she was desperate for some attention from me. Attention that I never willingly gave her.

The chickens have come home to roost, and roost they have.

"I know that you won't double-cross me, because if you do, your goose is cooked and so is Malcolm's. By the way, Malcolm is really a shitty attorney. I mean, I know that he's throwing my case, and he has been from the beginning, I just wish that he would be a little less obvious about it. The people in the media have begun to talk about him and his incompetence."

"It will all be over soon, won't it?"

I rolled my eyes. I hated this woman so much. Even if I didn't treat her very well, as I should have when we were younger, I couldn't believe that she was willing to see me go to prison for what she did. But that was the case, and I knew it. I knew it, and there wasn't a damned thing that I could about it.

Especially not now. Now that Serena was in danger, I really had to toe the line with Charlotte.

"So, why aren't you in jail right now? You talked to the detective, you told him that you killed Jordan, yet he didn't take you into custody. Why not?"

"Because, he seems to think that I might have a case for

self-defense. I admit, he's right about that. Why don't I try that angle with the jury? Think about it – you and Malcolm will still be off the hook, and, if it works, I won't be in prison. Everybody wins, and you still got your pound of flesh from me. Just my going through the stress of this situation should be punishment enough for all the transgressions that you imagined I committed against you."

"Is that what you think? That I'm just getting my pound of flesh from you?" She started to laugh. "You're very perceptive. You know, Slade, I probably would have dropped this entire thing, if not for that slut you're banging. In fact, I probably never would have framed you for Jordan's murder if it weren't for her."

I bit my lip. Charlotte knew about the fact that I had seen Serena well before she came up to meet me in Los Angeles? That I saw her when I went to visit a friend of mine in San Diego, and she was on the beach, sunning herself? I saw her and thought that she was the most magnificent woman I had ever set eyes on. How did Charlotte know all that?

Slowly, it all began to become clear. Everything. Malcolm and how he got involved with the whole thing. Why Charlotte was so clear that she wanted Malcolm to defend me. Did she also make Malcolm force Serena to stay with me? Was that all part of exacting the revenge on me? It wouldn't have been fun for her to just see me go to prison. No, she clearly wanted me to fall in love with Serena, and then my prison term would be that much more torturous.

Well played. Well played.

"Okay. It's time to come clean. I now know that you know that I saw Serena before I ever met her. How you know that, I don't understand. But your choosing Malcolm for this charade definitely has to do with Serena, doesn't it?

Or is it all a happy coincidence that Serena is working for the man whom you set up to murder Jordan and defend me for Jordan's murder?" I suddenly felt stupid for not seeing all of this before. "The only thing that I want to know is how you found out about my seeing Serena on the beach."

"Slade, I've had a tail on you for months. It's a good tail, too, because you apparently never suspected it. And yes, the tail told me all about the beautiful brunette you couldn't keep your eyes off of that day. He gave me pictures of her, and I matched her up on the Internet through Google Images. Her picture was part of the firm's website, so I knew that she worked for Malcolm, and the plan was in place from there. It was so easy to get it all set up, too. Malcolm was eager to work for me, and do whatever I asked of him. All he wants is publicity for his firm, and when I told him that I was going to frame you and that you were going to be his client, he was salivating. Absolutely salivating. It was almost all too easy."

My shoulders slumped as I drove. I looked behind me and saw Serena was tailing me on the highway. That was the only reason why I didn't completely despair in that moment – I was in love with Serena, and she was in love with me.

"And yes," she continued. "I knew that you would fall for her. I knew it from the moment I asked Malcolm to send her to your home. And damn, did you ever make my job easy. You fell for her immediately, and now, well, when you go to prison, you're going to see what it's like to have a broken heart. Your heart is going to be as broken as mine."

Hell hath no fury. Boy, is that saying true. "Okay. Listen Charlotte, as I said, you have your pound of flesh. The media has been crawling all over me from the beginning, I've lost a lot of business from this, and my very life and freedom are in peril. I would like to at least try for a self-defense acquittal for Jordan's death. If it doesn't work, it doesn't work. The jury will send me down the river. But if it does work, then…"

"You won't be punished the way that I want you to be."

"No, but I'll be plenty punished."

"And, what? You'll marry that whore? You and she will live happily ever after? No, Slade, I won't be okay with that. You know what you need to do, and that's plead guilty and go to prison for the rest of your life. You know the consequences if you don't. If you want to keep Serena alive, then you're going to have to dance the way that I want you to. I hope that I'm making myself crystal clear."

I shook my head. There had to be a way out of this for everyone, but I couldn't see it. Charlotte was a loose cannon, to say the very least. If I didn't do what she wanted, she would have Serena killed *and* she would turn in my mother for the homicide of Hugh all those years ago. She certainly had her ducks in a row on this one.

If I was less of a good guy, I would simply have Charlotte killed. That would solve all my problems. Then I would turn in the video of Malcolm bludgeoning Jordan, and everything would fall into place. Malcolm wouldn't be as dangerous to deal with as Charlotte. He didn't have the connections that she did, and he wasn't present when my mother was standing in the living room with a dead body. Charlotte had the connections to get Serena and she was there when my mother was standing over Hugh. That made her 1000 times more dangerous than Malcolm.

No doubt about it, if Charlotte were just out of the way, I probably could get out of the entire mess. And it would be nice to see that weasel Malcolm get what was coming to him too. I still couldn't believe that there were men in the world who would kill somebody just because he wanted publicity for his firm, but apparently Malcolm was one of those "special people."

"I don't want to talk to you anymore," I told Charlotte. "It's bad for my blood pressure. I can feel it rising up with every word I say to you." I couldn't believe that I was seriously entertaining thoughts about killing Charlotte. I remembered what I told Serena – that everybody is capable of anything. You just have to push them far enough.

I was pushed far -- extremely far. I needed to get off the phone with Charlotte right at that very second or else I may have turned the car around and went to that bitch's house and sliced her throat.

That was a dark fantasy that I was having right at that moment, and I didn't like it. Even though Charlotte was the last person who deserved mercy, I couldn't admit that I was truly capable of doing something like that.

"Okay. Listen. I need to be reading in the papers soon about your guilty plea. I need to see the expression on your face when you're all lined up to go to prison and be the butt-boy of an enormous black man. I need to see all the stories that will crop up about your life behind bars. All those Dateline specials and cable news channel programs that will breathlessly detail every aspect of this case and all the wonderful times you will be having in prison. Only then will I know that I really, and truly, got my just revenge on you. So, no, it's not okay for you to plead self-defense, because if the jury buys it, you're just going to live your life on the outside and get married to that whore. And that's the last thing that I want to see, Slade. You just remember that."

"How can I ever forget?"

At that, I hung up on Charlotte. I was getting closer to Serena's neighborhood, and I just wanted to concentrate on her. There really wasn't much time for Serena and I to continue to be together. I had about a week before I would be pleading guilty, and then it would all be over. Charlotte was right, too – I was going to have a broken heart. That was going to devastate me more than anything else once I went down for Jordan's murder.

I was going to prison. My entire life's dream would be ruined because my business would have to be sold to the highest bidder. I would make sure that my mother was taken care of from the proceeds of the sale though. I was going to be notorious and everybody was going to be talking shit about me for the rest of my days. I was going to give up my freedom and everything that I worked so hard for, all because of Charlotte and her sick and twisted mind.

Yet still, the only thing that I could truly think about was that Serena wasn't going to be in my life anymore. Somehow, that was the worst thing out of all of this.

Charlotte did know what she was doing when she made sure that Serena and I fell in love. She knew that my prison sentence was going to be that much more devastating now that Serena was in my life.

Stupid cunt.

Chapter Seventeen

Serena - Present Day

I arrived at my home just a few minutes behind Slade. He was standing out in the driveway waiting for me when I pulled in. "How did I beat you here?" he asked me with a smile.

"I guess you're just faster than me," I told him as I buzzed past him to open my door. I was shaking, so I dropped my keys. Slade picked them up and handed them to me.

"What's wrong?" he asked me as he gently took my hand.

I shook my head. "I can't get over any of this, Slade. It's like it's a horrible dream. There must be a way out of this for you."

"There's not. In the meantime, I really need to feel myself inside of you." He kissed me, and, for a brief moment, all was forgotten. In my mind, he wasn't in peril, and neither was I. He wasn't going to prison. He and I were going to be together, through thick or thin. I desperately needed that in my life, because it was the one thing that had brought me stability and happiness these past few months – being with him. It was a bright spot, a bigger bright spot than anything else had been in a long, long time.

"Slade, I…." I couldn't finish my sentence though. I put my head on his chest. The warmth of his skin and the beat of his heart were comforting to me. I couldn't imagine what life would be like if I didn't have this on a regular basis.

"Where are your brother and sister-in-law?"

"They're staying at a hotel in town. I'm probably going to be seeing them later if you would like to come." Actually, I hoped that he would turn that invitation down. I really needed to brainstorm with Luke and Dalilah about the Slade situation, to find out if there was anything that could be done to make sure he didn't plead guilty to Jordan's murder. I was already thinking of a few angles that would make sure that the judge didn't accept his plea.

"Mmmmm, that's tempting, but I really need to catch up on reports and the day-to-day running of the company. I've been behind on certain things, as you might imagine. It's not that big of a deal, because I have the interim CEO running the company right now, but I still like to keep on top of things. And now that I'm certainly going to prison for the murder of Jordan, I need to get a transitional team in place for when I'm no longer going to be there. It's going to be sad for the team, because we always worked together so well."

My heart started pounding when he was talking so casually about going to prison. I opened my mouth to say something to him about that but he seemed to know what I wanted to talk about, because he gently put his hand over my mouth. "No talking. Not right now. There will be plenty of time to talk and to cry and to do whatever it is that we need to do before I go away. But right now, that's not what I want to do. Right now, I just want to concentrate on you and me and that beautiful bed of yours. That very expensive bed of yours," he added with a smile.

At that, he picked me up in his very strong arms and carried me into the bedroom. He laid me down gently on the bed, and then crawled in next to me. "Now Serena, tell me a bit more about your fantasies and your past -- your sexual past." He gently put his finger on one of my many faint scars. "Your skin is fascinating. It's like a map of all that you've gone through. Tell me what you like and why you like it."

I felt shy, but, at the same time, I had gotten to know Slade well enough to know that he wasn't going to judge me. "I used to go to clubs. Underground clubs. Before I got therapy, I was carrying around a lot of pain. A lot of baggage and a lot of shame. I had no idea why. What I did know was that pain felt right to me. It always did."

"Right, in what way?"

"Right in the way that nothing else ever did. You have to understand, I never felt that I fit in with my family. They're all so aggressively normal. Or at least they were, before my mom was killed. But yeah, my brother Mark is studying marine biology here in San Diego, at UCSD. Christopher is a struggling musician. Amy is married to a guy who is on the fishing boat with my dad. And Luke is a successful artist. I don't think that any of them have serious problems except Christopher, and the only reason why Chris has problems is because he was there when my mother was killed. As you remember, she literally gave her life for him. That's a heavy burden for anyone to have to carry around."

Slade was looking at me, penetrating me with his beautiful green eyes. He put his finger on my forearm and traced along the edge of it, all the way to my shoulder. As he touched me, I felt the familiar heat as his fingers trailed the length of my arm. I closed my eyes, wanting to capture this feeling for all eternity. Soon, I might not have this in my life on a regular basis anymore, and I couldn't even begin to fathom what that was going to be like.

Stop, Serena. You're never going to find out what that is going to be like, because Slade isn't going to prison. He's not going to prison. You're going to make sure of it.

He put his hand in my hair and lightly kissed my forehead. "Okay, so, you felt like you didn't fit in. Is it because of your special abilities?"

I smiled, knowing that he didn't really believe in these special abilities. "Yes. I think that it started when I was very little, and I always saw people around me. I never quite understood that, because these people wouldn't stay around me. They would kind of go in and out of wherever I was. When I got a bit older, and could actually communicate with these souls, they told me things. One of the things that one of the ghosts told me was that he had been searching for years to find someone who would communicate with him, and he finally found me. He told me that he wouldn't tell the others that I could see him, but that word was soon going to get around, and I was going to be bombarded with messages."

Slade tried hard to not make a disbelieving face, but it didn't quite work. His expression was clearly one of somebody who was "calling bullshit." I was used to that though, so it didn't really faze me. He didn't say anything to me, though. His expression said it all.

Nevertheless, I had to keep telling him my story. "The

ghosts weren't the only thing that was bothering me during this time. I didn't know this until much, much later, but when I was a little girl, I was molested by my babysitter. I was only a one-year-old; so of course, I didn't know what was happening. And I didn't know anything about this, either, until I saw a hypnotherapist about why I was so dysfunctional. I mean, I knew part of the reason why, but I didn't know exactly why until I was hypnotized."

Slade wasn't disbelieving of this part of the story, and I was grateful for that. His expression turned from skeptical to pure grief as he put his hand on my shoulder and squeezed. He closed his eyes and I did as well. I felt the emotions from him, that of sadness and empathy, and I remembered, anew, why I was in love with him. For all his bluster, he was really a kind soul underneath it all.

"That must have been so difficult," he said. "I can't even imagine what that felt like to find that out. How violated you must have felt."

"Violated is a good word," I said with a nod. "And then, when I was a teenager…" I shook my head, trying so hard to get that incident out of my mind. It came so closely to when my mother was murdered, too. "I was a mess. I got DUIs, two of them in a span of one year, and I wrecked the car and tried to blame it on the passenger because I was drunk at that time, too. The prosecutor had threatened me, and had told me that if I got another DUI, it was going to be charged as a felony, and I was going to do prison time. So, I tried to make my boyfriend at the time take the blame for that accident."

I felt ashamed about that incident, and all the other things that I did during this period of wild rebellion. I felt even more ashamed about the fact that I was such a shit to everyone in my life after my mother died. I abandoned them all, because I felt so emotionally fragile that I couldn't deal with their grief, on top of my own.

But what happened to me right before my mother was killed was another matter entirely.

I felt my lungs constrict, which was the first sign of a panic attack. I suffered through panic attacks almost every day for years after my mother was killed and I was raped. Actually, the rape occurred right before she was killed, so I guess I should say that I suffered from panic attacks for years after I was raped and my mother was killed.

There were tears coming to my eyes, and I felt like I couldn't breathe. Slade was looking increasingly concerned, so he got up to get me a glass of water. "I'm sorry," I managed to croak out. "I get like this, where I can't breathe." I took a sip of water.

"Is there anything else I can get for you?" he asked me, his eyes filled with concern.

I swallowed hard. "In the hall closet, I have a bunch of inhalers. If you could bring me one, that would be a lifesaver."

At that, he dashed to the hall closet and, a few minutes later, he had an inhaler in his hand. I sucked on it, feeling the air expanding my lungs, and I felt comforted.

He put his hand on my back and rubbed. "What's happening?"

I shook my head. "I still can't talk about this without wanting to die. But there was a boy in school, his name is Derek. He was the one that all the girls wanted, the big man on campus. And he pursued me. Here was this jock, this popular guy who was the one who had girls dripping off his arm everywhere he went, and he started to ask me out."

Slade looked perplexed, and I could also feel his anger, which was clearly directed toward Derek and not to me. I was happy about that, because I was so tired of feeling like people were blaming me for Derek's attack.

"So, anyhow, I wasn't quite in his social status. In fact, I hung out with the goth kids. I was dying my hair black and wearing black clothing every single day. Black dresses with combat boots and black lipstick and eyeliner. They were a good group though, because they weren't judgmental, and most of the kids in my group got decent grades. We didn't stay out of trouble though, because many of my friends ended up in rehab for drugs and alcohol. But I certainly wasn't the kind of woman that Derek would date. He pretty much stayed with the cheerleaders and other popular girls."

Slade furrowed his brow, waiting for the rest of the story.

I felt my lungs constricting again, so I sucked on the inhaler again, and I immediately felt better. "So, yeah, this Derek guy asked me out repeatedly, but I never went. I always thought that maybe he was put up to it, so that when he took me out, there would be some dirty trick played on me, like with Carrie. That would make sense too, because there were always rumors going around that I was special like Carrie. Not that I could move things with my mind and set things on fire just by thinking about them, but that I had special abilities. I knew that those popular boys and girls hated anyone who didn't conform to their rigid views on who is acceptable, and I never felt like I was acceptable."

"But you finally went out with him?" Slade asked me.

"Not really, no. I was at a party one night, and he was there, too. He wouldn't leave me alone. I was trying to talk to people there, people that I felt comfortable with, but Derek was always there, everywhere I was. And I got pretty drunk that night too."

I started to visibly shake and I attempted to bring the

glass of water to my lips, but I couldn't. My hand was shaking too much, so I ended up spilling water on my shirt. Slade gently took the glass of water from my hand and put it up to my lips. I took a sip and then turned my head.

I was going to get through this, dammit. I was going to finally tell Slade what the source of my pain was. How deeply rooted it was. There was a part of me that was hoping that if I told him my story, and he knew how much I had suffered in my life, he would change his mind about his guilty plea. How would he be able to leave me when he knows how devastated I was going to be, and how much I was going to be suffering? How could he leave when he knew that my life was painful, and he was just going to be adding to it?

Those thoughts felt manipulative though, so I tried to shake them off.

"Go on," he whispered. He was still stroking my arm, trying to let me know that he was there for me. I closed my eyes, feeling comforted by his touch. I tried to concentrate on how he was making me feel, as opposed to concentrating on the memories that were flooding my brain, but it was very difficult.

"There were some woods around the house that was having the party. You have to remember, I grew up in a fairly rural area. I always tell people that I'm from Portland, Maine, but my dad's house is part of a small, wooded area that is considered to be unincorporated for the most part. Our town was so small that we had a courthouse in a large double-wide trailert hat was very cramped."

I was stalling because I didn't want to talk about what Derek did to me. I really didn't want to talk about the aftermath. Yet, I felt that I had to.

My heart pounding, I put my hand on Slade's

outstretched one, and he gripped it tightly. *I'm right here*, he was saying with his eyes and his gestures. *I'll always be here.*

Liar! He wasn't always going to be there for me, and a part of me hated him for this.

I took a deep breath and another sip of the water that Slade had given me, and went on with my story. "There were woods around this house. Woods that I knew. These woods were where I used to go whenever I was feeling out of sorts. This meant that I was out there a lot. Sometimes I met some of my friends out there and we'd smoke pot or drink or whatever. Most of the time though, I just went out there my own. I could communicate with the animals sometimes, and I never felt like I was actually alone. I always felt such a bond with animals and nature, and being out in the woods felt like home for me. Especially during that time of my life."

Slade's lips curled slightly in a smile. "I can picture that about you. Communicating with the animals. You're so good with your dogs. I swear that they know what you're thinking, and you feel the same way about them."

"I do. I do. I've always felt at one with animals, which is why I decided, early on, not to eat them." I smiled, too. "Despite what that bitch Charlotte said." I remembered that Charlotte had accused me of being a vegan just because it was trendy, and that rankled. She didn't know me. She didn't know the first thing about me.

Slade looked at the wall. He appeared to be consumed with some kind of memory. After a little while though, he just shook his head and returned his gaze to me. "Charlotte is a bitch, the worst kind," he said. "And you don't know the half of it. Anyhow, please Serena, go on with your story."

I *did* know the half of it. I knew how awful Charlotte really was. After all, she was blackmailing him to take responsibility for a murder she orchestrated. How much worse could she possibly be?

I looked at Slade and he appeared to be listening for the rest of the story, so I felt that I had to finish. It wouldn't be right to just leave him hanging.

"So, yeah, I was at this party, and Derek was sticking around me like glue. I eventually couldn't take it anymore so I went out into the woods. I had a joint and I was going to smoke it. The joint wasn't welcome at that party though, so that was one of the reasons why I left. The other reason was that I wasn't feeling comfortable. Some of my friends were there, but I felt like I couldn't really talk to them that much because Derek was always hanging around."

Slade smiled. "You were a typical teenager, leaving a party to get high. Most of us experienced that when we were younger."

"Yes." I took a breath and let it out slowly. "So, I got out into the woods, and I lit up the joint. And I heard a voice behind me. It was Derek, coming out to tell me that I had to share with him, or else he would report me to the cops when I left the party. He would report that I was driving impaired. Well, even though it was a weak threat, I already had two DUIs, and I certainly couldn't afford a third. I let him share the joint with me."

Another deep breath. "At first, everything was fine. We just shared the joint. Then he started asking me about why I kept turning him down. I told him the truth – that I felt he was only asking me out because he wanted to play some kind of a cruel joke on me. I told him that there was no other reason why he would be so interested in a girl like me. I didn't have a ton of self-esteem, but that wasn't the main reason why I thought that he couldn't really like me. I also thought that he couldn't like me because I was so different from him. He was the popular football player who didn't get the best grades, and I was the goth nerd who got straight As in my AP and college courses."

"You were a nerd?" Slade teased. "I never would have thought that about you."

"Yes, I was a nerd. I mean, I was a nerd in the sense that I did well in school and studied a lot. But I also listened to emo and punk bands, so my love for Muse, Pussy Riot and Death Cab for Cutie kinda made me not such a nerd. I guess I was a hybrid. I always did well in chess, too."

Slade's face brightened. "Chess. You never told me that. We need to play."

I smiled, and there was a part of me that hoped that Slade would allow me to drop the rest of the story. That maybe he would tell me that I didn't have to continue on with the story, and maybe we could just play a game of chess. After we ravished each other, of course. I could see in his eyes that he was still very interested in the two of us getting naked together. But I could also see that he was interested, very interested, in knowing what happened to me out in those woods.

"Seriously," he said quietly. "What happened out in those woods? I hope that you don't mind telling me."

I closed my eyes, feeling how it was for me and Derek. I felt his hands on my breasts and I felt his hot breath on my neck. I felt him overpowering me, and slapping me when I didn't want to comply. I tried hard not to get too caught up in these awful feelings, but I felt them consume me, bring me down. I felt the pain of him taking me, because I was a virgin at the time. I saw the blood that came out of me, and I saw me lying on the ground after he had already buttoned up his pants and high-tailed it out of there. He just left me there after he was through with me, as if I was a piece of trash. Which was what he made me feel like anyhow.

After he was through with me, I ended up spending the night in those woods. I literally couldn't get up. All around me, I heard the coyotes chortling and singing, I heard the owls hooting, and crickets and frogs everywhere. It was a veritable symphony, and I remember, clearly wishing that I could transform into one of those animals. I wanted desperately to be some kind of a shifter, so that I could go and find Derek and kill him savagely, and actually get away with it.

Slade had told me, on more than one occasion, that you don't know what you're capable of until you are put into a situation, and I knew what he was talking about. There was nobody that I wanted to slowly kill more than Derek that night or in the weeks afterwards. Then, when I started bleeding profusely in gym class, with clots being passed, I knew that something was wrong. The bleeding continued for the entire week, as heavily as it was that first day, until one day, the toilet was completely filled with red. I was terrified, not knowing what was going on, until I got on the Internet and looked it up. I saw that I was possibly having a miscarriage, in fact that was what was probably happening, and I felt even more violated. I ended up in the hospital, where the miscarriage was confirmed.

I mourned the loss of my innocence as much as I mourned the loss of this child, whoever he or she was to be. I lit candles both for my baby and my mother for an entire year. When I moved out and left the family, choosing to stay at the home of one of my friend's until I got into college, I lit those candles every single night. Nobody really understood it, but they didn't really question it either. After all, I was a daughter who was grieving for her mother. That much was known. What nobody knew was that there was a secret shame as well, that of getting knocked up through a brutal rape, and then losing that baby in the toilet of the gym.

Sometimes I had tried to communicate with that spirit of my lost child, but, for some odd reason, I was never able to connect with her. That made me feel even worse because I wanted to know that the spirit was at peace. I didn't necessarily know how that spirit would find peace, considering the way that this baby was conceived, but I prayed every night that she would.

Through it all though, I never said a word to anyone about what had happened. I withdrew from everyone, and I told everyone that I was depressed because of my mother. That was only half true. The other half was that I was reeling, and almost suicidal, because of what had happened to me in the woods. There were nights when I literally just wanted to end it all. Just drive up to the ocean, weigh myself down with rocks, and walk into the sea. Would I even be missed? My family hated me, for good reason, because I was a total shit in those days. I wasn't all that noticed in school, because I wanted to disappear, which is why I had my clever goth disguise – I felt like all the black makeup, hair and clothes hid me from everyone. That I walked around the halls of school playing the part of somebody else, because the real Serena couldn't bear to walk those halls with everyone else. The real Serena didn't want to be known.

"Serena," Slade said gently, bringing me out of my daydream. "You don't have to go on if you don't want to." He put his hand on my shoulder and lightly played with my hair. I sighed, feeling what I felt when I was with him – loved, protected, cherished. Like nobody was going to hurt me, ever again. I squeezed his hand and turned my head and sighed.

"No, Slade, I do think that I need to tell you this. My therapist in New York told me that this incident played a big part in shaping me and what I want from others. Why I feel the need to have some pain in my life. It's all a release for me, a release for the pain that I was carrying around with me. It's all a part of my wanting to suffer, too, because of the guilt that I was feeling for not stopping the murder of my mother. A lot of complex things are rolled into my psyche, and I wish that you didn't have to know about them or experience them, but I think that you will."

Slade bowed his head. "I had no idea. I knew that you had some secrets and some shame, but I didn't know all of that happened to you. What did you do? Did you tell anyone about him?"

I shook my head. "No. I felt so ashamed about it, I just didn't tell anyone at all. And I was very angry. I started to lash out at everyone, especially my family. I think that I was angry with my family anyhow because they never believed me when I told them about my gift. Or curse, it depends on how you look at it. But they never believed me, so I was angry with them. Then, all these things started to cascade – the rape, the miscarriage, my mother – and I felt that I was cracking up. I went to college at NYU, but, every night that I could, I went to an underground club. Nothing had ever felt more right to me than being whipped, bound and humiliated at this club. I think it was that when I felt pain from them, I forgot about my own internal pain."

Slade swallowed, hard. "I'm so sorry," he said quietly. "So very sorry. I wish that there was some way that I could take away your pain."

I looked at him, suddenly feeling shy about asking him what I was going to ask him. But, at the same time, I felt that I had to. "Slade, what about you? I feel that maybe you're a Dom, or you've had experience with that."

He smiled slightly, but it was almost like a grimace. "Yes. I've had some experience with that. I've needed to be in control because of my own experiences in my own life. When you're only 7 years old and you see your mother kill your father in cold blood, it does something to you. I don't think that you could possibly imagine, or maybe you could, what that is like. And what it's like to suddenly be forced to live with strangers, strangers who are cold to you. My mother is a native New Yorker, from a loud Italian family. She's vibrant and alive. Helen is the polar opposite of my mother. She's very WASPy, and she covers up her feelings with gin. She never gave me hugs or any kind of physical contact, unlike my mother, who always was warm and funny and…expressive. Emotional. So, yeah, when all that happened, I withdrew, just like you."

I nodded my head, suddenly seeing where his controlling nature came from. I guess I never thought of it like that, but it made sense – when your early life is that out of control, I would imagine that trying to regain control, anyway that you could, would be paramount. It would probably be the most important thing to think about.

It was my turn to put my arm around him. I snuggled my chin into his neck while I played with the hairs on the back of his head. I loved his hair, because it was so thick and dark and luxurious. "Well, I guess this all settles it. We're drawn to one another because we recognize each other. We know each other's wounds, and we know just how to tend to them. That's something that I've always craved – to be with somebody who knew me, who got me, and who knew how to help me feel something that's not totally destructive. I feel that I could be dominated by you, and

ANNIE JOCOBY

that you could inflict pain that wouldn't feel humiliating or degrading as much as it would feel like love."

Slade smiled. "Yes, but I'm drawn to you for so many other reasons. Mainly I'm drawn to you because of your fierceness, your independence, and not to mention that you're goddamned gorgeous. But, I admit, the fact that you and I have had similar experiences is a part of it." He smiled, putting his finger under my chin, which was a gesture that I loved. "But only a small part."

As he kissed me, I knew that I was going to have to talk to him about what I wanted from him. I knew what I liked and what I craved. My therapist told me that if I could experience the pain that I sought in a respectful and loving relationship, I would possibly be able to handle it. It was something that I wanted, desperately, to turn away from, because that path wasn't good for me, yet it was also something that I felt that I needed in some way. I hadn't gone to any underground clubs here in San Diego, because I was trying to turn away from that lifestyle, yet, here it was, being tacitly offered to me. I didn't want to turn that down.

"Slade," I said, after our lips parted. "I'd like to continue to explore that side with you. The other night, with the candle wax and the belt felt amazing. I'm not totally hardcore or anything like that, but I do like pain. In fact, I crave it. I love to be dominated, bound and gagged and flogged and made to do things that I would never admit, in a million years, that I wanted to do. Can we explore that?"

I felt nervous, waiting for his answer.

He seemed hesitant. "Serena, I would love to do all that with you. But I'm soon going to be gone, and, I'm sorry, but you and I probably won't be able to stay together. I don't want you to be pining away for me when I leave. I want you to move on with your life. I feel guilty right now, sitting here with you, because the more time we spend together, the harder it's going to be when I have to go away."

I was quiet, feeling rejected and rebuffed. "I don't understand, I guess. The plan was, all along, for you to take a dive on your case, wasn't it? Because if you didn't, Charlotte would go to the authorities about your mother? So, you've known, all along, that prison was end-game for you on this. So, why would you have ever started up with me if that was what was going to happen, and you wanted it to happen that way?"

He shook his head. "I don't want it to happen this way. I never did. And, the original agreement between Charlotte and me wasn't that I was necessarily going to serve time for Jordan's murder. It was that I was going to be punished by being dragged through the mud, and I hired Malcolm, who I know was the real culprit, as part of this plan. I knew that Malcolm was going to throw the case, so I also knew that there was a good chance that I was going to do time for Jordan's murder, but that was a stipulation that Charlotte put on all of it. She wanted there, clearly, for me to do time for the murder, but knowing that I would have excellent grounds for appeal due to ineffective assistance of counsel. That was her loophole, in her crazy head. She figured that I would serve time in prison, and get out with the help of a good attorney who would appeal because of Malcolm's incompetence."

"That doesn't even seem logical. If you appealed, and won on appeal, you would get a new trial, and then what? Presumably, Charlotte would have to allow you to get a decent attorney, one who was truly invested in helping you win, and there would be the possibility that she and Malcolm would be the ones who would end up in trouble for all of it. I don't think that she thought all of it through."

Slade was telling me that the plan wasn't always that he was going to necessarily do time for the murder, but he also knew that there was always a good chance that he would. So, his words weren't comforting me. Why would he get involved with me, knowing that there was an excellent chance that doing time was going to happen?

I asked him that, and he simply said "I couldn't stay away. I couldn't imagine not being with you. I couldn't not make love to you, kiss you, and feel myself inside of you. I couldn't not feel what it felt like to wake up with my arms tightly wrapped around you. I know it seems selfish, because I've always had the feeling that you aren't exactly whole, but I couldn't help myself. From the first time I saw you, I felt something. I don't even know what that something was, but I felt it. I think you did too."

Slade was right. I did feel it, right from the start. It was magnetic, electric and threw me for a total loop. It wasn't even that I felt that I had known him all my life, but that certainly was part of it. But it was also that I knew that there was something underneath all that cocky bluster that was just like me. Damaged, broken, unable to heal. Seeking something, anything, to make it all better.

And I was going to lose him. Soon. Once he pled guilty, there was no turning back. None at all. No way to appeal. He would be sitting in that prison cell for the rest of his life. And for what? Because he was too much of a good guy to risk his mother's freedom. He wanted to also save me. He was throwing himself on his own sword for the two of us. Here was a man who was literally willing to sacrifice himself to make sure that the people he loved were safe and protected.

I couldn't take it. I wasn't going to take it. I didn't care. I knew what I had to do, and I knew how I was going to get him out of this. He had no idea that I had a plan up my sleeve, and I didn't want to tell him just yet what was planned.

I sighed. "I did. I definitely felt it from you from the very beginning."

He was watching me, as if he was studying me. He wasn't saying a word. Finally, he spoke. "There is something that I need to tell you. I was on the beach down here in San Diego and you were there. I think that you were with one of your roommates. And I was..." He shook his head. "I can't even explain it. I couldn't take my eyes off of you. And, in a weird way, that's what put this whole thing into motion."

I felt stunned. I had no idea that he had seen me before I went to his house. I also didn't know what he was talking about when he told me that seeing me on the beach put the whole thing into motion. What did he mean by that?

"I don't understand. How did seeing me put this whole thing into motion?"

He sighed. "Charlotte is a wily one. She had a tail on me, and the tail saw me watching you obsessively that day. He took your picture and sent it to her, and she was able to find your picture on the Internet by using Google images. If you upload a picture, any picture, Google will match the image with any other image on the web. When she uploaded your picture, she was led right to the website of your law firm and your picture. Her whole plan fell into place after that. It was perfect for her the way it all fell into place."

I shook my head. "I still don't understand."

"She found out that you worked for Malcolm, and that's what led her to Malcolm and your firm. She was deliberate – she apparently wanted us to meet and fall in love, which would make my prison sentence that much worse to bear. Charlotte is just a sadistic bitch."

I let his words absorb and permeate. There was a part of me that couldn't quite believe what he was saying. But there was a part of me that could see how diabolical it all was. It wasn't enough for her to destroy his life. No, she had to make sure that he truly had something to lose when he went to prison.

Diabolical. That was the only word for it.

Chapter Eighteen

After Slade and I had our talk, I knew that I wanted the two of us to explore a side of me that I hadn't explored in a healthy way yet. He was experienced in the dominant-submissive lifestyle, as was I. We weren't virgins in that area, and I knew that we could do well together. I knew what I liked, and he probably felt the same.

So, we talked about it. It was the most respectful thing to do, and, really, it was the only way to truly explore a relationship like this. "If you're okay with the fact that we won't be together next week, then I would love to really try a few things out."

He seemed almost shy when he was talking to me about it, and I felt the same way.

I took a deep breath. "I would like to try things out as well." I felt nervous, for some reason, to admit that I was all ready to go in a way. I had purchased a St. Andrew's Cross some time ago, and I had it hidden away in the large walk-in closet that was in my room. I also had a spanking bench in there. "I'd like to show you some of the toys and things that I have."

He smiled, and I knew that he was going to be game for anything.

I went into the closet, and brought out the cross. It was lightweight, for it was made with hollow steel, although it was very large. My cross was about six feet tall and wasn't really a cross that people would think about so much as it was a giant X. At the top of the cross was two leather handcuffs that hung by some short but heavy chains. On the bottom of he cross was two devices that would secure my feet. "I'd like for you to chain me to this and blindfold me," I said. "And do whatever you want with me."

I could tell by the look on Slade's face that he was very excited about this. I also had the feeling that this was not his first time seeing this type of thing.

He came over to me and the two of us put this cross against the wall. I felt my heart pounding as I thought about what was about to happen. I was about to entirely give up control to him. Once I was on this cross, I was going to be rendered helpless. I was going to be at his mercy, so to speak. Granted, we had a safe word, but I was determined not to use it unless or until he did something that was over the line. I wanted to lose control. I wanted him to dominate me and make me submit to him.

He kissed me passionately, and I felt my netherparts tingle. "You trust me," he said. "That means a ton."

I nodded my head. "I do trust you. It takes a lot for me to trust anyone." I looked down at the ground. "But there's not a doubt in my mind that I trust you."

He got down on the ground and kneeled in front of me. He gently took off my one of my shoes and then the other. I spread my legs and his tongue gently massaged one of my calves and then made its way up my thighs. His hands wandered to the back of my skirt and he slowly but surely unzipped it, and then he brought down my panties. As my heart started to pound, I groaned as his talented tongue stroked inside of me. I put my arms above my head, wanting him to secure me on the cross.

He unbuttoned my blouse, button by button, as I felt my breathing get faster and faster. After he flicked off my bra, I was completely naked and he was still completely clothed. He reached into my toy chest, which was situated by the bed, and brought out a cloth blindfold and put that on me. "Don't forget your safe word," he said.

"Orange."

"Right."

He gently led me over to the cross, and turned me towards the cross and spread my legs. The fact that he decided to put me facing the cross excited me and scared me all at once. I anticipated that he would be using a whip or a belt on me, and my heart started to pound even more. The fact that I had no idea what was coming increased the anticipation and the adrenaline.

I was standing there, my chest facing the cross, my wrists secured to the top of the cross and my legs secured at the bottom. I found myself squeezing my eyes shut inside the blindfold, wondering what was going to happen. Slade had something up his sleeve, I knew that. Exactly what that was, I had no idea.

I heard him rummaging around in my toy box, and then he chuckled. "You do have some things in here," he said. "I had no idea."

I nodded my head, unable to speak. My breathing was coming too hard and I really didn't have words to say.

"I'll just start kind of light," he said. "You said that you don't want anything too hardcore."

"You can do whatever you want," I said. "I trust you that much."

I felt him rubbing something on my back, and I imagined it was some of the body butter that I had in the toy chest. I then felt his tongue slowly and languidly consuming the moisture that was on my back. "This is delicious," he said. "Just like you."

He swirled his tongue around the opening of my ass, and the sensation was tantalizing. Then his finger was in my ass, and I could feel wetness stroking inside. I took a deep breath and then gasped as I felt anal beads. One bead went in, and then another and another and another. The first bead was small, and the next one was larger and the next was larger still and so on. Slade put each bead in my ass slowly and deliberately, taking care to make sure that I could feel each bead as it went in. I swallowed hard, and felt a slight ache in my nether parts that told me that I was close to orgasm already.

"Don't come yet," he said. "I know you want to, but you have to hold back."

I nodded my head, but it was so difficult to stem the rising tide that was threatening to shoot throughout my body.

"If you come, when I'm commanding you not to, you're going to have to be punished," he said. "Now, hold still."

He pushed himself against me, and I realized that he was still completely clothed. He was covering me with his entire body, and his tongue was lightly grazing the back of my neck. Then, with one hand, he started to remove the beads. I shook my head, trying mightily to hold back my climax, but, when each bead was removed, it was a sensation that was so piquant that I knew that I couldn't hold back. I cried out, and Slade immediately put a ball gag over my mouth.

"I told you not to come yet," he said. Then I felt a paddle whack my bare cheeks. It stung, but it felt so beautiful and right. "You can come when I tell you to come, and not one second before."

Since I had the ball-gag covering my mouth, I certainly couldn't cry out anymore, so it stifled the outlet that I had. This made all the sensations that much more intense.

Slade's hands wrapped around me from the back, and they had the same type of body butter that I felt on my back earlier. It felt like some kind of massage oil, so his hands were able to glide around my abdomen. He stroked my stomach for several minutes, his hands kneading into my skin. I felt like he was teasing me in doing this, because I so wanted his hands to be exploring other parts of my body. But he was in no hurry - his hands were gentle on my torso as his fingers made circular motions. I swallowed hard, wanting him to explore my breasts and my netherparts with those talented hands.

The anticipation of what he was going to do was literally making me ache. The feeling in my lower extremities was that of extreme pleasure mixed with extreme pain. I felt a tightening of my clit, and I had to breathe harder and harder to try to contain the orgasm that kept threatening to burst. I knew that if I cried out that Slade would hit me again with the paddle, and that thought was delicious yet scary.

He fastened a leash and collar around my neck and brought my head down with it. Because my oxygen was being cut off, I was starting to feel slightly light-headed, but that enhanced the sensation of what he was doing that much more. He took of the ball-gag, and his sensuous lips met mine, devouring my own, his tongue exploring inside my mouth with increased urgency. The kiss lasted for a long time, while his hands were exploring my abdomen gently. When he finally started to gently massage my breasts, and put two clamps on my erect nipples, it was too much. I started to breathe in through my nose, trying to stem the tide, but the pain of the clamps, combined with the sensation of his masterful hands on my belly and the sensuous feeling of his lips on mine, finally brought me to one of the most powerful orgasms I had ever had.

Slade backed off of me, slipped the ball gag on and picked up the paddle again. "You need to hold your orgasms back," he said, as he thwacked my backside once, twice and a third time. Each of the slaps to my backside were harder than the last, and that pain radiated throughout my body. Ironically enough, the paddling made it much harder to contain the orgasm. I had to concentrate to try to hold back, but the endorphins were flooding my system, and holding back was literally painful.

His fingers found my clit, and while two of his digits pinched my engorged G-spot, his other fingers swirled inside me while I groaned. "Are you ready for this?" he asked, as I heard him tear into the condom packet.

I nodded my head. I couldn't possibly be more ready for his enormous manhood than I was right at that moment. I couldn't speak, though, as I still had my ball-gag on my mouth. He was right behind me, and he leaned up against me, his cock teasing my opening. I was dripping wet - I could feel my own wetness on my legs. Slade jerked my head back with the leash as he simultaneously plunged his manhood deep inside me, and my breathing started to come so fast that I thought I was going to hyperventilate.

"Now you can come," he said, and the release that happened after he said that was like nothing I had ever experienced. He finally took of the ball gag, and I screamed out loud.

"Holy fuck!" I yelled over and over and over again. Slade's cock was sliding in and out, and I was driven so wild with desire that I desperately tried to move my shackled arms and legs but couldn't. My breathing was so labored now that I was once again feeling light-headed, and my entire body was trembling.

His thrusting continued for what seemed like an eternity, and every thrust intensified my orgasm until it was almost unbearable. I had no idea what it felt like to have pleasure so heightened that it mixed with pain, but this sensation came close.

Finally, with a groan, I knew that he was sated as well. He was also breathing hard. Sweat dripped off his body, and his damp skin mingled with my own. I lowered my head, and he took off the nipple clamps. The real pain associated with the nipple clamps came after they were removed, and my two orbs were raw and sore. Yet I had never felt more alive than I did right at moment.

He carefully took me out of my restraints and I crumpled to the floor. I was spent, absolutely spent, and, when I looked at him, I knew that he was as well.

Slade gently helped me up off the floor, and I smiled at him weakly. "Oh my god, that had to be the strongest orgasm that I've ever had."

"Come over to the bed," he said. "I need to put some ointment on your beautiful ass, because you're going to soon be feeling the pain. I'm glad that you didn't give me the safe word, although I was afraid that you would."

We walked over the bed and I lay down on my stomach. Slade gently got some cream and rubbed my cheeks with it. It was soothing and cool, and he was right - I didn't feel the pain right at first, because all I could feel was the adrenaline coursing through my body. But my rear was starting to sting just a little bit. The cream was cooling everything off and I groaned in pleasure as his strong and sure hands spread it around my butt.

After a few minutes, though, I could feel that he was starting to get aroused again. He lay down on top of me and started to massage my legs. I could feel his breathing coming faster. "How about something more vanilla?" he asked me.

When I felt his manhood at my opening, I knew that I had to have him inside of me again. I was already swollen and wet, so he was able to slip his enormous cock inside me gently and smoothly. I bucked up, needing to feel him buried deep inside of me. I needed him to go as deep as he possibly could. As he gently thrust in and out, he stroked my back and kissed my neck. I felt another powerful orgasm coming, and I cried out loud.

He was silent as he thrust inside of me, but I could hear his heart beating. I knew that my own heart had the same rhythm, and it seemed appropriate. He was melded to me, inexorably and completely. There was no way that we could ever be torn asunder, no matter what happened. Even prison, god forbid, wouldn't be enough to truly separate us. I would always carry him with me, especially after this night.

He groaned and flipped me around to face him. His

sensuous lips met mine and I sighed. "I love you Serena. No matter what happens, never forget that."

I nodded my head. "I love you too."

He rolled over and lay behind me, is arms wrapped around me from behind. I gripped his hands with my own, afraid to let them go. I felt that if I released my grip that I would somehow lose him. He would just slip away.

The very thought made me ill.

Chapter Nineteen

After Slade and I had our night together, I knew what I had to do. I simply had to find a way to make sure that he stayed out of prison. That would mean that I would have to undermine him 100% and go behind his back and do something that he clearly didn't want me to do.

I knew just who was going to help me out with all of this.

The first thing I did, though, was get my dogs out of their pooch hotel. I went to the hotel, and picked them up, and they were as excited to see me as I was them. It was amazing to me how much they had grown in just the month or so that I had them. They were both plump dogs, stocky really, as Frenchies tend to be. Bella had more black on the tips of her ears than Gigi, but both dogs were fawn colored, with the trademark round eyes of a French Bulldog, and the bow-legged stance of these dogs. French Bulldogs tended to be short and squat and powerfully built, and these two dogs were starting to take on the look of a mature version of their breed.

I loved these dogs so much. I picked both of them up, and they both cried out and covered my face with kisses when they saw me. Animal behaviorists often said that dogs cannot feel love, only instinct, but I always refused to believe this. I *knew* that Bella and Gigi loved me, because I was in tune with how they felt. And I always felt pure happiness emanating from their little bodies every time I saw them.

I walked them to my SUV and put them in the carrier in the back, and then I called my brother.

He picked up on the third ring. "Serena, hey! Dalilah and I have been having a blast visiting your fine city. How's it going?"

"Great. What have you guys been up to?"

"We did the Zoo and Balboa Park, and tomorrow we're planning on taking a little dinner cruise. So far, Olivia has been amazing, and hasn't really given us any problems, so it's been a lot of fun. I could certainly be persuaded to move here. Especially when I get to New York and it's colder than a witch's tit in the wintertime."

"Just how cold is a witch's tit?"

"Pretty goddamned cold. You know that."

I smiled in spite of myself. I still had to pinch myself when I was talking to Luke, after how much he hated me for so long. I silently gave thanks to his fiancée, who I adored. "Listen, Luke, come over for dinner tonight. I just picked up a nice bottle of wine, and you know how well I can cook. I really need to see the two of you."

"Sure, what time?"

"Be there at seven if you can."

"See you then."

We hung up, and I went straight home. I let the dogs out in the backyard, and I got out a different bottle of wine than I was going to serve to Luke and Dalilah and poured myself a glass. I couldn't quite believe that I had finally come clean to Slade about all that had happened to me, and I couldn't quite believe how hot our sex was last night. I reached down and touched myself and felt a tingle when I did so. I couldn't keep my mind off of Slade and all that we had done the night before. He got me and he understood exactly what I wanted. He knew how rough I wanted it, and how gentle I sometimes wanted it. He was somehow able to give me everything that I wanted and needed, and there was just no way I was going to give any of that up.

If it was the last thing I did, I was going to keep that man out of prison. There was no doubt about that.

As I sat in my easy chair, I smiled when I heard the phone ringing with Slade's ringtone and his face appearing on my screen. I picked up. "Hey you," I said, still feeling slightly dreamy and tingly just thinking about him. "How are you?"

"I can't get you out of my head. I don't know what you're doing to me, but man, last night was incredible."

I smiled and said nothing. There were really no words for how I was feeling about him, at least no words that I could articulate right then. "It certainly was," I finally said. "I can't keep my mind off of you, either."

"I need you to come over here tonight."

"I can't. Luke and Dalilah are coming for dinner." I somehow felt guilty telling him that. After all, in his mind, the two of us were living on borrowed time. We needed to grab every single second we could and fill it with time together. Yet, I was telling him that I didn't want to see him, and he was probably wondering why I didn't also invite him to dinner. If Luke and Dalilah could make it for dinner, then why wouldn't he be able to as well?

He was quiet on the line for a little bit, and I worried. I

worried that he might just show up out of the blue, and that wouldn't do. I had some very serious things to talk to Luke and Dalilah about, and the topic was going to be Slade and how to get him out of his guilty plea. Needless to say, I couldn't also have Slade at the dinner party, because there wasn't any way that I could talk to Luke and Dalilah about him if he was there.

"Slade?" I said to him. "Did I lose you?"

"No, I'm here. I guess I'll see you tomorrow. Can you take the day off again?"

I had some vacation time coming to me, and, truth be told, I didn't want to be around Malcolm anymore. He turned my stomach. He was such a weasel, even worse than Charlotte. Charlotte was contemptible. She was wrong in the head, and her obsession with Slade knew no bounds. Yet, I could almost respect her more than I could Malcolm. Malcolm was nothing but a pathetic lap-dog. I almost felt a bit sorry for him, because he was so desperate to make a name for himself that he brutally murdered a man. I had no idea if Malcolm would do something like that under ordinary circumstances, but just the fact that he was capable of it...But, then again, as Slade said, anyone is capable of anything at any given time.

"I think that can be arranged. Let's go to the beach tomorrow, huh?"

"Tomorrow. What time?"

"I'll be at your place at noon."

"See you then."

As I hung up, I knew what Slade was thinking. He was wondering why he wasn't invited to come over tonight. And, like me, he was probably dreaming about our time together. The two of us were bonded, truly bonded, in a way that I never thought I would be bonded with anyone. It was almost as if we were seared together, and I felt alive in a way that I never thought that I would feel. He had awakened something in me that I didn't know was inside of me – the capacity to feel something that was right and beautiful, not scary and intimidating. The pain that he had inflicted on me last night was sweet and tender in a way that most people wouldn't even begin to understand. It was him giving me exactly what I wanted and needed, and I never thought that anybody would be able to do that for me.

I continued to sip my glass of wine, and then poured myself another. The dogs were at the door, so I let them in, and they leaped up on my lap, and within a few minutes, they were both snoring. I pet them absent-mindedly. My mind was filled with Slade, both in a negative sense and in a positive one. The positive thoughts were of last night. The negative thoughts were of what would happen if he really did plead guilty. I would still try to be with him, of course, going to see him whenever I could. But, knowing him, he would discourage me from continuing with him. He would want me to move on with my life.

I knew that I couldn't move on with my life, though. There was just no way. Slade had changed me indelibly. I didn't think that I could be happy with anyone else.

The depressing truth, to me, was that, if the worst happened, and Slade went away to prison, I probably wouldn't try to be with anyone at all. There are some people who are core-shakers – they're the ones who leave a print on your soul, a firm print that is there for the rest of your life. It's like putting your hands in wet concrete – in 1000 years, that handprint will still be there. It was the same with the core-shakers. I could live to be 1000 years old, and my soul would still feel bound to Slade's.

So, no, if he went away, I wouldn't just "move on." I

probably would still insist on being with him, even if he was behind bars. I would just have to convince him that I needed to keep seeing him, and I would have to take every chance I got to have conjugal visits.

I hated to think about this, but I was trying to be realistic. Luke and Dalilah, hopefully, would be able to help me think of a good plan, but if they didn't, then what? Slade was a stubborn man, and he was determined that he was going to go to prison.

And, in the back of my mind, I considered something else. What if I managed to intervene with Slade's guilty plea, and I was able to prove that Malcolm did it? What would be the consequences of that? Would Charlotte make good on her threat to kill me? Would poor Margot end up behind bars? And if Margot went to prison for whatever it was that she did, that Slade was clearly covering for, would Slade ever forgive me? Could I also prove that Charlotte was behind Jordan's murder?

This story was becoming ever more complicated, so I was anxious to see my brother and Dalilah and see if the two of us could brainstorm it. If anyone could help me see the solution to all of it, it would be them.

The hours ticked by, and I drank more and more wine as I sat in my easy chair in the sun room. I loved this room so much. It was filled with plants and flowers and there was one wall that was transparent and let all the sunlight in. My chair in the room was leather and plush and the most comfortable chair I had ever been on. There was nothing that I liked better than to come out here with the dogs and a good book and just relax. A nice bottle of chianti usually added to the experience.

Around six, I got up to make my food for the three of us. I had long since mastered the art of making vegan cheese that could stand up to the best vegan chefs. So, I made "cheese" enchiladas, where the cheese was actually made out of cashews. This particular dish was my specialty, because I also made a mean verde sauce, and I had even mastered making "sour cream" in the same way that I made the cheese. I was going to serve these enchiladas with a side salad with avocado dressing.

I was really happy about my cooking ability. When I was younger, and I decided never to eat animals, I was a bit worried about what I would be able to eat. But I soon was able to enroll in cooking classes that focused on veganism, and I was able to find out just how creative and varied the diet could be. Most people had a hard time believing that the cheese I made was actually made from cashews, and they often asked for my recipes. I was more than happy to give them these recipes, of course, but I didn't know how many people would be successful in recreating them.

Right at seven, my doorbell was ringing. Bella and Gigi barked anxiously, and I answered the door. Luke, Dalilah and baby Olivia were on my porch with a bottle of wine. I kissed both of them on the cheek and greeted the little baby, who was awake and surprisingly calm. "Come in, come in," I said. I was feeling slightly tipsy from all the wine I had been drinking.

They came in and had a seat. The baby started to cry, so Dalilah discreetly put a towel over her breast and fed the beautiful infant. "She's fussy," Dalilah said. "I don't know how my mother did it when I was this young. She was on her own for a little while, because she briefly divorced my father." Dalilah shook her head. "Luke has been a tremendous help, I'll tell you that."

I smiled. My brother was probably going to be the world's most perfect husband. He always had been a nice, sensitive sort who had just enough edge to keep him interesting. And he adored his fiancée and daughter so much. That was clear. They really were an amazing couple, and I was so happy for them. After all that they had gone through, they certainly did deserve their happiness.

Now, if only Slade and I could also be so happy....

"Something smells awesome," Luke said as he walked through the door.

"It's vegan enchiladas. Vegan cheese enchiladas."

"Vegan cheese enchiladas? I've never heard of such a thing."

"Luke, vegan cheese is sometimes made with soy, but the best kind is made with cashews," Dalilah helpfully told him. As her parents were both vegan, she was well-versed on the subject. "It's really quite delicious. I had vegan nachos at this place one time, and, oh boy, they were the best nachos I've ever eaten. Ever."

I put my hand on Dalilah's shoulder and squeezed. This girl got me more than anyone ever had, with the possible exception of Slade. "Dalilah's right, and just wait until you taste my reuben made with jack fruit. You would swear that it's the real thing. Honestly."

Luke shrugged. "I'm game for anything, especially since Dalilah has been talking about becoming a vegan herself. She told me that she wants to set an example for Olivia that animals are not for consumption because they have feelings just like the rest of us. As much as I like a good burger, I have to admit that Dalilah has a point."

I went into the kitchen and brought out the food and a bottle of white wine. I poured Luke and myself a glass, and Dalilah waved it off. "Breast feeding," she said with a smile. "As much as I would love to indulge in that with you guys. But this food smells amazing and I can't wait to dig into it."

I served everyone, and we all dug in. Luke's face said it all. "Good lord, Serena, these are delicious. How did I not know about this vegan cheese?"

"It's not something that you can buy everywhere, although I'll bet you can at the Whole Foods."

Everyone was enjoying their food, and Olivia was sleeping in her little bassinet by the table. Dalilah kept looking over at her as if she was mesmerized. "I just can't believe my good fortune," she said as she looked over at the baby. "There was a time when I not only wished that she didn't exist, but I actively wanted to…" She shook her head. "I still can't believe how close I was to going to that clinic. Talk about being desperate."

I knew what she was talking about. Nottingham was married to Dalilah, and he was a vicious and underhanded man. When she conceived Luke's baby while she was still married to Nottingham, there was always a distinct possibility that he would attempt to gain custody of the unborn child. Dalilah and her father managed to put a kibosh on that by hacking into Nottingham's computer and producing proof that he was involved with insider trading, and had been doing so quite prolifically.

This was what I wanted to talk to Dalilah about - her own hacking skills.

I cleared my throat. "I remember that time. Boy, that man was a piece of work, wasn't he?"

"Yes," Dalilah said. "But that's all in the past now."

I narrowed my eyes and drank some more wine and took a deep breath. "Okay. So…" I didn't quite know how to ask Dalilah what I needed to ask her, but I knew that it had to be done. Hacking was illegal, of course, and who knew how Slade was going to react? Or Charlotte? Luke and Dalilah owed me a favor because I went with Luke to an underground club to prove that the devious Nottingham faked injuries that he tried to pin on Luke, but I didn't think about that. I did that out of the goodness of my heart and because I really wanted Luke and I to become close again. Or close for the very first time – it all depended on how you looked at it.

"What's on your mind, Serena?" Luke asked me.

"Dalilah," I began, addressing her. "You're a computer hacker, aren't you?" I asked her that question, but I already knew the answer. She was brilliant, absolutely brilliant, and she had taught herself to hack when she was a young teenager. She had mastered that skill apparently, because she was able to hack her father's computer and she found some incriminating evidence that her father's best friend did something that was clearly immoral but not necessarily illegal.

She smiled. "Well, I wouldn't say that. I know my way around a computer, but I haven't hacked in years. I was really good at it, though. But when I came across that video of Nick forcing the suicide of that awful pedophile, I decided to give it up. I didn't want to invade people's privacy like that anymore."

She was referring to the video she found of Nick, her father Ryan's best friend, going to the apartment of Paul Lucas, who repeatedly raped Scotty, Nick's wife, and hundreds of other girls. Nick then forced the pervert to kill himself. It was all captured on videotape, because they wanted insurance in case the man didn't decide to do that on his own.

I closed my eyes and shook my head. I wished that she didn't say that about not wanting to invade privacy, because there wasn't any way that I could back down now. I had to ask her to do this, and she was going to be uncomfortable with it, to say the very least. I really hoped that she wouldn't get into trouble.

"Why do you ask?" Dalilah inquired as she bit into some more enchilada. "By the way, Luke is absolutely right. These enchiladas are phenomenal, absolutely phenomenal. I'll have to get your recipe sometime. You could open up a restaurant with this recipe alone. You'd have them lined up at your door."

"Well…" I was hesitant, but I had to push through. "As you know, I'm defending Slade Bridgewell. Or my team is, although whether or not Malcolm, who's the lead attorney on this case, is defending him is open to interpretation. I think it's more like Malcolm is throwing Slade under the bus."

I then told them the entire story, although Luke looked skeptical when I told him about how the spirit had contacted me and had told me everything. Dalilah didn't, though. She looked like she understood completely.

After I told them everything, they were quiet. Finally, Luke was the first one to say something. "Serena, I love you. I do. But you got this information from a ghost. Or so you say. Isn't it probable that you hallucinated that whole thing? You said that you were in a desperate situation without food or water for days and days. Believe me, your brain was deprived of what it needed, and it was going haywire. In that situation, I don't necessarily know if I would trust what you think you saw."

"I know, but Luke, Slade confirmed it for me that Malcolm did it. I guess you didn't listen to that part."

"Alright, so it was a lucky guess."

I rolled my eyes when he said that. Luke was always saying things like that and it pissed me off. "It wasn't a lucky guess, but that's neither here nor there."

Dalilah was studying me and she opened her mouth. "Okay, I'll do it."

Luke gave her a look. "You'll do what?"

"Whatever Serena needs me to do."

I smiled. Dalilah was the smartest person I had ever met, and her intuition was spot-on. I hadn't yet asked her for what I wanted her to do, but she gathered it from my story and the fact that I had asked her if she was still hacking computers.

"And what does Serena want you to do?" Luke asked. "She didn't ask you to do anything yet."

"No, she hasn't asked, but I know what she needs." She turned to me. "You need me to hack Slade's computer, don't you? You need me to hack it and see if I can't find his copy of the complete video that shows that this Malcolm person actually killed Jordan."

"Yes," I said after a long pause. "That's exactly what I need for you to do."

At that, Luke looked like he was about to blow a gasket. "Oh, no. No. Dalilah, you can't do that, I forbid you to do that. It's dangerous and you could go to prison. Prison, Dalilah. You'll miss our daughter's formative years." He crossed his arms for emphasis. "No."

She raised a single eyebrow at him. "Forbid me? Forbid me? You *did not* just say that."

Uh oh. I not only was now possibly putting her at risk, but I was causing tension between her and my brother. Maybe I shouldn't have said anything and tried to find a computer hacker on my own. "Listen, Dalilah, forget I said anything at all. The last thing I want is for this to be a problem for you and Luke."

But Dalilah wasn't listening to me. She was giving the evil side-eye to Luke, who looked like he was about to explode. That wasn't like him at all, because he had always been so even-tempered.

"I did just say that, and I mean it," Luke said. "Dalilah, I'm serious. After all we've gone through, you're willing to just throw it all away? Seriously? You might think that nothing is going to happen, but I'm here to tell you that you're probably wrong about that. Some of the best computer hackers get caught. What makes you think that you'll be any different?"

I cleared the table. "Do you guys want dessert now or later?"

"Now," Dalilah said.

"Later," Luke said at the same time.

"Luke, I've never allowed you to tell me what to do, and I'm certainly not going to start now. If I decide to do this, then I'll do it. I won't have you or anyone else telling me that I can't."

I bustled in the kitchen, bracing myself for World War III in the dining room. Why, oh why, did I decide to ask her this? She was going to do it, I knew that, but what was going to be the cost? If something happened and she got into trouble, Luke would never, ever forgive me. I just got him back. He and I were approaching the point where we were not just brother and sister but friends. And I decided to do something that could possibly put an end to our tentative relationship.

I came back out with the dessert I had made, which was an apple crisp made with soy butter. "Here it is, apples and nuts, just the way you like it, Luke. See, I remembered that this is your favorite. It's mom's recipe, but I modified it just a tad, because I know that she used lots and lots of real butter in hers."

Luke wasn't hearing me, and he didn't look at me or the

dessert. I put it down in front of him and one for Dalilah, and I sat down and stared at the apple crisp. "Oh, I know what this is missing. I have some coconut milk ice cream in the freezer. Wait right here, I'll go get it and scoop some on both of your plates. You can't have apple pie or apple crisp without ice cream, right?"

"Sit down, Serena," Luke said in a voice that I didn't recognize. "This apple crisp is fine on its own. What isn't fine is the fact that you're actually asking my fiancée to do something that might send her to prison."

I sat back down and stared at the apple crisp, my hands folded in front of me. And, for a long time, nobody said a word. Luke and Dalilah were glaring at one another, I was staring at that apple crisp as if I expected it to grow legs and walk away, and Olivia was still sleeping in her bassinet. The dogs came to the table and begged and whined, and I wanted to bring one of the dogs on my lap, which was what I often did when I felt the need to be comforted, but I knew that most people would find that gross, so I didn't.

After what seemed like an eternity, Dalilah piped up. "I'm going to do it, Luke, and you can't stop me. Serena needs help trying to nail this Malcolm asshole, and that won't be easy to do at all without that video. As she said, there weren't any fingerprints in that lab except Slade's and Jordan's. Malcolm cannot be a suspect, because nobody even knows that he's tied to Jordan, and maybe Charlotte can become a suspect because of her obsession with Slade, but Malcolm is probably in the clear. If you can kindly give us another way of bringing Malcolm down, I would like to hear it. If you don't have another way, then kindly shut the fuck up."

Luke bit his lip, and I knew what he was thinking. I closed my eyes and I felt the extreme anger emanating from every single pore. I shook off those feelings after I opened my eyes. I was surprised that laid-back Luke had such anger inside of him, although I probably shouldn't have been. At least not in this case – after all he and Dalilah had gone through, I was now asking her to do something that would cause him to lose her again. Me, the sister that he had hated for so many years. We were on good terms now, but the festering anger with my behavior over the past years was still there with him, I realized. It was just below the surface. As much as Luke was trying to be civil and trying to love me, there was still a ton of water under the bridge that caused him to not quite bond with me in the way that I wanted.

I was correct about the true reason why Luke was so adamant that Dalilah wasn't to help me. "After all Serena has done over the years," Luke said with measured tones that belied his white-hot anger, "she doesn't deserve for you to put your neck out for her like that."

Dalilah's eyes got wide and I saw that she was just as angry as Luke, and when I closed my eyes, I felt her anger even worse than his. This woman had a temper, I could tell. She was about to go Defcon One on Luke's ass. "Oh my god. Oh my god. Luke, you would be in prison yourself if it weren't for your sister. Seriously? You're going to play the 'poor me, my sister was mean to me for years' card? After what she did for you? If I can recall, Serena put her own neck on the line for you. She didn't have to go with you to those underground clubs and act like she was a detective. If anybody would have had any suspicions about either of you, you both would have gone to jail for impersonating an officer. And if she didn't pull that off for you, you would have been hard-pressed to prove that Nottingham framed you for beating him. You would probably be in prison right now instead of being an up-and-coming hot artist. So don't even tell me that Serena isn't worth my sticking my neck out now. I credit her for keeping you out of prison, and you should too."

Luke took a sip of his wine, and I could tell that he was trying very hard to be calm. "Her helping me is the least she could have done after how she treated me and our entire family over the years. I felt that maybe the score had been evened when she did that for me, not that it was something that should be repaid in kind. That just got her up to base-line level."

He was talking about me as if I wasn't even there at the table, and it stung. I knew that there was still some leftover resentment towards me, but I didn't necessarily know that it was still so strong. I guessed that I should have seen it coming, and I probably did see it coming, but wanted to turn a blind eye towards it. I wanted to believe that Luke and I were okay, but clearly, we still weren't.

"Goddamnit, Luke, how can you still be so petty? This is your sister. Your sister. She's made a lot of mistakes over the years, but she's clearly shown that she's a good person. She's always been a good person, but you just refuse to see it. She needs our help, and I'm in the position to give it to her. And, quite frankly, I'm eager to do it. I hate that I'm going to be this stay-at-home mother whose only role is Olivia's mom and your fiancée. Dammit, I was somebody when I was younger, and now I'm nobody. I have this chance to really make a difference to your sister, and I'm going to take it."

There it was - the resentment that underscored their relationship. Dalilah was an artist too, a very good one. When she was younger, she was phenomenal. She was on the cover of magazines and her work was shown around the world. I knew that she had mental blocks that kept her from again realizing her potential as an artist, but I thought she was overcoming them. After all, she was a part of Luke's artist co-op. I had wondered if she was still having problems with creating. After what she just said to Luke, I knew that was probably the case.

"And what is wrong with you being Olivia's mom and my fiancée, soon to be wife?" Luke said with gritted teeth. "I'm so sorry that you feel that's not good enough." His voice dripped with sarcasm and I cringed.

Dalilah then started to cry. It was just tears that were moistening her eyes, as opposed to her sobbing and throwing her napkin, but still, it broke my heart. "Nothing is wrong with that, but I want to be more. I just don't know why I still can't produce the way that I want to, but something is holding me back. But that's neither here nor there. If I can't produce art the way that I want to, the least that I can do is give back to those who have helped me in the past. And Serena has been a god-send to me." She took her napkin and twisted it, her delicate hands gripping the fabric tightly.

I closed my eyes and I felt that Luke's anger had drained away, and, in its place, was sorrow. Deep sorrow. "Honey, I know that you've been having problems with your creativity and your voice," he said, putting his arm around her back. "But you have to know that I just cannot lose you again. Not this way. We've gone through too much for me to see you go to prison and leave me again."

I realized that I was also crying. I bit my lower lip so hard that I drew a bit of blood, and I put my napkin to my mouth. There was a small red stain on the white cloth.

The two of them then sat there in their chairs, and they were whispering to one another. I couldn't hear them very well, but I thought I heard snippets of their conversation.

They were in their own world, and I wasn't in their bubble, and neither was Olivia. Nothing penetrated their little world right at that moment. I felt uncomfortable and knew they could use some privacy, so I got up and took the dogs into the sun room with me and sat on the chair. The dogs came up on my lap, and I petted them absent-mindedly.

I never wanted this. I never wanted my request to cause tension between my brother and Dalilah. And I certainly never wanted to be privy to their dysfunction. It was so uncomfortable being at that table and watching them battle it out and listening to them talking about me as if I wasn't even there. It was hurtful to know that Luke still resented me so much, and it brought me a great deal of pain to know that Dalilah was still struggling.

They seemed to have it all – a new baby, a tight and loving bond with one another, and Luke had wild success. But, like everyone else, if you peel back the curtain for just a second, you can always see the cracks. Look closer into anyone's relationships and you can see the fissures and fault lines that divide them. Sometimes I found it amazing that anyone stayed together.

After about a half hour, Dalilah came to find me. "We cleared the table and put the dishes in the dishwasher," she said, sitting down in the chair that was cater-corner to my own. "Luke is changing Olivia's diaper, and I wanted to come in here and talk with you."

"Thanks for cleaning up. I would have done it myself, but…"

"I know. And I'm sorry that you had to listen to all of that. Luke loves you, he really does. But he's also having problems with letting go of his resentment of you. I've tried to tell him that you're a good person who's had some hard knocks in life, and he does understand that. And, of course, we've gone through absolute hell and back in the last year or so with Nottingham. He's just being protective, a bit overly protective if you ask me."

"No. Not overly protective. I was asking you to do something highly illegal, and I regret that. I'll just have to figure out something on my own to prove that Malcolm was involved. I might be able to implicate Charlotte if I find out more about her background and her obsession with Slade, although even that theory is going to be far-fetched for the police to take seriously, let alone the DA's office. And, because this is such a high-profile case and the DA's office wants to nail Slade so badly, it's going to take a Herculean effort to get them to consider somebody else."

Dalilah nodded. "I can see that. This is the biggest case that office has had since OJ, and with the media attention on this, they want to come off as having bagged a big one, where they failed with the OJ case. So, you're right, you have to have a smoking gun to nail somebody else for Jordan's murder, and it certainly doesn't help that Slade confessed."

I sighed. The odds of nailing Charlotte and Malcolm certainly were long. The odds of nailing them before Slade came up for his guilty plea were non-existent. Without that videotape, there wasn't a damned thing that I could do to try to delay Slade's guilty-plea court date. I could find out about Charlotte's obsession, but her obsession was circumstantial evidence of her guilt, not a smoking-gun, and no prosecutor was going to try to get a continuance on Slade's plea on circumstantial evidence.

I needed that videotape. Slade wasn't going to cooperate with me, so I was going to have to obtain it illegally. If Dalilah couldn't help me, then I was going to have to find somebody who could. I guessed that I could Google "computer hackers" on the Internet to try to find somebody who could obtain the videotape.

That was a joke, of course. If Dalilah couldn't do it, I had no Plan B.

Dalilah took a deep breath. "So, there's really no way for Slade to avoid prison without that videotape?"

"No. Think about it – his lawyer, Malcolm, is the one who actually killed Jordan. Obviously, Malcolm is going to be complicit in these shenanigans. If his lawyer doesn't try to talk him out of it, then the guilty plea will go through. Even with the videotape, it will be dicey. But I would have to send it to the prosecutor's office and hope that they do the right thing with it." That was still a long-shot. The prosecutor's office would have discretion on whether or not to accept the guilty plea. That would mean that they would have to do the right thing if they had the videotape on hand. If they decided not to do the right thing, they could still accept the guilty plea, videotape or no videotape. I silently prayed that wouldn't be the case.

It was all working against Slade – the obsessive media attention about the case, Charlotte's evil plot, everything. The prosecutor's office could very well ignore the videotape, on the grounds that they really wanted to bag the big fish. It was like Gary Condit all over again. The congressman was having an affair with a young intern who was murdered in the woods. The media pounced on the poor guy, ruining him and his career for life. He was guilty until proven inno-cent, just like Slade. It turned out that a random serial killer murdered Chandra Levy, the intern, but that was little-reported. The only thing that the public remembers about that whole debacle was Condit, the affair with Chandra, and the fact that Condit was clearly guilty of her murder.

That was how media attention affected things. In this

case, it might prove more important to the prosecutor's office to nail Slade than to actually get at the truth. That videotape was our only hope, but even that was a long-shot for so many reasons.

"Luke and I are obviously going to have to talk about this," she said. "He's in the other room and he's calmed down, but he still doesn't like the idea. I've told him that I know what I'm doing, or I can at least learn how to hack with today's security protocols, and that even if the worst thing happens and Slade discovers what I did, I doubt that he will turn me in. Maybe I'm naïve about that, but he sounds like a really decent guy, and I can't imagine him going to the authorities if he catches me doing that to his computer."

"That's a good point. An excellent point. He'll be furious, for sure, but I don't think that he'll want you prosecuted." I got quiet for a bit. There were other things that I was worried about. "But Dalilah, the security on his system is going to be like Fort Knox. He has to have amazing security because of all the patents he has pending with his drugs. Corporate espionage is a real thing, and it's something that he has to safeguard against. His system is going to be very secure. It's going to be like hacking into the government servers. I know that you're absolutely brilliant, but I also know that hacking isn't your full-time gig. Are you sure that you can pull this off?"

"No, of course I don't know that for sure, but I'd like to try." She sighed. "Truth be told, I'm kinda bored and, pardon the cliché, but stuck-in-a-rut. Don't get me wrong, I love my family. Olivia has been a dream baby so far, and Luke, is, well, he's Luke. He's the love of my life, and I didn't think that it was possible to feel the way that I do when I'm with him. I can't even explain it, except to say that he's really my soul mate. Yeah, we argue and fight, because he's very headstrong and so am I. But we get each other."

After that, she got quiet, and I knew that more revelations were coming. "There's a 'but' in there," I said. "You love your life 'but'…"

She shrugged. "It's kind of the same thing as before I met him. I've been frustrated by my inability to motivate myself to do something real. I mean something real outside of my maternal and wifely responsibilities. I don't know what it is – I was starting to get my artistic voice back, I really was. I was producing stuff that I thought was as good as the things that I was producing when I was a young girl. But, with Olivia here, my focus has shifted, which is good and bad. Good because I love being her mother. Bad because I don't want that to be my only role in life. When I was a very small child, my parents were convinced that I would cure cancer. When I got a bit older and was getting so much recognition for my art, they thought that I would become a world-renowned artist. Now, nobody is saying much about me doing anything important for the world. I guess I feel that if I helped you that maybe that would somehow help me retrieve a piece of me that seems lost."

I laughed a little as I took another sip of my wine. I scratched Gigi's ears, and she raised her muzzle to me while she closed her eyes. Her back leg thumped against her belly, and this made me laugh some more. "Sorry, I don't find this funny, at all. Your dilemma isn't funny in the least. But the reason why I laughed is that I'm asking you to do something illegal. Are you sure that's the hill you want to die on?"

"No, but it will be a start. It will get my brain working again, and sometimes, when your brain gets working in a creative way, any kind of creative way, it helps unblock you.

Hacking Slade will be difficult and will take all my intellect, abilities and creativity to figure it out. My hope is that once my brain is working towards something that isn't family-related, it will become unblocked and I can start to get back to who I was, or who I was going to be. Unlock my potential again."

I nodded. I knew that Dalilah was having on-going problems with being artistically blocked, and I felt for her. She was a brilliant, brilliant, woman, which put pressure on her from all sides. Luke certainly wasn't helping with his over-protective nature, although I knew that he helped her in other ways. He was very supportive of her art career and always encouraged her.

"Well, talk some more to Luke tonight and see if you guys can come to an agreement. If you can't, you can't. I don't want this, or anything else, to come between you guys. You and Luke have been through too much already. The last thing I want is for there to be some kind of relationship issues that I caused."

"Shhh, don't talk like that. Luke and I are fine. We'll survive anything, because in the end, we're very strong together and weaker apart. He needs me and I need him." She patted my hand. "Anyhow, I wanted you to know that I'm on your side. If I can convince Luke to give in, I'll be on your project as soon as I can. I know that time is of the essence, and if he has as tight security as you think that he does, it will take me days to figure this out. I know that we have less than a week before Slade comes before the court. So, I need to get started immediately."

We stood up and I hugged her tightly. I was closer to her than I had been to any woman, ever. I would have even said that I was closer to her than I had been to any person, ever, but that wasn't entirely true. I was seared to Slade. He was a part of me that I simply couldn't ever let go. God forbid he went to prison, but if he did, I would stay faithful to him no matter what. I loved him that much.

That's what love was – for better or for worse. I never knew what that meant until Slade. Now I did, and there was no way that I could ever give that up.

"Dalilah, you mean the world to me," I told her. "Thank god my silly brother found somebody like you. Without you, I don't know where he would be."

"Oh, he would be fine," she said unconvincingly.

I knew better. He wouldn't be fine. He would probably still be broke. Dalilah sacrificed a lot to make sure that Luke got his shot in the limelight. She married a beast whom she hated, because the beast blackmailed her into it by threatening to sabotage Luke's career if she didn't. That same beast, though, was responsible for Luke getting the shot of a lifetime that eventually led to his current success. It took a lot of twists and turns before that happened, though. In the end, Nottingham, the potential instrument of their destruction, really was the instrument for Luke's success. It was ironic how it happened, though.

"So," I said to her. "When will I hear from you about yay or nay?"

"Tomorrow. Luke and I are going to talk about this seriously when we get back to our hotel room."

"Are you sure you can't stay here? I have that guest bedroom that's all nice and cozy and ready for the two of you."

"We will, but not tonight. Tonight, we need some space to talk about this."

I hugged her again. "Well, make sure that he's really and truly on board with all of this. If he has any doubts about it, then don't do anything. I certainly don't want to be the thing that drives the two of you apart. And make sure that he's not grudgingly accepting it. I've had experience with that, and it always comes back to bite you in the future. You know, he'll finally say 'sure, let's do it.' Then, in every fight you guys have in the future, he'll use it to throw back in your face. I don't want that, and I know that you don't either."

"Oh, I know about that. That's something that every couple has to face – the thing that's tucked away, just waiting for the right moment to strike. So yes Serena, I'll make sure that he doesn't have any hesitation. But, of course, if something happens and I do go to prison..."

"Luke will never forgive me. I know that." I knew that, but I was willing to take that chance, anyhow. It was that important to me. If there was another way, any other way at all, I certainly would never take that kind of chance. But desperate times called for desperate measures, and these were certainly desperate times.

I felt terrible, though, that Dalilah was taking that chance as well. She was doing it for me, and only for me. Well, for herself as well, according to what she said earlier about unleashing her creativity, but mainly for me. I loved her more than I could love any family member, and she wasn't even blood.

We went back into the dining room, where Luke was busy holding a fussy Olivia. The little girl was crying, and Luke was bouncing her up and down and talking softly to her. I smiled at the sight of my brother and his new baby. I also felt a pang, knowing that I was putting a wrench, a possible wrench, into their happiness. I wished that it could be helped, but I knew that it couldn't be.

Damn Slade and his loyalty to his mother and to me. Damn Charlotte for doing this. I hated Malcolm for doing this as well, but I realized that he was nothing but a pawn in Charlotte's sick games. One man was dead and another man was on the ropes, all because the woman was sick in the head. Sick and psychotic.

"Well, we better be going," Dalilah said, with a hug and a kiss on the cheek. "It's getting late and Olivia is getting fussy."

Luke gave Olivia to Dalilah and looked at me sheepishly. "I'm sorry about what I said earlier," he told me. "You caught me off guard. I don't still resent you."

"Yes you do," I said with a smile, so he didn't think that I was too angry about what he said. "But that's okay."

"No, Serena, I..." Then he shrugged. "I guess there is still some resentment there, but I'm working on it. Dalilah is right – you saved my ass in the Nottingham business. I couldn't have done it without you. You put your own self on the line there for me. I'm not saying that I'm ever going to be on board with Dalilah doing this for you, but, at the same time, I know that it has to be done. At any rate, we're going to talk about it."

"That's all I ask," I said, giving Luke a hug. "Now you two get that little one to your hotel room, and I'll be seeing you soon, okay?"

Luke nodded, looking a bit perplexed. "You really have changed," he said. "How did you change so much?"

"Years of therapy." I wanted to tell Luke about my secret pain and all that I had gone through, but I didn't really have words. I didn't really want to open up to anyone about the rape, although Dalilah knew about the molestation when I was a baby. That was something that I just discovered through hypnotherapy, so, because it was something that was fresh, I did want to talk about that with people I felt close to. For some reason, I had always felt close to Dalilah, as if she were my sister. I had a sister, Amy, but I never felt close to her. She was so different from me, and we never did find common ground. So Dalilah was really the sister that I never had in a way.

We said our goodbyes, and I cleaned up the kitchen. There really wasn't too much to clean up at that point though, as Luke and Dalilah had apparently done most of it, bless their hearts. There were a few dishes, and I put them in the dishwasher while the two dogs stood at my feet. They tended to follow me everywhere, anyhow, but especially when I was in the kitchen. They knew that I would possibly give them a treat. They stood at my feet, looking up at me expectantly, Gigi's tiny non-tail wagging and Bella's entire body doing the same. Gigi barked a tiny little bark, a sound that was so cute and precious that I felt that I had to give them both a little something. I went to my ceramic cookie jar and got them both a greenie, and they took it eagerly into the next room to eat it on their dog beds.

Tiny things make those two happy. If only it were the same with humans. We humans were messy, complicated and sometimes ruthless. We were jealous and irrational. And sometimes, as with the case of Charlotte, we were just plain nuts.

As I did the few dishes that were still not clean, I pondered. Charlotte was not a suspect in the case, and I didn't know how to make her a suspect in the case. It was mind-bending. She had kidnapped me and almost killed me, yet there was no way to prove any of that. If I could prove it, it would go a long way to show that she was behind everything. The fact that Malcolm was the perpetrator made the whole thing infinitely more complex.

How was I going to nail them both? I couldn't go to Malcolm and ask him to investigate Charlotte as a suspect.

That would send off alarm bells, and I probably would end up fired from the firm. I was going to have to, somehow, someway, show that Charlotte was unhinged enough to have somebody murdered, just to frame the man with whom she was obsessed.

And I was going to have to do it completely on my own.

Chapter Twenty

About 2 AM, I awoke with a start. I was feeling just a bit hungry, but I didn't really need to eat, so I didn't wander into the kitchen. The dogs were snoring on my bed, and they both looked up at me when I awoke. They were light sleepers, as dogs usually were. I guessed that was instinct for dogs – if they weren't light sleepers, their ancestors would have been in trouble in the wild. It was a survival mechanism.

Bella and Gigi sleepily wagged their tails, before putting both of their little heads down and the snoring began again. I smiled as I sat there in the dark, willing myself back to sleep. After a few minutes, though, I knew that I was going to be awake for awhile, so I got out my laptop.

This was the first quiet moment I had since the kidnapping. The first moment where nothing was going on – no guests coming over, no Slade wanting to see me – and it was the first moment where I decided to investigate Charlotte online. It was remarkably easy to do, at least under her stage name. Just typing in "Charlotte Boswell," brought up a multitude of pages. Her IMDb page, her Wikipedia page, and tons of articles about her rise from supermodel to the Hollywood world. Critics were saying that she was one of the few models who could actually act. She had been in just two independent films, but they had been carefully chosen for her to play against type, and she had apparently knocked the socks off of some of the major movie critics.

The consensus was that she was the one to watch in the coming years.

Not that any of this was interesting to me. I was so out of touch with the Hollywood scene and with movies in general that I barely knew who she was. I was a bit surprised that she was becoming so acclaimed, but I really shouldn't have been. Of course she was an amazing actress – she was crazy. The roles that she had taken on, that of a junkie in a Gus Van Sant film and as a prostitute in another independent film, by a director that I didn't recognize, were suited for somebody like her.

I noted that her next project was as the lead in a big-budget David Fincher movie, and I felt both impressed and depressed. I didn't like movies that much, but I did appreciate David Fincher. They were often dark and gritty, yet highly stylized in many ways. He was a massively popular director from the time he directed *Sev7n*, a movie about a serial killer that featured, as a penultimate scene, a woman's head in a box. *Fight Club* was actually one of my all-time favorite films, one that I had actually bothered to watch several times. *Gone Girl* was an excellent book and was adapted well by Fincher. No doubt about it, Fincher was A-List, and the fact that Charlotte was not only going to be working with him, but apparently was one of the leads in his upcoming film, impressed me immensely.

Yet it depressed me, too. How could a morally bankrupt

and crazy person such as Charlotte achieve such heights? How was that fair? I thought about the people who struggle just to get through the day, or couldn't make ends meet, yet they were good, kind, upstanding people. Charlotte was a woman who had somebody brutally killed, just because she was a "fatal attraction" for Slade and wanted Slade to spend his life in prison. Yet she was the one who had achieved fame and fortune.

Maybe Slade was right after all – there was no God. If there were, such scenarios as Charlotte achieving fame and fortune wouldn't happen, and all those good people who were on the streets or starving would have the fortune that Charlotte had. Maybe not the fame, because not everyone wanted that. But they would have her fortune, in a just world ruled by a just God.

I tried to shrug off the metaphysical musings and hunker down. Her movie career and past career as a sought-after supermodel were interesting, but they weren't what I was after. I was really after the dirt. The dirt that she might have tried to cover up. I needed to find an in-depth article that would maybe provide me some clues as to who she really was.

I hit upon a *Vanity Fair* cover story about her, and I knew that this was something that might give me some clues. I knew that *Vanity Fair* stories were comprehensive, factually correct, and had none of the bullshit tabloid-style hype that other magazine articles dished out. I got up and got a glass of wine, and sat down in my easy chair in the sunroom and started to read the lengthy article.

I scanned the parts that talked about her movie career and rise to fame. I was more interested in her early life, and the article didn't disappoint. Her birth name was Carlotta Garancino. The article didn't say that she was a mafia princess, though. Not that it surprised me that the article wouldn't say something like that. I would imagine that Charlotte, or Carlotta as it were, dictated what could and couldn't be in the magazine, and that would be something that she would definitely want to keep out. I knew how the game worked – if a media outlet wanted to get access to a person in the future, they played the game and made sure that certain facts don't become known. That was how major actors stayed in the closet.

As I read about her daily life and her struggles, I sarcastically played a violin for her in my head. She whined about how her life had changed since she was offered major roles in major films, and she tried to sound self-deprecating about unflattering pictures of her without makeup that had shown up in various tabloids. She had nothing to be self-deprecating about, though – those pictures showed that she was gorgeous even without a stitch of makeup. I looked them up while I read the article, and she truly was luminous. She explained that her father was a restauranteur in LA – is that what they're calling it these days? – and her mother was a banker. I read between the lines there – the restaurant was a front for the illegal business, and her mother was probably the private money launderer. After doing a number of mafia cases for the firm, I knew how the racket went. Illegal dollars had to be "laundered" so that they became legitimate, and restaurants were a key way of doing just that. The drug money and the money gained through other illicit means were funneled into the business, which was necessary, because, otherwise, the IRS would become suspicious about how X person had a yacht, a mansion and five sports cars, yet no reportable income.

I wrote down the name of the restaurant that her father owned, which I recognized as being one of the best Italian restaurants in Los Angeles. That was certainly a place to start.

The article was interesting in its own right, but it didn't necessarily shed light on what I was looking for. Then again, maybe it did, because I knew Charlotte's real name. Carlotta Garancino.

I felt impatient. I had to find something on her that could possibly lead the investigation into her direction. I knew how to bring down Malcolm – all I needed was the complete videotape. I had to assume that the videotape would identify Malcolm, because otherwise, there wouldn't have been a reason to destroy the portion where Jordan was killed. So, find the videotape, and Malcolm goes down. But how would I get Charlotte as well? Would Malcolm give her up? If he didn't, then it was vital that I find the dirt on Charlotte to show that she was behind it all.

Just then, the phone was ringing. It was Dalilah.

"Hello," I said. "Dalilah, how are you? And why are you awake at this time of the night?"

"I'm okay, and it's really morning. I couldn't sleep. Listen, Luke and I have been talking. We can't come to an agreement. I'm so sorry. I really want to do this, but…"

My heart sank. I had a little over a week to get this, and I had no idea where to start. Who else could hack?

"I understand."

She paused. "It's not the end of the world. My father's security team is awesome. They're the ones who were able to help me out when I needed it. They can help you as well."

"Really?" I couldn't believe what I was hearing. Perhaps all wasn't lost? "Can they do it in the time frame that I need it?"

"That's the rub. I need to get in touch with them and see what their workload is like."

I swallowed, hard. It was wonderful news that Dalilah had the contacts that I needed. But would they be able to come through for me in time? "Okay. Call them and let me know, and how much it will cost."

"I will. Don't worry about the cost. They're on retainer with my dad, so they'll do anything that I ask them without charging me."

"Dalilah, I know what a retainer is, and somebody is paying. Your father most likely would the one here. I insist on paying. I haven't even met your father, so it would be completely taking advantage of him if I didn't pay anything."

"Serena, my father literally has more money than he knows what to do with. Literally. I want to do this for you, so please let me."

I hated feeling like I owed somebody, so I protested some more until Dalilah threatened to not call them at all if I didn't give in. "Seriously, Serena, I want to do this. I won't take money from you, and neither will my father. Now, if you want me to call this firm, then I want your word that you won't try to pay them."

I sighed, feeling defeated on that point. "Okay and thank you. You're such a godsend."

"Don't thank me yet. I don't know yet if they can do it in the next week and a half. Hopefully I'll know within the next few hours, though, if they can do it in the time frame that you need it."

"Thanks so much." I felt awkward asking her for something more, especially since she was insisting on my not paying the firm for doing all of this. But I needed to do it.

"There is something more that I need. I almost hate to ask this from you, but I feel that I need to."

"Go ahead."

"I need some dirt on Charlotte. There's something in her background that might link her up to this whole thing. Getting information on her is less crucial than getting information on Malcolm, though. It's less important than getting that videotape. It's important, but not as time-sensitive. I hope that makes sense."

"Of course. What's her full name?"

"Carlotta Garancino. I found this out by reading an article about her this morning. I couldn't sleep, so I got up to find out more about her, and that's what I found out."

"What kind of things do you need?"

"Anything you can find. I would try to subpoena the information about her, but that would be impossible, considering the fact that I can't tip Malcolm off that I know what he did. If I asked him to issue subpoenas for Charlotte, the jig would be up."

"Okay. I'll have them do it. Since time is not necessarily of the essence with this one, it shouldn't be a problem."

"Thank you, Dalilah. I don't know how much I can thank you for doing this."

"Anything for you, girl."

We got off the phone, and I immediately felt like the clouds were about to part. There was a chance that the whole thing was about to come together.

I prayed that I was correct about that.

Chapter Twenty-One

That morning, Slade picked me up to go to the beach. I had everything together – the umbrella, the sunscreen, the snacks for the day, and the dogs. The plan was to go to Coronado, where there was a dog beach, and spend the day. We had also talked about going to a dog-friendly restaurant for dinner. I had to admit that I was looking forward to this day, which was a chance just to lay back and relax. Just to try to forget about the Sword of Damocles that was hanging over our heads.

He got to my house, and I went over to him and gave him a hug. I found that I couldn't let go, no matter how hard I tried. To my surprise, the tears came out of nowhere, and I sobbed into his shoulder. *I can't lose him. I just can't lose him.* "I'm so sorry. I don't know what got into me."

He continued to hold me even after the tears abruptly stopped. "Serena, I understand. This is tearing me up as well. I don't show it, though."

I looked at him. "Why don't you show it?"

"It's just not in my nature. But I'm in just as much

185

agony as you are about all of this. I would like there to be a way around it, but I really can't see it."

"I can. Call her bluff. See if..."

He kissed me full on the lips when I said that. Then he stared at me for a few minutes while he ran his fingers through my hair. He kissed me on the forehead while his strong arms wrapped tightly around me again. "Don't be naïve. Charlotte would be okay, and I probably would have been able to call her bluff if it weren't for my feelings for you. She knows me well, too well, and she knows how I feel about you. She understands that what I really want to do is make things permanent with you. All these years, she hasn't really felt threatened. She's always had it in her head that maybe she and I were endgame after all, so she hasn't done anything negative. But she knows that you're different. So..."

"Well, let's not let this whole thing ruin our day together." I was so looking forward to the beach, which was something that I loved to do year-round. It was the main reason why I moved from New York to San Diego. I tried to get to the beach when I lived in New York as well, but it wasn't the same as actually living within walking distance. Coronado wasn't within walking distance, although it wasn't far, either.

We packed up the car with the umbrella, a cooler, boogie boards, two chairs and the two dogs, and set off.

On the drive there, Slade held my hand and kissed it from time to time. I didn't have to close my eyes to know what he was feeling. It was written on his face and I could tell by his actions. He loved me, and I loved him, and he was feeling that there wasn't a damned thing that could be done to prevent what he was going to do. I knew that there was, but I didn't tell him that. He would have made me stop the car and he would have gotten out. He would be that angry if he knew what I was planning.

We arrived at Coronado along with another line of cars, passing through the stations that used to take tolls for the Coronado Bridge, but now were defunct. I wondered why they didn't just take these stations down, because they were very confusing. The first time I saw these stations, I didn't think that I could enter the island, because I didn't have change nor my debit card on me, so I was surprised that I could just sail on through without having to pay anything at all.

The winding road took us through the town, which was one of the cleanest towns that I had ever seen. There was plenty of green grass and parks, and there wasn't any litter on the streets or graffiti on any wall. Nobody was ever seen panhandling. People lined the streets, heading to restaurants, bars or shops, which lined the streets. This was a touristy part of town, due to the enormous "Hotel Del," a large white hotel with distinctive red cupolas, made famous by the old Billy Wilder movie *Some Like It Hot*, which was partially filmed at this destination. The main part of the old hotel was red and pyramid shaped on the bottom, yet was round. The rest of the hotel looked like a castle, with the red pointy cupolas that pointed high in the air.

I loved coming down here, because it felt like being a part of history. I could imagine Marilyn Monroe, Jack Lemmon and Tony Curtis wandering around the halls of the Hotel, and walking these very beaches.

The dog park was on the far end of the beach, next to an air force landing base. Which meant that, from time to time, enormous planes would land, coming in close to the people on the beach. That was somewhat exciting for me too, because I always loved being close to planes that were landing. It was somewhat thrilling.

We walked to the beach, hand in hand, and I let Bella and Gigi off the leash when we got to the dog beach part. They immediately started excitedly sniffing around, and another dog came up to make friends with them. The dog ran off, with Bella and Gigi running after her at top speed, barking all the way.

Slade couldn't help but smile, and neither could I. I smelled the air, which had the distinctive odor of the beach, and I felt instantly calmed. The water was surprisingly violent, which I didn't necessarily associate with Coronado, as this water was more shallow than other beaches around the city, so the waves were usually small in these parts. Then I remembered that there was a powerful hurricane in Mexico, which probably affected the surf in this area. Since Slade and I were planning on boogie boarding, it was fortuitous that these waves were better than normal.

It was the middle of the week, so there weren't a ton of dogs around, but there were about 20 or so, running around. I usually saw the same breeds when I came out here – Frenchies, Pugs, Labradors, Boston Terriers, and Pit Bulls. There were other random breeds, such as enormous French poodles and the occasional wolf-mix, but, by and large, I could tell which breeds were the most popular in the world by coming to the dog park.

After setting up the umbrella and our chairs, we sat down and got out some water and snacks. I stretched my legs out in front of me, putting my toes in the warm sand. I drank some of the contraband wine that we snuck into the place. Since alcohol wasn't allowed on any beach in San Diego, we couldn't just drink it openly, so we put the wine into containers that weren't clear and drank straight out of the containers. It wasn't that big of a deal here, though, since this part of the beach wasn't patrolled, nor were there any lifeguards on duty.

I watched the dogs frolicking for a while, and then got up, with our boogie boards. "Let's go," I said. It looked like the surf was rolling, and it was going to be an excellent day for this kind of fun. Slade got his board, and we raced into the water.

For the next hour or so, we boogied on our boards. I caught wave after wave, and some of the waves I rode all the way into the shore. This delighted me, as I felt like I was flying. The two little dogs were watching us from the shore, and Gigi would tentatively try to get into the water, before the waves would crash over here and she would back away, shaking her little head. After a little while, they made some other dog friends and forgot all about us, although I always had my eye on them.

Slade, for his part, was game, although I had the feeling he would rather be on a surfboard. He had told me that he was an excellent surfer, although he rarely had time to do it anymore, especially now that he was in the middle of the fight of his life. But he made do with the boogie board, and he was quite good at getting the right wave at the right time and riding it in.

After about an hour, we were ready for lunch, so we went back to our umbrella and opened up our picnic basket. Inside the basket were sandwiches, chips, fruit and coleslaw, the latter two packed in ice. There were also little plates and plastic utensils. I placed a sandwich and some chips on each of our plates and then dished out some coleslaw and fruit as well.

We ate in silence for a few minutes and drank our wine. He tentatively gave me his hand, and I took it. He squeezed my hand, and words didn't have to be spoken. This was a perfect afternoon. The temperature hovered around 80 and there wasn't a cloud in the sky, the dogs were running around like two chickens with their heads cut off, and the surf was perfect. Most importantly, we were sitting next to one another.

I wondered, I honestly wondered if we would ever have another day like this one. Would Slade be in prison in a few weeks? If he wasn't in prison, would he speak to me again when I got that videotape and halted his guilty plea? Would that videotape even do the trick? Even that wasn't a magic bullet. If the prosecutor wanted, she could pretend that the videotape didn't exist. It wasn't going to be authenticated, and it would be obtained by illegal means. Malcolm certainly wouldn't sanction it. The prosecutor could authenticate the video easily enough, but the fact that the video would be obtained illegally would make it difficult to introduce as evidence.

If that happened, then I would have to send the video to the media. That would blow everything up. Everything would be blasted to smithereens. The media would probably do the investigations that the police and prosecutor, thus far, had refused to, and they probably would be led to Charlotte somehow.

Once the cat was out of the bag, would my life be in danger? Would poor Margot be put through the ringer for whatever it was she did 10 years ago? If that happened, would Slade ever speak to me again?

So many questions were clouding my brain, and I tried desperately to shake them off. I wanted to just concentrate on this day, this perfect day. It wasn't going to last. Perfect moments never do. But I needed to have this day in my head and embed it into my memory. I wanted to be able to carry it with me whenever times got tough in the future. That was important.

Slade noticed how quiet I was. "What's on your mind?" he asked.

I couldn't tell him. I didn't know how to explain it, even if I wanted to tell him. So, I simply said "just thinking about how perfect this day is."

He smiled, and I could see that his eyes were weary behind that mirthful expression. "It is a perfect day. Thanks for thinking of this."

"Well, I thought it was important that I be able to include the dogs in this outing. I don't think that they've been to an off-leash park before. I know that I haven't brought them, and they were little tiny puppies when I got them, so I doubt that they went before they came into my life."

"They're making the most of it."

Indeed they were. They were still running around, socializing with other dogs. I saw other dogs come up and sniff them, and they would do the same. Then they would take off chasing each other or another dog, before resting in the sand. They were hilarious to watch, since their bodies and legs were so squat. I was always amazed how small dogs with short legs could be so damned fast, but I knew that they were. I had a dachshund growing up, with the shortest legs possible, and that dog could run like the wind. She would dart outside the door every time somebody would come to visit, and I would always be the one to chase her down. Even though I had always been athletic, I had a hard time catching her.

"What's after this?" Slade asked.

"Well, I thought that we would go to Vigilucci's to eat

on their outdoor patio with Bella and Gigi. They have amazing food and they are dog friendly too."

That was one of the best things about being in San Diego. Since there were so many restaurants with outdoor seating areas, there were a lot of restaurants that welcomed dogs. It was very important to me that I include those two girls in most everything I did, because they were truly a part of my family. When Luke and Dalilah went home, and god forbid, if Slade ended up in prison, they would be my lifeline.

———————

After about five hours of sitting beneath that umbrella, watching the waves and the dogs, and boogie boarding, we headed to the bathrooms to get changed for our dinner. Then we packed up the dogs and went to Vigilucci's.

We were seated in the outdoor patio, again under an umbrella. The chairs were black wicker, and the table had white table cloths with wine glasses at the ready. Slade ordered a bottle of wine, and an artichoke hearts appetizer, after clarifying that the artichoke hearts were made with oil and not butter. I felt embarrassed, just a little, when he also told her to hold the cheese.

"I feel bad. I know how much you love cheese," I told him.

He shrugged. "Life's a bitch," he said with a smile. "How can I ever survive not having cheese on my artichoke hearts?" Then he paused. "I doubt that I'll have cheese with my artichoke hearts in prison. Or artichoke hearts for that matter."

It was then that I truly saw the sadness behind his eyes. I thought that I had seen it earlier at the beach, but not like now. When you have a perfect day like this, with sun and fun shared with the one you love, followed by an extraordinary meal at a beautiful restaurant, it would be so hard to even contemplate having to give all that up. To know that you have to trade your beautiful mansion in Los Angeles, complete with a full staff of help, for a tiny prison cell would be devastating. Days like today, that I had taken for granted, would be gone forever. There wouldn't be fancy Italian food in prison, only the gruel that they have served to them by people with hair nets on. In place of a butler, there would be a beefy prison guard with a night stick. No more Vividus bed, which is the most comfortable bed in the entire world, literally. In place of that would be a tiny cot and a thin sheet.

Most devastating, though, would be the fact that we couldn't be together.

He squeezed my hand. "I'm trying not to think about it, but goddammit, it has been a great day. It's just starting to hit me."

I knew what he was saying. While he was talking, I suddenly became anxious. I hadn't heard back from Dalilah as to whether or not her father's security team could get that videotape. She promised to text me the moment she found out if they could do it in the tight time-frame that I demanded. Thus far, I hadn't received that text.

The waiter came around with our food and wine, and Slade ordered scallops for himself and capellini with toma-toes, garlic, and basil for me. I had to admit that his dish sounded truly amazing, as the scallops were served with risotto and sweet corn, and I briefly wished that I wasn't a vegan. I hadn't had a touch of animal products in years and years, and I wasn't about to start now.

We drank our wine while the dogs snoozed at our feet.

They were pooped after their day of fun, and the sounds of their loud snoring brought a smile to my face. I looked around, and there were people everywhere with their dogs. I hoped that my dogs' snoring sounds weren't bothering them. Nobody seemed to notice though, so I felt comforted.

"This is a cute place," I said, looking around. "I haven't been here before."

"Me neither. Then again, I haven't spent that much time around here before meeting you. I guess that you changed my life in more ways than one."

I raised an eyebrow and smiled. "That's a good thing."

"It's a very good thing." He took my hands and looked into my eyes. I felt my heart quickening, as it always did when he looked at me like that. He was seeing my soul; I knew that, just as I was seeing his. It was a strange thing really, being able to get one another the way that we had. Our sex games the other night bonded us even tighter than ever, if that was even possible.

"What are you thinking?" I asked him.

"Just thinking about seeing you naked in about an hour or so." He sipped his wine, and I knew what else he was thinking. He was thinking about seeing me tied up with a gag in my mouth while he lightly flogged me with a cat o' nine tails. I was thinking the exact same thing.

I felt a pool of moisture between my legs, and my body suddenly felt like it was on fire. I couldn't wait to get him alone later on that night. There was nobody who had ever made me feel the way that he did, and I doubted that there ever would be. How could there ever be somebody who made me feel so alive? I had lived my whole life without feeling the way that I did with him, and losing that seemed inconceivable. Inconceivable.

"I have to admit that I was thinking the same thing. I really need to feel you inside of me."

"You will. Trust me, you will."

Although the sun had gone down, and the evening had cooled off, I felt warmer than ever.

The food came around, and we dug in. We ate our food in leisure, sipping our wine with it, and holding hands from time to time. We filled the silence with idle chit-chat, while both of us knew what was on the mind of the other. It was written all over his face, and when I closed my eyes, I felt it. The white-hot lust emanated from his every pore. The other night had awakened something dormant in both of us, and it had sprung to life, consuming us in its wake. I felt that I had to be with him soon like that – naked in more ways than one. Our bodies would be naked, but our souls as well. It was unspoken that it was going to be a necessity for both of us to be exposed in that way, so that if the absolute worst thing happened, and Slade had to go away to prison for the rest of his life, we would each have something to cling onto when times got desperate.

After we ate our meal, we headed to my car, the dogs trailing behind us. They were sniffing the ground and the flowers and the trees. We were walking slowly, him with this arm around me tightly, me with my head on his shoulder. Neither of us wanted this time together to end, although both of us knew that it had to. Not anytime soon though, since I had taken that week off of work. Of course, that didn't mean that I was going to be with Slade the entire time. Rather, I was going to hopefully be meeting with Dalilah's father's security team. Ryan, who was Dalilah's father, was supposed to be talking with them soon. At a moment's notice, I was going to be flying to New York City, and then back to Sacramento to finally take the California

Bar. It was going to be a stressful whirlwind, but, if all went according to plan, it would be absolutely worth it.

We came to my car, and got in, securing the dogs in the back in their cage. I dreamily put my car into drive, and we headed back to my place. But, halfway back, Slade said "let's go to my house. I have a surprise for you there."

I felt tingly as I imagined what that surprise could be. I simply nodded my head, unable to speak. I was suddenly overcome with emotion, as the reality of the situation flooded through me.

He just smiled and continued to grip my hand. "You'll like it, I promise you."

"I know that I will." I didn't want to speak the words that were in my head, because if I spoke them out loud, they would become real. What I was thinking was that, in a little more than a week, there was a real possibility that all of this would be over. That I would only be able to see him, if at all, during weekly visits to the state prison. I swallowed hard, trying to not ruin this perfect moment after a perfect day. I concentrated on the road and the sound of Bella and Gigi in their kennel, snoring as usual. I tried hard not to let my mind wander to what was possibly going to happen.

Stay in the moment, Serena, stay in the moment. Or else the moment will be ruined. I wanted, more than anything in the world, for the moment not to be ruined, so I tried to think of the things that comforted me. Like the sound of the snoring puppies, and, since it started to rain lightly, the noise made by the gentle wiper blades. The whoosh of the water on the streets. "Finally, some rain," I said. We desperately needed the rain because of the drought that had been plaguing our state for years.

I finally looked over at Slade, who was smiling at me lazily. His beautiful green eyes were half-closed, and the grin lit up his beautiful face. I could read his emotions on his face, as usual, and I didn't necessarily see that he was thinking the same thing I was. It was as if he were completely divorced from reality. Maybe he was, or maybe he just didn't want to think about it. I willed my own brain to turn off so that I could concentrate only on him. "I know," he said, apparently responding to my comment about the rain. "Thank god, huh? I don't know what's going to happen to this state in a few years. We might all have to move out and go to someplace where it actually rains on a regular basis."

"Sometimes I miss thunderstorms. Actually, that's one of the things that I miss the most about living in New York, along with the change in seasons. I used to love to walk or run through Central Park when the leaves were changing. There wasn't anything like it in the world, really. It's funny how you take certain things for granted." Then I smiled. "However, I don't miss what came after the leaves changing. The bitter cold, the snow piled up on the sidewalk. The enormous mounds of snow that would line the streets after the plows went through. I hated trying to get to the subway in wintertime." I shook my head. "I guess it's a trade-off. I don't get my changing leaves, but I also don't have to deal with cold and ice."

"I think that I know what you mean, but not really. I'm an LA boy, born and raised. I never got to see snow unless I went to the mountains in the wintertime. Sometimes Helen and Scott would take me to the mountains so that we could see the snow, but I wasn't really that much into it. Of course, we also took vacations to various places around the globe, but it was usually during the summertime. The one exception was when we all went to Switzerland to ski one Christmas. That was a lot of fun."

"How well do you ski?" I had never been skiing myself, but I had always wanted to.

"Pretty well, I guess. I learned on that vacation from school that year, and I was on the black diamond course by the end of it."

"No fear," I said. "I admire people like that. Just see a mountain of snow, and conquer it."

"You can't let things defeat you or intimidate you. Any psychologist can tell you that you have to face your fears, no matter what they are, or they will control you."

"You don't have any major fears?" I asked him. I knew that the one thing that I was terrified of, absolutely terrified of, were spiders. If a spider invaded my home, I usually had to leave or call somebody to come and take care of it. Just the sight of one of those creatures paralyzed me with fear. I tried to think of sweet Charlotte, from the book *Charlotte's Web*, saving the pig Wilbur from certain death, but I just couldn't associate that sweet spider with the ugly creatures I encountered on a regular basis. It wasn't a rational fear, as everybody always told me that the spider was more afraid of me than I was of it, but that didn't matter. Arachnophobia was real, and I was afflicted with it.

Now of course, when I heard the name "Charlotte," I would never again think of that spider, but of Charlotte Boswell, who really was a spider in her own right. She had Slade trapped in her giant web, and it was up to me to try to get him out of it.

Slade shrugged. "I don't know, I guess I have some irrational fears. Not of heights or bugs or anything like that, though. I guess that I really fear being torn from the people I love. It happened to me once before, when I lost my mother to prison for all those years, and it's about to happen again. But there's nothing that I can do about that."

Instantly, he looked really sad. He looked out the window, staring at the rain, and I put my hand on his neck and squeezed.

"It's going to be okay," I told him. "I promise."

He had a look on his face that made me concerned, because he was probably wondering if I had something up my sleeve. "Serena, it's not going to be okay. And I hope that you're not plotting something that you think is going to make it all okay. Trust me, if you do something to screw up this guilty plea..." He shook his head. "My fear will come true, only I won't be losing you because I'm going to prison, I'll be losing you because you're going to end up dead and my mother in prison. I know that you think that you'll be doing a good thing, but trust me, it won't be."

I tried to laugh off what he was saying, so that he would be thrown, but all I could do was make a small sound. I felt that I was about to nonverbally confirm his suspicions, so I tried to concentrate on the road and change the subject. "Another fear that I have is of heights. I've somewhat conquered that though, by forcing myself on really high Ferris wheels and rollercoasters. I've even gone on a balloon ride once or twice. But for the life of me, seeing those old photographs of men sitting on beams high atop the city, just eating their lunches, gives me the willies." I was referring to the famous photographs of the men in the 1930s who worked on the Empire State Building. One photograph showed about twenty men on a beam eating, and others showed men taking naps on those beams, or working on affixing bolts. In the background was the city, and it appeared that these men were hundreds of feet in the air. I knew that there weren't any casualties in building that structure, so I knew that these men were safe, but it still gave me the heebie-jeebies. They truly were a part of the greatest generation. Nowadays, skyscrapers were mainly constructed with cranes, and the men who worked on them had safety harnesses, but it appeared that the men in the old pictures didn't.

Slade was silent when I was speaking, and I was afraid that our moment was truly over. There was something that I had said that tipped him off, and he wasn't happy. He seemed to be brooding. Then, just like that, he appeared to snap out of it. "I don't want to ruin the little time we have together by interrogating you. But just know that anything you do to throw a wrench into the works won't be appreciated. As long as I make that known, I'm going to drop the subject from here on out. I trust you, Serena. I trust you to respect my wishes, and realize that I'm not blowing smoke up your ass. If I thought, for one second, that there was an alternative, believe me, I would be taking it. I wouldn't leave you for all the platinum in the world if I didn't have to."

I smiled weakly, knowing that if I said something in that moment, it would come back to haunt me. I couldn't lie to him, so I just said nothing at all. I hoped that would be good enough, so that he would just forget this part of the conversation had ever happened. When I looked over at him, he was smiling again, and it seemed to be genuine, so I hoped that the bad moment had passed.

Chapter Twenty-Two

We finally arrived at his house, and I got the dogs out of their kennel, and the two of us went inside. "I can't wait to see your surprise," I said.

"Well, perhaps it's not such a surprise after the other night," he said. "But I have a room of my own that you probably will love."

I smiled, knowing what he was saying. I could just imagine what his playroom looked like.

I wasn't disappointed. He, too, had a St. Andrew's Cross in this elaborate room. He also had a spanking bench and handcuffs that were attached to the wall. I looked over at him and he raised an eyebrow. "Tonight I'm going to fuck you against the wall, but I want you to face me this time. I want to look you in the eye."

I felt totally excited when he told me that. I loved being blindfolded the other night, yet I also craved having the connection with him that came from the two of us looking at each other in the eye while we made love.

"Here," he said, handing me a leather catsuit. It had

cutouts for the breasts and my netherparts. He also provided me a pair of high-heeled leather boots. "I think that you would look delicious in this outfit."

I took off my clothes, making sure that Slade had a good look at me while I was doing it, and zipped up the catsuit and put on the black high-heeled boots. I felt like one of the Doms I used to see in the clubs I used to go to. When I got into the outfit, Slade grinned. He seemed amused and lustful, all at the same time. "As I knew you would, you look ravishing."

He kissed me and then pushed me against the wall with some degree of force. He clenched my head with his hands and his lips, so electric and on fire, completely devoured mine. Our tongues were interlocking and he leaned up against me so that I could feel just how hard he was. I already was feeling warm, because of the suit, but his kisses almost burned my skin. The heat in my body was starting to become unbearable.

Then, when Slade pinched my already-erect nipples, sending tingles of electricity and pain throughout my body, I cried out. He smiled. "You can come," he said. "I won't force you to hold back this time."

I simply nodded, as he lifted up my arms, high above my head, and secured them with the handcuffs that were attached to the wall. I loved the feeling of being helpless and controlled. I didn't know why I loved that feeling, but I did. It was the biggest turn-on for me that I could have possibly imagined.

Slade bit and sucked each one of my nipples as his hands wandered down to my netherparts, which were exposed in a cut-out at the bottom. He lightly pinched my clit, sending waves of pleasure and pain that radiated throughout my entire body. Then he smiled and unhooked me from the wall. I didn't quite know what to expect, as I felt unbalanced, but I soon realized what was going on. Slade had another St. Andrew's Cross that was on the floor, and he carried me over to that and lay me down on it. He secured my wrists and my legs to it, so that I was splayed helplessly, my legs spread far apart, my arms above my head.

I soon realized why he changed his mind about having me secured against the wall. He unzipped his cock, and it sprung free. He straddled my neck and fed me his manhood, inch by inch. My mouth tightened around it, sucking hard. I opened my throat, trying to take him all in, but I knew that was impossible. There was simply too much there. I was game, though, as he gently fed it to me while he groaned in pleasure.

I licked and sucked hard on his shaft, and I could tell at some point that he was close, so he immediately withdrew it from my mouth. He lay down on top of me and kissed me passionately while he fingered my clit. I felt like I was going to explode because the whole experience was just so sensuous and so right. I loved being confined, and I loved knowing that I had zero control over what was going to happen.

"This is probably not the right time to ask you," he finally said after he was done kissing me as I lay on the floor. "But what are your hard limits?"

I smiled. "I'm game for anything but humiliation. That means no golden showers or anything like that. I also don't necessarily enjoy being confined like in a box, although I love to be handcuffed of course."

He raised an eyebrow. "And that's it?"

I nodded. "That's it."

He kissed me some more and got up and went to his toy

box, which was just within reach. "I don't want to get into anything hardcore," he said. He had a jar of something in his hand, and I recognized it as being honey butter that was packed on ice. He put some of that in my inner folds, and, as his fingers caressed and massaged inside of me, I felt like I was already holding back on an orgasm. I tried to hold back on it, though, because it was too soon. Slade was right - when you hold back your orgasms, and you finally are "allowed" to come, it's a powerful sensation, more powerful than anything I had ever experienced in my life.

But, when his tongue started to lick up this butter, I couldn't hold back any longer. I groaned with pleasure, and the orgasm that was threatening earlier reached its crescendo and started to radiate outward from my nether-parts. I gasped, biting my lip, trying to hold back, but I couldn't. I cried out, and Slade immediately put his finger inside of me and swirled it around. He crawled down to where my breasts were and put each one in his mouth while he sheathed his cock and entered me slowly. It was almost painful to receive him at that point, because my clit felt like it was absolutely on fire. He thrust in and out, stroking slowly and deliberately, but picking up speed, so that he was fucking me hard. I swallowed and tried to control my breathing, but it was no use. I burst again, and I felt Slade cock pulsating, so I knew that he did as well.

He smiled and unhooked me. "This is just a taste my beautiful Serena," he said as he picked me up. "Now let's get to my bed and finish off the night."

He picked me up and carried me to his bedroom and turned off the lights. For the rest of the night, we made love - kissing, exploring and feeling each other in the night. I don't think that we got a wink of sleep, and that was okay, because sleep wasn't necessary. What was necessary was that we had to make every second count.

And count it did.

At some point, though, we were finally sated and both of us got some much-needed rest. Slade was wrapped around me from behind, and I had never felt so satisfied and happy in my entire life.

Chapter Twenty-Three

The next day, I woke up next to Slade in his bed, and found myself saying "our bed" in my head. I felt that he was so much a part of me by then that it was truly "our bed," and "our house," even "our dogs."

Stop Serena, I thought to myself as I looked at the sleeping Slade. He was sprawled out on his stomach, dead to the world. *You have to stop. You don't know what is going to happen in the future. Start thinking of him as being an integral and indispensable part of your world when you're more certain on the future.* This was an odd thing for me though, to be thinking so deeply about the beautiful dark-haired man next to me in bed. I had never in my life thought of anybody in quite those terms before. I had a difficult time getting close to anybody, for obvious reasons, and now, all that I wanted was for this man to be permanent. The irony was that our future was far from secure, and that there was a real possibility that I was going to have to see him, in the coming years, only during conjugal visits or talking on a phone with him behind a partition and me sitting on a hard metal stool on the other side of the wall.

I got up to make breakfast, and feed the dogs. I realized that I hadn't gone for a run in quite a while, because I had been recovering from my attack. My whole body felt the neglect. I missed the endorphins, the feel of crisp air of early morning in my lungs. I felt the need to smell the sea while my legs pounded the sand while the seagulls flew overhead. The entire experience of running in this city was something that I yearned for, and I hadn't done it in awhile. Yet, I felt that as long as Slade was a free man, he was going to be my focus. Running would only take away from that.

Again, I was "that girl." The girl who gives up what she loves so that she could spend time with her man. But, in this case, it was justified. Slade wasn't necessarily going to be around in another week and a half. I had the California Bar in a matter of days, and I was going to have to find an excuse to possibly fly to New York if Dalilah gave me the word. There was too much going on, and my daily run was suffering for it.

Slade came into the kitchen as I was making turkey bacon and eggs for him and cereal with flax milk for me. His hair was wild and just slightly askew and he was dressed only in boxer-briefs. This was my favorite look for him – it was almost primal the way that his puffy lips, strong jaw and gorgeous eyes looked in the morning, before he combed his hair and put on clothes. He wrapped his strong arms around me from behind while I stirred around the eggs, and I could feel his hard-on on the small of my back. He put his face in my neck and breathed deeply, not saying a word.

"Good morning sleepy head," I said to him. "I'm making breakfast, as you can see. But how you can eat baby chickens is beyond me, not to mention beautiful birds." I didn't make him pork bacon, because that was the one thing that I really couldn't countenance – I loved pigs, and I understood them. I knew how much they suffered. Slade did too, because ending gestation crates for the animals was a passion of his. I remembered that he held a charity ball in his house to address that cause.

"You're right. I love animals, and I'm not going to make a joke about loving eating them. I really should become a vegan like you." At that, he spun me around and planted a kiss full on my lips. "Last night was awesome, as usual." His hands wandered to the small of my back before resting on my butt. I was backed against the counter before he hoisted me up and I spread my legs.

"This is so unsanitary," I teased him, as his head went between my legs. His tongue leisurely found my clit, and his fingers swirled around inside of me. I moaned as he tore off my panties, and pulled down his boxer briefs and entered me.

"I know it's unsanitary," he teased back. "We're going to have to bleach this counter," he said with a smile. "But goddamn, you feel amazing right now." He lifted up my shirt, which, by now, was the only thing that I was wearing, and he sucked on my breasts as he stroked in and out. He kissed me passionately while he was fucking me hard, with my legs spread high in the air. I threw back my head and cried out as he brought me to orgasm, my inner thighs clenched around his taut waist. "I love you, Serena," he said. "I love you more than I ever thought I could ever love anybody."

"I love you too, Slade," I said as he rapidly stroked in and out. This was so hot, this spontaneous fucking. I loved this almost as much as I loved the more kinky stuff that we had been experiencing with each other. I felt real and raw and powerful.

He came inside of me, which was fine, as I was taking birth control pills, and I was reasonably certain that we were officially monogamous. He kissed me some more, putting my face in his hands, and I sighed. I jumped down off the counter, and smiled at him while I looked at the eggs, which were getting slightly overcooked. "Now look," I said. "Breakfast is burned. Guess we'll have to go out to eat. Darn."

Slade just shook his head. "Watch and learn," he said with a grin. He went to the refrigerator and got out the eggs and put a sauce pan on the stove and filled it with water and a little bit of white vinegar. While he hummed a song, he cracked the eggs into a bowl and waited for the water to start to boil. Once it did, he slid the eggs into the water and set the timer for two minutes. In the meantime, he got out some English Muffins and put them into the toaster. "Let's see, it looks like you didn't damage the turkey bacon too much," he said, as he examined the meat that was cooking on a skillet. Then he went back into the fridge and took out a lemon that he cut it in half, an egg yolk and some butter. I watched as he casually combined these three ingredients into a thick yellow sauce that made my mouth water, in spite of myself.

In two minutes, the eggs were just slightly cooked and the English Muffins were done. He assembled these onto a plate. "Eggs Benedict," he said proudly. "One of the first things I learned to cook when I was a small lad."

I had to smile. Even if I couldn't try that food, it looked scrumptious and, for a brief second, I found myself wishing that I wasn't a vegan. It smelled wonderful too. "You're quite the cook."

My own breakfast consisted of cold cereal with almond milk, strawberries, and orange juice. It looked positively pitiful in comparison to Slade's beautiful meal, but it couldn't be helped.

The two of us went to the sun room and sat down with our food. Slade smiled at me warmly, yet lustily, while we drank our juice and ate. "Man, I'm going to miss this," he said as he dug into his eggs. "A perfectly cooked egg, freshly squeezed orange juice, and the most beautiful woman the world has ever seen. Not to mention dogs." Bella and Gigi were at our feet, looking up at us with pathetically cute expressions. Slade reached down and pet them, and their little non-tails started rapidly wagging. "Somehow, I don't think that I'll be getting Eggs Benedict and freshly squeezed juice where I'm going."

He fed Bella and Gigi a bit of his bacon, and the two dogs eagerly lapped up this morsel.

"Don't do that," I scolded, swatting his hand lightly. "They're going to get fatter than they already are."

"They're fine. Frenchies aren't exactly known for their slim frames."

True that.

"So," I said, taking a deep breath. I was going to ask him what he wanted to do that day, aside from having sex, but I was interrupted by a text -- from Dalilah.

"So, what?" he asked me. "What were you going to say?"

I opened my mouth to speak, but nothing came out. I was completely distracted by the text, which simply said *they can do it. Call me.*

I shook my head, trying to remember what it was I going to ask him. But I couldn't. All I could think about was Dalilah's text, and the fact that I was not only going to have to answer her text, but I was going to have to think of an excuse to go home, alone. If Ryan's security team was going to be able to do what I needed them to do, I was going to have to hightail it to New York City. It was Wednesday, and the Bar was on Saturday, and Slade was scheduled for a guilty plea in exactly one week. There wasn't a day to waste.

"I don't remember. Listen, Slade," I said. "Yesterday was a lot of fun. All of it. But, if I ever hope to pass the California Bar, and become an attorney here in the Golden State, I need to study. So, after breakfast, I'm so sorry, I have to get on it."

Slade's face immediately fell, and I felt terrible. He looked hurt, a little crushed even. "Okay," he said, digging into his eggs silently. His mood was definitely solemn, and, in a few minutes, he didn't look hurt so much as pissed. "No, it's not okay. You never even mentioned having to study earlier. I had assumed that we would spend as much time as possible together before I..." His voice trailed off and I shook my head.

How was I going to pull this off? Slade was going to track me, that much was clear. His face said that he was suspicious about why I suddenly was trying to give him the brush-off. He would know where I was, and he would know that I in New York. Yet, there was no way, no earthly way, that I could ever tell him where I was going. I was just going to have to get up there without my cell phone, which would probably send Slade ballistic.

It was certainly a dilemma. There wasn't a way that I could slip out of town without him either knowing or getting pissed because he couldn't figure out where I was. And he might even start to think the worst – that Charlotte had nabbed me anyhow. No matter, I was going to have to put him off, and get to New York with Dalilah and Luke on

Ryan's plane. I was also going to have to face the music when I got back, and I had no clue what I was going to tell him.

I had a family emergency? Nope, he would want to know why I didn't include him.

I had to get away to some peace and quiet to study? That wouldn't work – he would want to know why I just didn't tell him that and why that would necessarily mean that I was away from my phone.

He was now glaring at me. I tried to smile to show him that everything was okay, but that only made him avert his eyes. "Well," he finally said, after a silence that permeated the entire house. "I guess you need to be going. Thanks for breakfast." He threw down his napkin, and, just like that, he got up from the table.

I followed him into the bedroom, where he was hastily dressing. "Slade, I'm sorry, I would love to spend more time with you, but…"

"But what? You told me, time and again, that you didn't really need to study. That you know those topics like the back of your hand. That you passed New York without having to really study, and trust me, New York is one of the toughest in the country. Even tougher than California. I personally think that you have something up your sleeve, and if it's what I think it is…" He shook his head. "It better not be. That's all I have to say."

I started to feel panic rising in my throat. I should have known that Slade was no dummy and could figure out what I was up to. Then again, maybe he was just being paranoid that I had somebody on the side.

"Wha-wha-what do you think I'm up to?"

He said nothing, but just finished dressing. "I'm serious, Serena," he said, as he stood up. "Back the fuck off. If you don't, you're going to send so much bullshit cascading onto your head, you won't even know what hit you. And trust me, I won't be able to save you next time."

At that, he left the bedroom and I followed him into the living room. He went to the front door. As he left, he shouted at me over his shoulder, "Lock up when you leave." I couldn't follow him outside because I was still dressed only in my underwear. So, I watched from inside the house as he pulled away and drove off.

I was shaking as I texted Dalilah back. "Meet me at the airport in 30 minutes," I texted, and then I got dressed and got the dogs kenneled. I would drop them off at a doggie hotel near the airport, which was only about 20 minutes away.

She texted me back right away, giving me instructions for how to find her father's plane.

I dropped off the dogs, and then headed to Lindbergh Field. The airport was situated just off of downtown San Diego, which I thought was a pretty crazy place for it to be. The planes flew low over the buildings, and I had always heard that it was a dangerous place to land. Still, it was convenient, and ordinarily, I would have been fascinated to see planes landing so close to the street. But I wasn't thinking about that. I was thinking about how Slade seemed to know what I was doing, and how pissed he was. Was this going to be the end of us? If Charlotte made good on her threat, would his mother go to prison? Would I be the target of a mafia hit?

My hands were absolutely shaking on the steering wheel. I felt a well of panic rise and fall steadily. I knew that I was doing the right thing, but at what price? I was going to be unleashing the fury in a very unhinged woman who would stop at nothing to get what she wanted.

I didn't have my cell phone. I couldn't bring it, obviously, because Slade would definitely be tracking me and he would know just where I was. I guessed I really shouldn't have been too concerned, because he already knew what I was up to, but I didn't want to take the chance that I would have to wait on Dalilah and Luke, and Slade would show up at the airport and raise a stink.

I went to the terminal that had the private planes, and Dalilah and Luke were already there. "We both got a hotel near the airport," she explained, giving me a big hug. "I'm so happy that this can happen. Trust me, this security team is amazing. They can do anything, anything at all. They've hacked into the government servers and it didn't take them all that long. They're the best in the business."

"I hope so," I said. "Slade's server, I'm sure, has a ton of security. He has to have amazing security, just because of what he does. He has to ward off corporate espionage."

"Well, my grandfather was a billionaire and extremely powerful and extremely paranoid. He got this security team to protect him, and I've been amazed at what they have been able to accomplish."

I gave Luke a hug too, and looked at baby Olivia. She was a beautiful child, just sleeping in her carrier. Oh, how I wished that life was as uncomplicated as it was for her. The only things that she had to worry about were when her diaper was going to be changed or when she would be able to nurse. There was nothing else in her world but those two things.

She'll find out soon enough how cruel the world can be. I hated that I was feeling so cynical, but this whole process was bringing that out in me – the cynical bitch. There were people in the world, like Charlotte, who ruined everything for the rest of us.

"Hey, while they're at it, can this security team do something else?"

"What's that?"

"Can they find out information about Charlotte? I really would like to know if there's anything in her background that we could use against her. When the shit hits the fan, we might need leverage."

"Sure," Dalilah said. "We could do that."

"Thanks."

I had no idea what sort of information would constitute "leverage" when it came to a woman like Charlotte. Maybe there was nothing at all that we could find out. Or maybe there was nothing that would make a difference in this situation. I didn't know, but I really wanted to find out.

We climbed aboard the plane, which was a beautifully appointed jet with leather seats and a mini-bar. I had never in my life been on a private plane, and I was very impressed. "Man, I could get used to this," I said as the sky hostess brought around mimosas and smoked salmon on crackers for Luke and Dalilah. I begged off, however, not able to eat the salmon and not feeling like drinking.

Dalilah smiled. "My grandfather was a very wealthy man, and he wasn't exactly good to my father, so he bought him this plane."

"Did you know him?"

"Not really. I heard that he had a deathbed conversion, though, which gave my dad closure on all that he did to him." She looked out the window as the plane flew high in the sky. I did the same, and saw the cars start to look like ants, and then saw as the land started to resemble a checkerboard. I tried hard to swallow my anxiety, as I imagined what Slade was thinking as he tried to track me and couldn't. He was going to be infuriated. He might even call it quits. I had no idea what was going to be in store for me when I got back to San Diego, and I didn't really want to think about it.

"You okay?" Dalilah asked me. "You're looking kinda pale."

"I'm fine. I just don't know what's going to happen with Slade and me after all of this goes down. Assuming that we'll be able to get our hands on that videotape, that is. He's going to be so angry, and his mother might be at risk. Not to mention myself." I tried to quell the lingering doubts that were filling my head. I knew that I was doing the right thing – so why did it feel like the wrong thing?

"Maybe that woman is bluffing," she said.

"There's only one way to find out, I guess." Of course, the way to find out was going to end up in disaster for everyone involved. I wondered if I could find any way possible to blackmail Charlotte into not doing what she was threatening to do. Lord, what had I come to – thinking about blackmail, illegally hacking into computer systems, lying to Slade...I had tried so hard to turn over a new leaf when I moved to San Diego, yet scandal seemed to follow me wherever I went. It hung on me like a cheap suit. I wondered if there was ever a way to get away from it.

"Well, we're going to be on this plane for awhile, and there's nothing that we can do until we get there. So, let's try to take our mind off of it for now. I have some movies to watch, or we could play some cards."

"Actually, that would be fine, but I really need some sleep." After all, I got very little sleep the previous night.

So, I closed my eyes, and to my surprise, I actually started to drift.

Chapter Twenty-Four

Slade - Present Day

Serena had something up her sleeve, and I didn't like it one bit. While I didn't necessarily know what she was up to, I had some idea. She was going to try to find the one piece of evidence that would exonerate me. I loved her for doing that, but, at the same time, I hated her for doing that as well.

I wasn't going to be blindsided. I was going to have to find out if I had any options if the whole guilty plea were blown to smithereens. So, I called Charlotte.

"It's me," I told her. "We need to talk."

"Huh. Don't tell me you're backing out."

"I'm not. But we still need to talk. There might be a problem. I don't know, but I need to talk to you all the same."

"Slade, you know what you need to do."

"I know. But listen; there might be a kink in the works. I need to talk to you, and I need to talk to you now."

"Okay. Come up and meet me at my home."

I hung up without a word. I was apprehensive, more than apprehensive about everything that was going to happen. What I needed to do to make sure Serena and my mother were safe if Serena decided to take it upon herself to do the one thing that I didn't want her to do.

I drove up the coast, thinking the whole time about Serena. I loved her more than I thought I could love anyone. Going to prison was going to devastate me, mainly because I couldn't be with her. Yet, there was the distinct possibility that I wouldn't be able to be with her anyhow. I knew what Charlotte wanted from me. What she really wanted, if she couldn't see me suffer, was to be with her. I couldn't stand to be in the same room with her, yet...I shook my head. There had to be another option. There had to be some way that I could still be with Serena, and secure her safety and the continued freedom of my mother. I only wished that I still had something to hold over her head. Something good.

She was dangerous. Of course, I always had the option of turning her in for the murder of Jordan. She would most likely beat that charge, but, even if she didn't and she ended up in prison, Serena would be dead for sure. Charlotte would make sure of that. She would put a hit on her faster than you could blink an eye.

Turning her in was out of the question. There had to be something else.

The pit in my stomach was twisting, inside and out, as I continued my drive up the coast. I had to play the game on her level, because she held all the cards at the moment. I hated that feeling, but I knew that she was not only more ruthless than I had ever contemplated being, but she was also more powerful. Like it or not, she had the one of the most powerful mafia families in the area at her beck and call. They were second only to the Bianchis, in terms of power. Serena wasn't an enemy for them, so ordinarily she wouldn't be a target of a hit, but Charlotte was the daughter of the godfather, so she could make it happen. Only if I stayed one step ahead of her could I prevent this, assuming that Serena was going to do what I thought she was going to do.

I could try steely determination and see if she blinks first. In other words, I could call her bluff and tell her that I would send that videotape into the proper authorities, and work with Malcolm to ensure that he rats on her as the mastermind, and see what happens. That was one option, one that I had considered, but one that I dismissed pretty early on. The downside to that was abundantly clear - she probably would just have Malcolm taken out so that he couldn't say a word, and then there would be no tying her to the crime. Then nothing would stop her from laying waste to both my mother and Serena. This made her dangerous.

I could work with Malcolm first to have him give testimony to the prosecutors about his involvement, after I turn in the videotape to show that he did it, all behind Charlotte's back. But if I did this behind her back, she would be infuriated to the point where Serena and my mother would be in danger immediately. If the authorities would go up and arrest her after this happened, she would immediately send word to her father about what she wanted to make happen, and I had no doubt that it would happen.

Which left me with my other dilemma – how to prevent Charlotte from putting a hit on Serena and turning in my mother, even after I took the fall and went to prison. I had to believe that wouldn't happen, because she would have gotten what she wanted out of this whole mess, which would mean that she wouldn't have motive to hurt them. I had considered speaking with Malcolm about an insurance policy, should things go wrong, but I wasn't at that point just yet. The last thing that I wanted was for Malcolm to go behind my back and tell Charlotte that I was speaking with him about him rolling on her if anything happens to Serena and my mom. If that word got to her, she would uncork her vengeance.

I had thought about all of these scenarios in my head before, but they were even more present in my brain as I sped up the coast. Charlotte had secured the best trap that she possibly could, and I was in it completely. I had to accept the fact that my going to prison wasn't going to 100% secure the safety of Serena and my mother, but it gave both of them the best chance.

But Serena had something going on, and I was just going to have to work with that reality. I had to see if there was any option that would save both of them, should Serena somehow, someway, find that videotape, thereby putting a kink into the works.

I finally arrived at Charlotte's mansion, which was situated high in the Hollywood Hills. It was secluded and surrounded by iron gates and armed guards. I flashed my ID and told them that Charlotte was expecting me, and they nodded and waved me on. I drove through and then got to her door. A doorman, who evidently was expecting me, opened it as I approached. "Miss Boswell is in the sitting room," he said. "She is meeting with her agency, but she is expecting you."

I nodded, and he led me through the maze of the house and opened up the door. Charlotte was sitting behind a desk, and there were five people around her. She saw me and immediately dismissed them. They looked at me, a bit stunned that I was there, evidently, and they left.

Did she just make a mistake? She had her publicity people there, meeting with her, and obviously didn't tell them that I would be arriving. They looked like they had no idea that she and I were still in contact. A kernel of an idea started to form in my head. It was a long-shot, as any idea in this arena was, but I just might have found my Ace in the hole.

"Slade," she purred. Whenever she spoke with me, she used her huskiest voice, one that was reserved just for me. She projected this voice very well, however. "I would have to say that this is a pleasant surprise, but, then again, it's not a surprise, is it?"

"No," I said. My mind was flashing to those publicity people. Was there a rat in there who would sell their hottest client to the highest bidder? I shook my head. Even if I could get a whisper campaign going that Charlotte was involved in Jordan's murder, it would only increase her cache in the eyes of the public. And it would bring her a ton of publicity. Any publicity is good publicity, I had to remember. A whisper campaign wouldn't do it. I would have to definitely tie her to Jordan's murder, and I was going to have to do it in a way that she didn't know what was happening; as impossible and dangerous as that would be.

"So," she said, gesturing to the leather-backed chair in front of her desk. "What brings you up here today? I have a bad feeling that things might not be going according to plan."

"They are. I have my guilty plea teed up for next Wednesday." I swallowed hard. It was gut-check time. I looked her in the eye, trying to discern what she was thinking, but it was impossible. She was slippery, and she always had been.

"You know, Slade, I wish that it didn't have to come to this. I never wanted to see you behind bars. But I also certainly don't want to see you in the arms of another woman. As you know, I would rather see you behind bars than to be married to anybody but me." She looked, at that time, like a vulnerable girl, not a heartless villain. That was her acting skills, though. They were honed to a T, especially now that she was Hollywood's "It" girl. I knew that she had a real future in Hollywood. Not only did she have the looks to rival any supermodel, and she was a supermodel herself, but she was undeniably dynamite on the big screen. I had to grudgingly accept that fact after seeing her in the Gus Van Sant movie, and seeing her dailies in her David Fincher movie. She was a star.

I drummed my fingers on the desk, wondering how far I needed to take this and how to play it. "How is your movie coming along?" I asked her, trying to buy time.

"It's great. The film is getting a ton of early-release buzz, so it's an exciting time right now."

"Are you the next Rooney Mara?" I asked her. Rooney was one of the women that got all the early buzz for another Fincher film, *The Girl With the Dragon Tattoo.* Unfortunately, that film didn't live up to its own early buzz and was a disappointment at the box office. Rooney's fortunes apparently fell with the prospects of that film. She was amazing in it, though, so it was a shame that nothing much happened with her career.

She narrowed her eyes. "That's a shitty thing to say." Then she sat up straight and looked at her nails. I was getting to her, sensing her fear. *She's afraid of failing. She's afraid that I'm right. She's afraid that she's going to fall flat on her face in front of the world.* How was I going to use that to my advantage?

It was always vital to find an enemy's weak spot, and I think that I found hers; her ego. It was fragile. She desperately wanted the public to love her, and she desperately wanted to be a huge star. The next Jennifer Lawrence. I looked in her eyes and saw that she already imagined herself in front of the Academy, accepting the award for Best Actress. I also saw in her eyes the fear that she would be an also-ran before she even got the chance to begin. The next Rooney Mara, if you will.

"Cut to the chase, Slade," she said, her voice changing from kitten to pissed-off she-lion. "Why are you here?"

I drummed my fingers on the desk, a plan suddenly starting to form. "I wanted to tell you in person that I am going to plead guilty on Wednesday. I wanted you to look me in the eye so that you can be assured that this will happen. The last thing that I want is for you to get itchy trigger fingers and pull the plug on this whole thing prematurely."

She leaned back in her chair, evidently satisfied with this explanation. Then she got up from behind the desk, and slinked behind me, unbuttoning my shirt and putting her fingers on my chest. I felt my skin crawl at her touch, and I immediately took her hand off of my chest.

"I'm sorry," she said in a tight voice. "I thought that maybe you were really here because you wanted to see me."

"No," I said, realizing that I was probably riling her up. "I'm not here to see you. I mean, I am here to see you, but not for the reason that you thought. I simply wanted to talk to you face to face, to reassure you that everything is going according to plan."

She sat back down behind her desk, evidently disappointed. "Okay, Slade, well, you've seen me. Now I would like for you to leave."

I stood up. "Okay."

"I need my publicity people back in here, so, when you go, please tell them that I need to speak with them some more."

Oh, this was becoming too easy. "I will."

At that, I went out into the hallway, where the team was sitting around on chairs. They looked bored and put-out that Charlotte was so willing to dismiss them to speak with me. I caught the eye of a young blonde who bit her lip shyly and looked up at me with seductive eyes. I knew that look. I had seen it all my life in the eyes of females. I knew the power of having a lot of money and the looks to go with it. I wasn't full of myself, but I knew.

"You guys can go back in there," I said. They all stood up to go, but the young blonde hung back, looking at me. I smiled at her, and she looked like she was going to melt into the floor. "You know," I said, addressing her, "I can always use somebody new on my own publicity team. Why don't you give me your card?"

With shaking hands, she nodded her head, and, without a word, gave me her business card. "Sarah Fuller," it read, and I recognized that she was a part of the largest talent agency in the business. Her eyes never left mine as she walked into the door. Then she finally disappeared, and I thought that maybe, just maybe, I had found my 'Ace in the Hole'.

Chapter Twenty-Five

Serena - Present Day

We finally landed in New York, and the oppressive humidity hit me in the face. "Oh, summer in New York. I can't say I miss this." San Diego was hot, but it wasn't usually humid. Not like this, anyhow. I felt like I couldn't breathe. Then again, that could also be because of the situation that I was in. I felt like I was trapped in a box, and there was no way out. Any way I looked, any way I turned, there was peril. If the security team was able to retrieve the video, there would be peril. If they couldn't, there would be worse peril.

Heads I lose, tails you win.

Dalilah was sensitive to my mood, of course. She was carrying little Olivia in her carrier, and she caught up with me as I was rapidly walking down the concourse towards the gate. She put her arm around me. "It's going to be okay," she said. "I promise you."

I wished that I could believe her, but I couldn't say much

of anything at all. I was too in my head about all that was at stake. Not to mention about all that was going to happen when we got back. "Let's just head over there and see what happens."

"Okay."

At that, we walked into the airport and jostled with everyone else until we got to the street, where there was a limousine waiting for us. A man immediately got out and put our bags into the trunk, and we sat down in the leather seats. I breathed hard, in and out, in and out, trying to calm the rising panic that was in my chest and radiating throughout my body. I had never before felt like this.

Dalilah put her hand on mine sympathetically. "I know how you feel. I felt the same way when Nottingham had me in his evil clutches. It worked out, and it will work out for you too. You and Slade are meant to be, and nothing will come between you."

Luke, for his part, sat in the front seat, and turned around and smiled at me. "Serena, you got this. Look at all the problems Dalilah and I had, and we're solid; the other night not-withstanding."

Dalilah just shrugged when Luke referenced the epic fight they had about whether or not she was going to hack the computers for me. "We go round and round sometimes, because we're both stubborn. I think that this compromise that we made really is best for everyone. I'm an amateur, these people are absolute pros. It's what they do."

I nodded and looked out the window. The sky was grey and the city seemed dirty to me. I never really noticed it before, but since I had been living in the land of palm trees and beaches, it all seemed different. I thought that I would miss New York more than I did. While I wasn't a "native

New Yorker," I had lived here for long enough to consider myself a part of the city's fabric. Yet, when the car got going and we immediately got stuck in traffic and people were honking and yelling, I cringed. I saw none of this in San Diego. There was traffic there, but not like this. Nobody honked their horns and screamed out the window, and there wasn't usually gridlock.

Luke smiled. "Welcome home, Serena. I bet you missed this."

"No. How do you guys still live here?"

"Where else are we going to live? This is where it's at. This is the scene. You guys might have palm trees and beaches, but we have life. Not to mention the epicenter of the art world. It's all a trade-off."

"I guess I'm really not in the mood for all of this." I wanted Slade to be next to me, and I wanted all of this to be over. I needed to be able to see all of it in the rear-view mirror, much like Dalilah was currently seeing the Nottingham situation in the rear-view mirror. The Nottingham situation was a nightmare for her – he had forced her into marriage by blackmail, and Dalilah had gotten pregnant with Luke's child while she was still married to that bastard. There was a long time when she feared that Nottingham was going to try to take custody of the child, until she found a way to blackmail him into giving up his rights to the baby. Luke was the biological father, of course, but Nottingham was the father by law. It was a mess, an absolute mess, and thank god, she was able to straighten it all out.

Blackmail. That seemed to be the only way to get things done with diabolical people. Perhaps that would be what we would be able to do with Charlotte. That would be the dream – find out something about her that would cause her to back the hell off.

The limo slowly crept along until we reached an enormous high-rise building. "This isn't where you guys are living now, is it?" I asked, looking at the gleaming glass structure.

"No, I wish. I mean, we're doing okay, but we can't afford to live in a building like this. This is the headquarters for my father's security team. Ralph, the limo driver, is going to drive our bags to our apartment and drop them off."

At that, Ralph got out and opened the door, and we walked onto the sidewalk. Then we went into the magnificent lobby, passed through without a side-ways glance from the security guard, who evidently knew Dalilah and Luke, so I was okay, as well, and we took the elevator up to the 75th floor. My stomach went *whoosh* along with the elevator as it climbed and climbed. "We should have eaten," I said. There was food on the airplane, of course, and it seemed to be good food, but I wasn't in the least bit hungry at that time. Of course, it was salmon that was served on the plane, and I didn't bother to ask about vegan options.

"We will. We'll get breakfast as soon as we're done here."

"Done here? How long will this kind of thing take them?"

"Not as long as you might imagine. I'm telling you, these people are pros. They know what they're doing."

We got to the suite and we went back to the office, without the receptionist even trying to stop us. She greeted us, of course, calling Luke and Dalilah by name, but she didn't make us wait at all. I supposed that was because Dalilah knew everyone here quite well and why shouldn't she? This was her father's security team. Her father was extremely wealthy and powerful in his own right, having inherited billions from his own father. He had put this to use by passionately throwing himself into animal rights, which brought a special place to my own heart. I loved the work that he was doing, not just domestically, but abroad. He was slowly, but surely, changing the way that the world saw animals, and he was an absolute god-send to all the suffering creatures in the world.

We walked into the office, where we were greeted by Lars, who was the head of the team, Dalilah explained to me. "Dalilah," he said, giving her an enormous hug. "It's so good to see you."

"And you, Lars," she said.

He gave Luke the same hug, and shook my hand warmly. "You must be Serena." The man was tall and blonde and very Nordic. He spoke with a slight accent, very slight, and was dressed casually in jeans and a t-shirt that showed his muscular arms. His face was marked by enormous dimples, and he seemed to be a very jolly man. He immediately put me at ease.

"So, I guess that you need something from me?" he asked, directing his question at me.

"Yes. I need a video that's apparently on one of my boyfriend's computers. Slade Bridgewell."

"Yes," he said. "I've been working all morning, and I've already pinpointed all of his servers around the world. His firm has offices in China, India, Venezuela, Spain, Italy, Germany, and even in Sweden." He grinned when he said that. "He has offices in Stockholm, of course, but also in Gothenburg, which is my hometown. Good taste, putting offices there."

"Good," I said, feeling encouraged that he was already

so far into the project. "How difficult is it going to be to retrieve this video?"

He shrugged. "It would be extremely difficult for most people, but I'm not most people. I've been able to retrieve information from places that you would never even imagine. Your boyfriend has the kind of security that I usually only see at the very highest level of national defense. That's understandable, of course, considering the business that he does. But, do not worry, if I can retrieve information from the Department of Defense, I can retrieve it from him. I'm working on the encryption right now. Give me the afternoon, and I should have something for you."

"Thank you," I said. I still felt sick. We were breaching Slade's security protocols. This was such a violation. Slade always told me that he feared corporate espionage anyhow, and I was opening him up to this.

I cursed having to do it this way, but I knew that there was nothing else that could be done.

"Can you do something else for me?" I asked Lars.

"I'm sure I can. What do you need?"

"I need for you to try to find out any dirt on Charlotte Boswell. Birth name is Carlotta Garancino. I have this gut feeling that there is something out there that Slade maybe doesn't know about, and it might be something that would give me insurance against her."

"Sure. I can find out if she's been institutionalized or been in rehab or committed a crime or anything else that you need to know. I imagine that is the kind of information that you've been looking for?"

"Yes. Something along those lines. The woman is too crazy to not have sought some kind of professional help along the way."

"You got it. Is there anything else?"

"No, I think that if you could find that out, along with the video, we should have what we need to put this whole thing to bed."

At that, we all left the office, after giving our pleasantries and hugs.

"That wasn't so bad, was it?" Dalilah asked on the elevator.

"No, he certainly has a sunny personality. That helps."

We got to the lobby and went through the doors. "Let's find a place to eat," I said. "I'm really in the mood for something good."

We ended up at the *Candle 79*, a popular vegan restaurant. I ordered the black bean-pumpkin seed burger, and Dalilah got the zucchini enchiladas while Luke got the spaghetti and wheat balls. "This is the one thing that I miss about New York," I said. "This city has some kick-ass vegan restaurants. We don't have nearly the same selection in San Diego."

To my surprise, I found myself starving. Not to mention, in the mood to drink. I needed something to take the edge off, so I ordered a Bloody Mary. Dalilah looked at me with longing in her eyes. "I wish I could join you," she said. "I love motherhood, but sometimes I don't like the sacrifices so much."

Luke put his arm around her, and nuzzled her neck. "You're such a great mom. Olivia is such a lucky, lucky little girl."

I was happy to see that they were, once again, in a good place. After that awful argument they had at my house, I had my doubts. And I knew that Dalilah was frustrated with not being able to be at the same level, professionally-wise, as Luke. Still, as I sat across from them, I felt nothing but satisfaction and happiness emanating from both of them.

I found that I couldn't say much to the two lovebirds across the table. I was too much in my own head. Everywhere I turned, there seemed to be roadblocks. Not just roadblocks, actually, but land-mines. Even after the waiter brought my "burger," which was a delicious black-bean concoction with pumpkin seeds, mesclun, onion, avocado and chipotle ketchup, with a side of fries that were made with polenta, I could barely say anything.

Dalilah, of course, was picking up on my mood and kept looking over at me with a worried expression. She put her hand over mine. "It's going to be okay. I can promise you this. Lars is the very best of the business, as are the people he has working under him. He's an absolute genius."

For Luke's part, he also knew that I was worried, but he wasn't able to find the words that Dalilah did, so he simply said "hey, after this, let's go to my gallery. We can also visit your old neighborhood, for old time's sake."

I smiled. "Let's." That was all I said.

We ate the rest of the meal in silence, aside from Olivia waking up and crying, which was followed by Dalilah breast-feeding her at the table, with a cloth over her breast. I didn't finish my meal, although it was delicious. I just didn't have the appetite.

The waiter came around, and I wanly pulled out my credit card to pay for the meal. Dalilah and Luke tried to pay for their parts, but I waved them off. "Don't even insult me," I said. "After all you guys have done, this is the very least that I could do."

They let me pay, both of them thanking me, and we got up and got into the limo that was apparently summoned by Luke when I wasn't paying attention.

"Take me to the Thiessen Gallery," Luke said, giving him the address.

We pulled up there after about 45 minutes of gridlocked traffic, and went in. This was a beautiful gallery right in the Village and close to where I used to live. The ceilings were about 12' high, and the windows were enormous and let in the light. I walked along the hardwood floors and admired the paintings and sculptures that were on exposed-brick walls. I didn't know a whole lot about art, but I did know what I liked. I knew what moved me. I couldn't begin to say that this artist was evidently influenced by this movement or that movement, or what medium they used, but when something drew me in, it drew me in. I guessed that was what art was really all about.

I got to the area where Luke had hung his latest work on the wall, and I stared at these paintings. It was amazing how much he seemed to be like me inside. The painting was of a desolate place, evidently an abandoned city street. There was a lone figure on the sidewalk – a ballerina, complete with a tutu. She was graceful and beautiful, with a long neck and the signature powerful thighs of a prima ballerina. She was on pointe, her head was cocked and her arms were curving in front of her. She looked like she was performing *The Nutcracker* for the Bolshoi Ballet. She was in the middle of a performance in the middle of the deserted street.

Beauty in devastation. That was what I got out of it. It made me think about Slade and I, clinging on to one another while the world fell apart around us. That was beautiful, really, how we felt about each other. It was pure and it was what was right. Everything else was wrong, but this was completely right.

Luke came over to me as I was standing there, looking at the painting. "That's one of my newest ones," he said.

"It's combining two of the themes that I've explored in the past – artists and desolation. It's meant to say that, in any kind of ugliness, there is always something beautiful. You just have to look for it." He looked kinda shy, talking about his work. "I conceived of this project when I thought back about my life with Dalilah and how Nottingham brought us together. He's so black and ugly, yet he brought something that is absolutely beautiful into my life."

I smiled, and tousled his hair. "I'm buying this," I said, going over to the counter where there was a woman who was ready to take any form of money for these art works. I gave her my credit card and explained where to have it delivered. The price was $10,000 and I was impressed that my little brother could command such a high price for his stuff.

Luke came over and put his arm around me. "Serena, you don't have to pay for this, silly."

I raised my eyebrows. "Oh, but I do. You've gotta get paid. You have a wife and daughter, and every dollar counts. Again, don't insult me."

"At least let me give you a discount."

I just shook my head and said nothing. "It's a beautiful piece, and I'll be honored to hang it up in my living room. I think even Bella and Gigi will love it, not to mention…" I was going to say the word "Slade," but the pang in my heart reminded me that Slade might not want a thing to do with me after all of this. Invading his privacy, opening him to espionage, retrieving a video against his will, subjecting myself and his mother to danger…There were so many transgressions I was committing against him. I knew that it would all be worth it in the end, but that fact didn't make doing it any easier.

I paid for the painting and then walked around some

more. To my surprise, I found myself getting lost in these pieces of art. I wasn't even thinking about Slade and about how awful everything was at that moment. I was only thinking about the pain and beauty that was on every canvas in the gallery. There were some enormously talented artists with this co-op, that was for sure. There was a reason that this gallery was one of the hottest in the city these days – it wasn't just that Henry Jacobs had endorsed it, although that certainly was a factor. It was that these artists put their heart, soul and blood on the canvas. They did the same with the sculptures. They were laid bare for all the world to see.

I wondered what it was like – to have the need to create. To have it as your lifeblood. To feel that if you didn't create, you would wither away and die. I knew that art was a catharsis, much like running was for me. It was a passion, not an occupation. I never knew something like this – I was never much of an artist. Hell, I wasn't an artist at all. I could draw stick figures, and that was about it. I had never taken up an instrument and learned to play. I remembered that Slade was an amazing piano player, and I felt envious of that. I could write, but I really reserved that particular talent for creating amazing legal briefs that usually won the day in court.

I had my one catharsis, running, but I didn't really have an emotional one. I didn't have a way to put my guts on a page or a canvas or a piano. I didn't have the kind of creativity that my brother Luke did, or my brother Christopher, for that matter. Christopher was as amazing as Luke, really, except his medium was the guitar, not the canvas. He and Luke both also had a gift for song-writing. They had collaborated on songs before, and Luke had attracted the attention of some major musicians with some of his work. It helped that he was in touch with Liam Gallagher, Dalilah's cousin, who was a prominent record producer in London. Liam had taken a shine to Luke last year, when Luke and Dalilah stayed with him while hiding out from Nottingham.

Dalilah came up to me as I was studying another painting that was an abstraction. I was drawn to this riot of colors and trying to interpret it. "Luke told me that you bought one of his paintings. That one that you bought is my favorite, too."

"Great minds think alike, huh?"

"Yes."

"It's amazing the talent that's on display in this gallery. Luke did very well coming here. And you, too. I guess you'll be back here after you get your maternal footing?"

"That's the plan. When Olivia gets a little older, I'll just bring her in here while I create. I can't wait, either. I've been itching to get back into it, but things have just been too crazy. Nothing against you, of course. We love helping you."

I sighed. "I know. I just wish that I could get out of my own way with this one. I wish that I could believe that it will all work out, like it did for you two in the end, but I can't see a happy ending with this. I just can't. Charlotte is too much of a loose cannon, and, since she's a mafia princess, she can get anything that she wants. She will use force to get it. Must be nice to go through life, knowing that you can do whatever you damned well please."

"I know what you're saying."

I turned around and looked at her sad face. I knew that she knew what I was talking about. Nottingham was the same way – he looked at the world as his chess board, and the people in it as his pawns. He used his money, power, and influence to get the "little people" to bow down to him. As far as I knew, he didn't use violence to get his way, as Charlotte apparently did. Yet, the result was the same – he couldn't be controlled, and, for the longest time, he let Luke and Dalilah know that. They got out from under him by showing that he was a criminal, an inside trader, and used that to blackmail him. He was a greedy fuck on top of everything else, and that proved to be his undoing.

I never quite understood men like Nottingham. He was a billionaire, yet that wasn't enough for him, apparently. He routinely dumped stock according to inside tips, or bought them on the same basis. This wasn't yet known to the feds, but Dalilah was able to find this out through Lars and his team. She used this information to blackmail him into giving up his rights to her baby girl.

I prayed that Lars could do the same for me. *Please find some good dirt on Charlotte. Some dirt that will make her play nice.* I shook my head. It would have to be some amazing dirt, considering that, if Slade doesn't pay the price for Jordan's murder, Charlotte probably would. She was behind it all, and that house of cards would come crashing on her head if Slade was exonerated for this murder. Self-preservation was always a powerful thing, and that had to be on her mind.

Dalilah walked around with me, with Olivia in a sling on her chest. The little girl was sleeping, as usual, her little thumb in her mouth. I smiled. "Has Luke ever thought of doing a portrait of you and Olivia like this?" I asked her. Dalilah looked just like a picture, standing there, gorgeous without a stitch of makeup on, with an infant lying against her.

"Oh, yes, we've talked about that. In fact, I think that we will be doing just that, as soon as everything calms down."

"How long do you think all this will take?" I asked her, while I stared at another picture. This one was a photograph of a person - a waitress who was standing at a counter with a dreamy look in her eyes. She wasn't necessarily happy with her station in life, but she didn't seem entirely dissatisfied, either. She seemed contemplative, as if she was thinking about the future, and it was going to be brighter than her present. Like me. I was hopeful, despite all the odds being against all of this.

"With Lars, it really shouldn't take that long, maybe a couple of days, maybe a couple of hours. He has told me that Slade has many, many layers of protection that are going to be difficult to crack. As for getting dirt on Charlotte, that might be a bit easier. Hospitals and rehab centers have a lot of security, but Lars has experience with that. He knows how to get into databases as well."

I wondered how I would use that information, even if Lars was able to get it. Threaten to sell her out to a tabloid? Tell her current director, David Fincher, about it? I knew that there was often an issue with addicts and others, as far as insurance went. It was difficult to get insurance on people who had drug offenses and were addicted, which was why some talented actors had problems getting work when they had a reputation of being a drug addict. Robert Downey Jr. came to mind. He was severely addicted in the 1990s, to the point where he was in prison. Not jail, but prison. You have to be a hard-core addict to end up in the big house. He was able to come back, of course, in spectacular fashion and became one of the most well-respected actors in Hollywood. Not to mention one of the most bankable.

But Charlotte wasn't Robert Downey Jr. She was new on the scene, and hadn't yet built up the cache that he had when he made his comeback. He had been nominated for an Oscar before all his drama occurred. Charlotte had made one well-regarded movie, and was currently being spotlighted as the one to watch; the next Jennifer Lawrence. But she hadn't quite gotten there. Something major in her background could be scandalous enough to stop her rise.

Besides, if there was some scandalous dirt on her, wouldn't Slade know about it and use it against her? Maybe, maybe not, it all depended on when it happened and how close he was with her when it did happen. He wouldn't be able to get these records either, because such records are confidential and impossible to get for ordinary people. Lars wasn't an ordinary person, of course, so he would be able to find information that Slade wouldn't.

We walked around some more, and Luke found us in a few hours. "You guys ready?" he asked.

"We are," I said. "At least, I am. By the way, I'm really impressed with this gallery. It really has come a long way since you guys have been able to get so many benefactors and financiers on board."

"I know. Our co-op is attracting some of the very hottest artists in the city too. We've had to turn some pretty amazing people away." He shook his head. "Let this be a lesson to you, Serena. You can go from the very bottom to the very top in a short period of time. That's what happened to me personally, and that's what happened for Dalilah and me as a couple."

I paused. "We're doing the right thing, aren't we?" I asked him.

"We're doing the only thing, it sounds like. If it's a choice between this or prison for Slade, I think you know the answer to your own question."

We left the gallery and hailed a cab, since nobody had bothered to call the limo. Our plan was for me to pay a visit to my old neighborhood for old time's sake, and then maybe get dinner a little later on before checking into our hotel. It all sounded like a wonderful time, and it would be, if I didn't have so much on my mind. But I did have a lot on my mind, too much, and I couldn't get my thoughts off of it.

But I was going to try to forget about it for the evening, or else I was going to go crazy.

Chapter Twenty-Six

Slade - Present Day

As much as I didn't want to do this to Serena, I knew that I had to. That blonde was giving me signals that told me that she was really into me, and she could be an invaluable source of information. She was on Charlotte's publicity team, but that didn't mean that she was loyal.

So, I called her that evening. She had given me her card, which had her cell phone on it. She picked up, not recognizing my number, apparently.

"Hello, this is Sarah," she said, answering the phone.

"Hi, Sarah, this is Slade Bridgewell. We briefly met…"

"Yes," she said, her voice sounding anxious. A little too anxious. "I was hoping you would call. I mean —"

"I was thinking that you would want to hear from me. Listen, can we meet for a drink?"

"I'd love to."

"Good. Let's meet at the Seven Grand," I said, referring to an old-school cocktail and whiskey bar downtown. The place was classic, with dark wood paneling, and discreet. It would be the perfect place to meet and pick her brain. "At eight. I'll buy you a drink or two." I didn't refer to dinner, and I deliberately made the time for after dinner. I didn't necessarily want her to get the completely wrong impression, although she probably would.

"I'll be there."

I briefly thought of the implications for gallivanting around LA, where the tabloid press ran rampant. But it couldn't be helped. I was going to have to try to get some information from Sarah about Charlotte and hope for the best. Serena left me no choice but to try to do things underhanded.

I walked around my house, which was huge and relatively empty. There were still some staff around, of course, as I had to maintain my home no matter what happened, but I was used to people wandering about. Before I met Serena, I had a lot of parties where people would stay the weekend or the entire week, just because I didn't want to be alone. It was comforting for me to be around people. I had no idea why I was like that, except to say that there was a part of me that was very lonely. It had been rough to grow up the way that I did, with a mother in prison and adoptive parents that were very remote. It didn't help that my adoptive sister, Alice, had the hots for me from the time we were young teenagers. She wasn't my ally, because she was always trying to manipulate me into bed, as sick as that sounds.

Serena actually brought something to my life that I had never had – a sense of stability. Our connection was powerful and I didn't want to break it for anything in the world. Of course, there were so many things that were threatening it, between Charlotte and...well, it was only

Charlotte that threatened us -- Charlotte and her sick machinations.

As much as I was angry with Serena for apparently going behind my back and doing things that I explicitly told her not to – and I was quite certain that was where she was right at that moment, trying to find evidence to exonerate me – I loved her for doing that, as well. I was at war with myself on this one – she was putting herself and my mother in danger. That infuriated me. Yet her heart was in the right place, which softened the blow.

Eight o'clock rolled around, and I found a place to park and went into the bar. It was already alive with people, and I hoped that I could be anonymous. I was wearing a baseball cap and had dressed down. I looked around, and nobody really noticed me coming in. I kept my head down, and hoped that people still wouldn't notice, and looked around. I spotted Sarah in a back booth, waving to me, and I went over.

"Slade," she said. "I was hoping you would call me."

I sat down. "Well, I knew that I had to get to know you. By the way, do you mind ordering the drink for me? I don't want to be too conspicuous." It was less of a problem in San Diego, being out and about, although it was still a problem there. But in Los Angeles…there were paparazzi everywhere you turned. I was always a prime target for them, too, as they loved to portray me as the playboy without a care, while my partner was dead -- murdered by me.

"Of course, what do you drink?"

"Scotch neat," I said. "They have some good ones here. Order me a Macallan double-malt," I said, looking at the menu. It was $100 a glass, but I knew that it would be worth it.

The waitress came around, and Sarah ordered.

"So," she said seductively. She was the typical woman who was around Los Angeles – fit, with firm runner's legs and very large breasts, which were probably fake, but would be damned impressive if they weren't. Her eyes were big and blue, and her face was like a gorgeous Barbie doll. Of course, in LA, one never knew just what was real and what was fake. Her features were perfect, perhaps a little too much so. At any rate, she looked like a woman who went after the man that she wanted, and usually ended up getting him. "What caused you to give me a call?" She sucked on her straw suggestively with her full lips, and I felt her foot lightly brush my own.

I was going to have to play this just right. I didn't want her to know right away that I was using her for information. "We had a moment at Charlotte's house," I said. "And I knew that I had to get to know you better. A lot better," I added with a suggestive raise of the eyebrows.

She giggled lightly. "I was thinking the same thing. I mean, I know that you're in trouble and all of that, but…" Then she lowered her voice. "I always thought that you only dated the A-listers, so I was surprised that you would give me a call."

I used to date A-listers, but I'm totally off the market now. Lock, stock and barrel. "You're not an A-lister?" I asked lightly. It was meant to be flattery and a light joke all at once.

"No," she said. "My clients are, though. Like Charlotte." At that, she rolled her eyes, and I knew that I was getting somewhere. I had this feeling that she was not a loyal publicist, and I was beginning to find out how right that was.

"What was that eye-roll about?" I asked her.

"What eye-roll?"

"When you said that Charlotte was your client, you rolled your eyes."

"Oh. Well, she's fine, really. A little demanding, but not any more so than any other actor or actress in his town. I do have some good ones, though. Some of the people that you read about who seem to be the nicest people really are; others, not so much. We manage their image down to a tee." She shook her head. "Sometimes I don't get the actors and actresses who have a harsh reputation. Why their manager and publicist don't lock those things down, I have no clue. It's so easy to kill a story – just threaten the magazine or website with no access to the star forevermore, and they always dance. Especially if it's somebody big."

After that, we chatted for awhile about different things. Nothing too serious, because I needed to back off, just a little bit. I was gathering information in my head as I spoke with her. Information that might help me get what I wanted out of her. I tried to keep the sexual innuendo to a bare minimum, but she didn't do the same, as she made suggestive comments to me, again and again. I glided over them effortlessly though, not giving her anything in that regard.

After about an hour of small talk, I took a sip of my Scotch, and wondered if the time was right to prime the pump. I had just met this woman, yet I was getting the vibe that she was ready to talk. There was something about her demeanor that told me that she was.

What she said next gave me my opening.

"Anyhow, I'm ready to leave the business. I'm tired of these prima donnas and their attitudes. They're not real, anyhow. None of them are. That's why they're actors." She laughed a little, drinking her own Tanqueray and tonic. "If you think about it, how could you really be an actor if you had your own soul? How could you constantly become somebody else? Although some of the people in the business are genuinely nice, great people. They don't work for me, but I know of them."

She was getting drunk, I could tell. Her eyes were starting to become unfocused, and she was slurring her words. Her hands were shaking, just a little. She was a tiny woman, really, probably didn't weigh more than 115 lbs, even though she was around 5'6". She had apparently adhered to the LA code of "thou shalt not get fat." Her frame was that of a small bird, and, with her jacket off, I could see how scrawny her arms were.

"What about Charlotte?" I asked her. "Is she one of the prima donnas?"

"Oh, god yes. She's one of the worst ones. The very worst ones."

"What have you heard about her?"

"What have I heard about her or what do I know about her?"

"What have you heard about her?"

"That she's crazy. Literally crazy. As in, not Hollywood crazy, but Norman Bates crazy." Then she laughed. "Oh, that's a dated reference, huh? But she is, according to the people who work more closely with her than I do."

I narrowed my eyes. "Who are your contacts in the media? If I gave you a story, would you be able to get it to the right people?"

"I have contacts with all the magazines in town, and some major nation-wide ones as well," she said, naming off all the biggies – *Vanity Fair, Elle, Time, Vogue, Rolling Stone,* and *The New Yorker* were some of the ones that I was hearing from her. "So, yes, once I quit this hell-hole, I certainly could blow up a good story about her. If I have some excellent proof of whatever it is you're saying, of course. I wouldn't just take anything as a story. I would get sued for slander so fast..." She shook her head. "And I would never want to cross that woman without some solid proof. She would hang me out to dry, and so would all those magazines. They're respectable. Of course, if you want to make shit up, feel free – *The National Enquirer* and *The Star* will take anything these days," she said with a giggle. "Oh, I shouldn't say that. They're actually good at making up shitty headlines to make you buy the magazine, and then you get into the article you find it's nothing like what the headline promises. That's their MO, and I've been sucked into that more than once."

I knew something about Charlotte, something that I knew would alter her "It Girl" image forevermore. But did I have proof of it? No, no I didn't. I didn't necessarily know how to get my hands on proof of it, either. That was something that I was just going to have to talk to Serena about when she got back from wherever she was. I didn't know where she was right at that moment, unfortunately, as she had apparently left her phone at her house. I knew that she wasn't at her house, too, because I had driven by there more than once. She was out of town, up to no good, and I knew why – she was trying to find information that would exonerate me. That was the only good explanation for why she would up and leave, right before I was going to plead guilty, and right before she needed to be in Sacramento for the California bar.

"Why do you ask?" Sarah asked me. "About Charlotte? Do you have something that would blow up her image in the press? Right now, her publicists and managers are keeping a tight rein on her in the press. They're not letting anything get out that would damage her. She's going to be a big star, according to everyone, and her team is going to make that happen for her." She smiled devilishly. "Oh, how I would like to puncture that balloon." She rubbed her hands together. "I would never work again in this town, but I don't want to. After what I've gone through out here, I'd really like to just go back to my hometown of Atlanta and become a personal trainer."

I could barely believe my good fortune. I had found the one woman who was ready to leave the business and was therefore ready to talk. She had excellent media contacts, and she was drunk. It was a perfect storm for getting a story about Charlotte to blow up wide. That might be the one thing that I could hold over her head to make her back off of Serena, my mother, and me; maybe. Malcolm would have to be dealt with however, because Charlotte wouldn't go to prison for anything. If Malcolm was going to roll on her, she still wouldn't let me get out of pleading guilty to Jordan's murder, even if I went to Sarah with a story that I had about her.

I shook my head. I was close, but it wasn't going to work. I still had no proof of anything, and I had no idea how to get it. I was running out of time, too. And there was the issue of Malcolm. If I didn't plead guilty, and Malcolm was on the hook for that murder, then Charlotte would be, as well. That would be enough for her self-preservation instincts to kick in. I couldn't see her letting me off the hook for anything, even a bad story that would hit the press and ruin her burgeoning career.

"Yes," I said. "Anyhow, it's getting late. I have to go into the office tomorrow and see how things are going." This was true – I was going to go into the office and check on everything. I had been Face-timing with the crew the entire time I was in San Diego, and doing as much work from home as I possibly could, but it was time to actually go into the office and meet with everyone.

She raised her eyebrows. "Was it something I said?" She put her hand on mine. "I was hoping that we could take this conversation to my place or yours. I heard that you have a gorgeous place in Malibu. I would so love to see it."

"Maybe next time."

She raised her eyebrows again, more suggestively this time. "You're saying that there will be a next time?"

I was going to have to play this with finesse. I couldn't completely shut her down, because she wouldn't use her media contacts for me if I needed her to. If I could find the information about Charlotte that I was looking for, Sarah could be invaluable to me. Yet, I didn't want to lead her on. I certainly couldn't sleep with her – that would be violating what I had with Serena.

"Of course, there will be a next time. I would really like to get to know you."

"I was hoping you would say that."

We got up and left the bar. I walked her to her car and gave her a hug, and she tried to kiss me, but I turned my head so that her lips landed on my cheek. She looked embarrassed, and got in her car, which was a Lamborghini. I shook my head. A girl who drove a Lambo wouldn't want to be a personal trainer in Atlanta. She might have to down-grade to a Chevy or something. Maybe she was all talk, and I was getting my hopes up for nothing. She might just sober up in the morning and wonder what she did, and try to call me and take everything back.

I was walking a tightrope on this new plan. If everything

fell into place, I would have the perfect blackmail scheme for Charlotte.

It was a long-shot -- at best.

Chapter Twenty-Seven

Serena - Present Day

We got to my old neighborhood, and walked around. I loved this place and did kind of miss it. I used to live in a brownstone that was right on a tree-lined street. It was a place where I loved to run, especially in autumn, when the air was crisp and the leaves were brilliant. At the moment, it was summertime, and extremely hot, but it was still a beautiful place to live. We stood in front of my old home, and I wondered who was living there.

"Do you miss it?" Dalilah asked.

"Sometimes," I said with a shrug of my shoulders. "It certainly is a different vibe than a beach community. There are trade-offs wherever you go, I suppose." The one thing that I did love about this place was the communal feeling. On my old block was an Indian restaurant, several galleries, a vegan joint and an antique shop. My new neighborhood featured mostly houses on my block, and, across the street, there were mainly bars, restaurants, fast food places, and drug stores. The beach was within walking distance though, so that made up for the fact that my new place had much less of a funky boho vibe than my old place.

We walked along the streets, passing runners, people with dogs, and others who were just out for a walk. Again, this was an energy that I really missed. There were plenty of people on the beach, of course, but on my actual street, it was pretty quiet. When I stepped out of my new house and got into my car, I didn't necessarily encounter anybody. On this street, my old street, I would always see somebody when I left the house. That was always a source of comfort for me.

I sighed. I had made my choice, and I knew that it was a good one. It had brought me to Slade. As much of a mess as that had turned out, I did truly love him. I hadn't fallen in love like that with anyone else. I hadn't had anyone else "get" me the way that Slade had. I was grateful for that.

"Ah, kid," I said, putting my arm around Luke. "I do miss this neighborhood, but I'm anxious to get back. And I'm really anxious to see what Lars has to say."

Dalilah joined us in lock-step. "Serena, we'd like you to visit us as often as possible. As much as Luke and I have had a good time visiting you in San Diego, I think that you're right. This is the kind of vibe that we really can't leave, either."

I smelled the air, catching the scent of curry. I hated Indian food, really, but this smell still made me feel like I was home. I shook my head. I wasn't home. Home was in San Diego. Home was with Slade. He was my home.

I was so conflicted as I walked along that street that day. On the one hand, I felt comfortable here. On other, I was missing Slade and I was on pins and needles.

I took a deep breath, smelling the air and wishing that

things were different. That I was visiting here on a nice trip, and not because I goddamned had to. Not because I was spying on the man that I loved. This was not a nice trip, really.

A day went by, and then two. I was really on edge because I was going to have to be in Sacramento the next day for the California bar. I was still confident that I would pass it, that wasn't a problem. Taking it as distracted as I was…that was a problem. And it was also a problem that I didn't know if I would be back in time. Lars apparently was hot on the project, and I had called him several times. Every time I called, he would just say that he was working on it, and he would get back with me. "This Slade has some really tight security," he would say. "The tightest security I've ever encountered," which was saying a lot, considering he had hacked into the Department of Defense more than once.

Luke, Dalilah and I hung out and tried not to address the elephant in the room. We saw movies and drank wine and caught up. We talked about everything under the sun – movies we had seen, politics, current events, gossip – and we tried not to talk about what was really on everyone's mind. Slade. And, to a lesser extent, Charlotte.

Finally, the call came from Lars. "Oh my god," he said. "I can't even believe it, but I got it. I've been working around the clock. I can't believe the number of security protocols he has. He must be one paranoid son-of-a-bitch."

I was excited, yet apprehensive. "He has a reason to be paranoid," I said. "But you got it? The video?"

"Yes. It's hard to tell who was beating that poor chap to death, but I was able to isolate it, and you can tell who is underneath that hoodie very well. He tried very hard to hide his face, but I was able to make it very clear. It is clearly not Slade. I don't know who it is, but it is not Slade."

I let out a sigh of relief. The long nightmare was almost over. Maybe. I knew that this would only buy some time. There was going to be a long process of authenticating this video and "proving it up," for the prosecutors and the judge on the case. But if I provided this piece of evidence, at the very least, the judge would suspend Slade's guilty plea. That was all that I really wanted – to buy some time for him. And I did it. I did it. I let out a long breath.

"What about Charlotte? Were you able to find any information about her?"

"Oh god yes. That was fairly easy. Talk about a walking nightmare, that one."

"Okay," I said, feeling more and more excited. "Tell me about her."

"I got her psychiatric records, and the girl has been unhinged since the age of 12. She was a part of a murder's club when she was in 7th grade. She and some friends killed a teacher. She only served time in the juvenile hall, because her lawyer convinced the jury that she was bullied into doing this. From the sounds of it, though, I would say it was the other way around. It's really crappy, but, somehow, she only served about 3 years in the juvenile hall, and her record was expunged. She must have had an amazing attorney."

I felt excited. This was really getting somewhere. "Did you get your hands on her diagnosis?"

"Yes. Borderline personality disorder and antisocial personality disorder. In other words, it sounds like there is no cure for her. I know something about psychiatric disor-

ders, and I know that if you have either one of these particular ones, you don't come back from that."

I wondered if anybody in Hollywood knew the truth
about her. And I also wondered what would happen if
anybody found out the truth. Would she be able to find
work again if everyone knew that she was dangerous, and
she had been from a young age? I knew that starlets got
away with all kinds of things...but not really. The ones who
really went off the rails, such as Lindsay Lohan, couldn't
find work, no matter how talented they were.

Even if she couldn't be pinned for the murder of
Jordan, with these records, I could certainly ruin her in the
chosen profession. "What else did you find out about her?"

"That's enough, really. I think that you can do a lot of
damage with these psychiatric records."

"Yes, I certainly could." I rubbed my hands together,
feeling, for the first time in a long time, a sense of relief. I
could see the light at the end of the tunnel, finally. "Thank
you so much, Lars. You've done some amazing work."

"Well, it was a challenge getting that video. Even for me.
One thing is for sure, this Slade really didn't want that video
being found. Or anything else being found, for that matter."

I knew that he was right about that. He found it,
though. Now, I was just going to have to figure out how to
use it judiciously.

And I had to pray that Slade didn't hate me forever for
finding it and using it.

And pray that I didn't pay the consequences.

Or Slade's mother.

Chapter Twenty-Eight

The next day, with a copy of the video in hand, I got on a commercial airline and headed to Sacramento. I said goodbye to Luke and Dalilah with a hug, and said goodbye to New York City. I had to face my life back in California, and I was going to have to do it alone.

They were sad to see me go, of course. Despite the dark cloud hanging over our heads the whole time I was visiting them, we did have a good time. We talked until late in the night, and I got to know little Olivia, who was growing every single day. I was going to miss them, but, at the same time, I was looking forward to this next part of my life. I was going to take down that psychotic woman Charlotte, and I was going to get Slade off the hook. It wasn't going to be clean, and it wasn't going to be pretty. I knew that going in. But, it was going to happen, and that was all that mattered to me.

Dalilah tried to convince me to take Ryan's plane back to California, but I begged off. "I've been flying commercial all my life, and I'm not about to stop now," I said. "I love you for offering, though."

"Well, be careful. You're messing with an obsessive, psychotic woman. It's not going to be easy. Believe me, I know. I've been where you are."

"An obsessive psychotic woman who is going down," I said. "And she's going down hard. I might be going down with her, though. That's the price I may have to pay, and I'll pay that willingly."

At that, I got a cab, after saying my goodbyes to my brother and future sister-in-law, and I flew to Sacramento for my Bar Exam.

That weekend, I took the Bar, and I knew that I probably passed it with flying colors. I was slightly rusty on certain areas of the law – constitutional law was one that was always changing, because the Supreme Court was always making new rulings – but, by and large, I knew what I was talking about. The multiple choice portion took the entire first day, and these were difficult questions regarding the core areas of law – criminal, property, constitutional, torts and contracts. The second day was the essay portion that covered state law and also common law. I wrote and wrote and wrote on the essay questions, and I really had to think about the multiple choice answers, but I felt that I did the best that I possibly could.

After it was over, I boarded a plane for Los Angeles. I was finally going to face the music, and I was dreading it. Slade had warned me, again and again, not to meddle with his affairs. I therefore knew that Slade wouldn't be the first person I would be seeing.

I was going to pay a visit to his prosecutor.

Better to ask forgiveness than permission.

The second I touched down in Los Angeles, I made an appointment to see Slade's prosecutor. His name was Raphael De Los Santos, and he had a reputation for being a hardass. This was all going to be difficult, I knew, because Raphael was salivating about bagging a big Kahuna such as Slade. He was not going to want to accept this evidence. That was a given. He was in the papers already, as the California Bar was recognizing him as the one who brought Slade to his knees. I wished that I would have been dealing with the federal prosecutor, because she was much easier to handle than Raphael was. But I wasn't dealing with her. I was dealing with Raphael, who had Slade's case, and I knew that I was in for some brow-beating and intimidation.

I got to his office and knocked lightly on the door. He wasn't expecting me, so I didn't know what kind of reception I would get. He looked up, his dark brown eyes regarding me warily. He was behind a stack of files and was poring over one when I showed up.

"Serena, "he said. "I'm surprised to see you. What's up?"

"Raphael," I began. "I need to postpone Slade's guilty plea."

He shook his head. "No can do. Unless you have Jesus himself to testify on his behalf, that guilty plea is going ahead as planned. Is there anything else I can do to assist you?"

I cleared my throat. "Trust me, when you see the

evidence I have that will exonerate Mr. Bridgewell, even you will dance."

He raised a skeptical eyebrow. "I doubt it."

I showed him my flash drive. "This will change your mind. Trust me."

"I don't trust you, but that's really beside the point."

"Me?" I asked him, pointing to my chest. "I can't imagine why you don't trust me."

"I don't trust you because I've been in touch with the federal prosecutor's office, and they've informed me that you've already tried to pin this murder on two different mobsters. It's not their MO, and I don't see the motive. So, whatever you have better be a smoking gun, or there is no way that I'll ever allow you to interfere with Mr. Bridgewell's guilty plea."

"Just let me show you what is on my flash drive," I said. At that, I popped the flash drive into my computer. "I have the part of the video that was missing; the part that proves that Slade had nothing to do with Jordan's murder."

"Right. Listen sweetheart - if you think that I'm going to give up on prosecuting Slade, then you've got another thing coming. He's going down for Jordan's murder, and rightfully so. As I said, unless you have testimony from Jesus himself, testimony that exonerates Slade, then I will have to respectfully ask you to leave my office. I have files to look at before the next arraignment docket."

I booted up the computer and waited. I held my breath as I watched Raphael's reaction to what was unfolding in front of him. At first, he looked annoyed and bored, because the beginning of this portion of the video was Jordan, who was working in the lab, apparently peacefully. Soon, a hooded man showed up, and Raphael cocked his head and narrowed his eyes. The hooded man took a base-ball bat and whacked Jordan, who was standing right in front of him, holding up his hands. Jordan looked stunned and started to crumple to the ground, but he grabbed onto a table. He looked at the hooded man with a look in his eyes that said bewilderment and shock. He started to yell for help, but the hooded man whacked him again, this time aiming for his head. The hooded man didn't stop, however, as he savagely pummeled poor Jordan, again and again and again. Eventually, Jordan crumpled completely to the ground, and he was soon still.

The hooded man then went over to Jordan and felt for his pulse. He apparently was satisfied that Jordan was gone, and he left.

I looked over at Raphael, who looked like he was think-ing. He had his pencil to his mouth, and he was staring at the computer, which now had a blank screen. Finally, he spoke. "Okay. Listen. There are many issues with this video. Number one, you can't really tell who is whacking Jordan. Number two, I'm going to need to authenticate this. You could very well have taken the video of Jordan's murder and had it cleverly doctored."

"You have this video taken to a professional and have it blown up and isolated. You will clearly see who is doing the whacking. Hopefully, that same professional will be able to tell you that this video is authentic and not doctored. Now, I don't know how long it will take you to do all of that, but I hope that you and I can agree to at least postpone Mr. Bridgewell's guilty plea until you can have a chance to do your due diligence."

He sighed. "Why did you have to do this? I was this close to finally closing this beast of a case."

I rolled my eyes. "Yes. How dare I try to free an innocent man. How dare I try to keep a man out of prison for the rest of his life for something that he didn't do."

"Don't get on your high horse. Okay, I'll agree to postpone that guilty plea. I'm not going to guarantee you anything, though, until this video is authenticated and I can identify who this hooded figure is."

"Thank you," I said, standing up. "My team will…" I shook my head. My team will what? Malcolm was the guilty party. He wasn't going to agree to this continuance. I couldn't appear in court until I got the results of the Bar Exam back. I was going to have to tell Raphael something, and I didn't know exactly what. "Actually, could you just ask for the continuance?"

He narrowed his eyes at me suspiciously. "Why? You know that the judge is going to want to speak with both parties before he's going to approve of any continuance."

"You'll see why when you blow up that video recording."

He looked perplexed. "What's that supposed to mean?"

I took a deep breath. He was soon going to find out that Malcolm was the one on the video. I might as well just come out with it. "Malcolm murdered Jordan," I said.

He looked stunned. As if somebody had punched him in the gut. "What's that supposed to mean?"

"What do you think that it means? Malcolm murdered Jordan."

He shook his head. "That's insane. I've known him for years. I mean, he's kind of an odd duck in a lot of ways, but I could never imagine him doing something like that."

"Oh come on. You're a prosecutor. You, more than anyone else, understands that one never knows just who will come out and do something like this. There's no way to say that person A or person B is capable or incapable of crime

X. Anyone is capable of anything at any given time." I was starting to sound like Slade in saying that.

"I know that." He looked at the computer screen, which was blank. "But Malcolm? I've had drinks with him. He and his wife watched my kids a couple of times." He visibly shuddered. "I would like to think that he wouldn't do something like that. Besides, what motive did he have to do that?"

"I don't want to go into all that." Charlotte was going down for the murder eventually, but I had no proof that she was behind it, and I didn't want to complicate the issue. She was going to be next, that was for sure. It was just too soon to tell Raphael this.

"You know something," he said, his eyes narrowing again. "You need to tell me right now what you know."

"It will all come out in due time," I said. "I want you to investigate this video, and, well, I don't know what will happen next, but I can imagine."

"You know what will happen next. If this video is authenticated, then Malcolm will be arrested. Mr. Bridgewell will have the charges against him dropped." He shook his head and started to speak in Spanish. In English, he said "I've worked this job for 20 years, and I thought that nothing would shock me. But this is a different thing. This has shocked me. I guess I just never thought that I would personally know somebody who would do something like this. That sounds amazingly naïve of me to say, but, man..."

"I know," I said. Raphael was a good, upstanding prosecutor. I didn't always get along with him, but I knew that he was ethical. He looked like he was genuinely upset to hear that Malcolm was guilty of this murder.

As I left his office, after shaking his hand, I knew that

there was no going back. Whatever was going to happen was going to happen. I couldn't put the horse back in the barn.

It was freeing.

It was also terrifying.

Chapter Twenty-Nine

When I left Raphael's office, I knew that I had to face the music. I called Slade from my car, turning on the bluetooth. He picked up on the first ring.

"Serena," he said smoothly and calmly. "How was the Bar Exam?"

I wasn't anticipating this kind of low-key reaction, so I was taken aback. "It went fine," I said. "It wasn't a big deal. I mean, it was stressful to sit there for 16 hours over two days, but it is what it is."

There was a long, uncomfortable pause. I wasn't sure how to interpret his reaction to my calling him. I thought that he would have jumped down my throat about not being in touch with him these last few days, but he was so casual...I shook my head. There was something going on, and I didn't necessarily like it.

"We need to talk," I said, feeling more than apprehensive. "As soon as possible."

He took a deep breath. "I agree. I'll be over in 30 minutes."

"Make it two hours."

At that, I got off the phone and headed down the coast towards my house to wait for him. What I did was going to change everything between us. I dreaded telling him, more than I had dreaded anything in this world. Was he going to blow up at me? Would he hate me? I doubted very seriously that he would be surprisingly happy. That would be the best outcome, of course, but I thought that wouldn't be possible.

I wanted to get my dogs out of their pooch hotel, but I left them there for the time being. I had to get to my house before Slade got there, and there wasn't time to stop and get them. I didn't want to make things worse by making him wait for me to get home.

A couple of hours later, I pulled up to the house and went in, and sat down in my special place – the chair in the sun room, and drank a glass of wine. I couldn't believe how nervous I was to see him. I almost felt like getting sick, but I held it in. *It's going to be okay. Slade will forgive you. And, even if he doesn't, you did the right thing.*

I soon heard him pull up outside my house, so I went to the living room and opened the door for him. He looked extremely intense. His eyes were penetrating, even more than usual. He was dressed casually, in a pair of jeans and a t-shirt that showed every ripple of his muscular arms. I still felt the same way I always did whenever I saw him, but I wondered if he was also going to feel the same.

I closed my eyes, trying to feel his emotional vibe. To my surprise, he didn't seem to be just acting nonchalant. He seemed genuinely calm to me. I didn't know what was going on, but it seemed as if he was resigned to whatever it was that was going to happen.

I invited him in, and he came into the living room and crossed his arms in front of him. The two of us just stood there, staring at one another. I wanted so badly to tell him what had happened, but it didn't seem like the right time.

He finally spoke. "Where were you these past few days?"

I didn't try to lie. There wasn't a point. "I was in New York, and then I was in Sacramento for the bar."

"New York." That was a statement, not a question. "What was there?"

I took an enormous breath and let it out slowly. "I hired a security team. Actually, I didn't hire them, but they worked for me. They're on retainer with Dalilah's father. But they…" I wanted so much to tell him. Just come out and tell him. But I was terrified.

"They what?"

I shook my head. I couldn't bring myself to say what had happened.

"Serena, I've had a security breach. Why do I feel that you had something to do with that?"

"Slade, I-"

"Just stop. Stop. I know what you did." He shook his head. "Did you think that you would be able to just get away with doing something like that without me knowing about it? I haven't had a security breach in years. There's good reason for that. Now, you go out of town and there's a security breach. The video of Malcolm murdering Jordan is missing. Only it's not really missing, of course. But it was duped." He shook his head. "What were you thinking?"

I drew a breath. I still wasn't quite sure if I was on solid ground with Slade, or if there was a storm that was coming. He seemed to be incredibly calm about this news, but I knew that there had to be something more. It all just seemed way too easy.

"Slade, I…"

"I know. I know what you were thinking, and, believe me, I've been wrestling with it. At first, I felt incredibly violated. I couldn't believe that you would go against my wishes, and I really couldn't believe that you would willingly open up my business to that drastic of a breach. I had to get my own security team to come to the office, in the middle of the fucking night, to fix it."

I narrowed my eyes. I wasn't expecting him to worry about the security breach first. I thought that the security breach would be an afterthought, and that he mainly would be concentrated on the fact that I found the video.

"I'm sorry…"

He shook his head. "Listen, Serena, there's nothing that can be done about this. I have a feeling that you've already done what I expressly told you not to do."

I hung my head and swallowed hard. He was making it easier on me to tell him, in a way. Yet, I still felt strangely guilty. "I did. I turned that video over to Raphael."

I looked at him, and I closed my eyes. I sensed that he still had a strange calmness about him. I still didn't sense fury, which was what I had been bracing myself for.

"Okay," he said. "What's done is done. Now, we have to figure out how to fix it."

I felt on much better footing. "Charlotte…this murder isn't her first. She killed a teacher when she was in 7th grade. Some friends of hers helped her. She served three years in juvenile hall for it, and she was diagnosed with borderline personality disorder and antisocial personality disorder. She did it then, and she did it with Malcolm.

Something tells me that there probably are other bodies that we don't know about that she has gotten away with."

I looked at Slade, and didn't see surprise on his face. "I'm not surprised," he finally said. "There was talk about that for years. I didn't hear about that until after she and I got together, and after she started blackmailing me. I thought it was all rumors though."

"Can we use this against her?"

He smiled. "I think we can."

I cocked my head at him. He looked like he knew something I didn't. "Tell me more."

"I did something that hopefully won't make you angry. If it does, I apologize in advance, but desperate times call for desperate measures."

I furled my brows. "What would make me angry?"

"I took out a woman. Her name is Sarah, and she's part of Charlotte's publicity team. But she's perfectly willing to sell her out to the highest bidder. The ironic thing is the story of Charlotte and the teacher was the story that I wanted to sell to her, but I have no proof of it. Do you?"

"I do. Lars, the man who hacked you, was also able to find her private records. The expunged juvenile record and the psychiatric evaluation. They're authentic records."

He put his hand on his chin and looked at me. A smile started to creep around his eyes. "Show me these records."

I went into the other room and got into my leather satchel. Inside it was a manila folder that held Charlotte's records. I went back into the living room and handed him the documents.

He took the folder from my hands, and sat down on the couch. As he read them, that smile that was creeping around his eyes started to get bigger and bigger. He rubbed his hands together as he read.

He finally looked up at me. "I think we have her."

Chapter Thirty

I went over to join him on the couch. "Do you think this will do it?"

"Yes. I do. I was able to pick the brain of Sarah, and she told me how carefully Charlotte's image is managed. There's no way that she'll be able to have a career if this gets out. That's the most important thing to her right now – becoming a huge star."

I started to feel hopeful for the first time in a long, long time. "What's in the way here? There's something, I know there is. It can't be as simple as all that."

"No, of course it's not. It does give me leverage, though." He looked at me a bit longer. "The problem is Malcolm, of course. He's going to squeal like a stuck pig when this all goes down. Charlotte won't do anything that will put her in danger of serving time." He paused for a long time. "I don't see this going any other way, Serena. She's going to rub out Malcolm, and she's going to do it quickly. I think that I need to give her a head's up on what's coming, but only after I negotiate with her. This bargaining chip will go a long, long way, but it's not quite the smoking gun."

"I don't understand. Why give her a head's up?"

"Because, Serena, if she's blindsided and Malcolm gives her up, she'll have nothing to lose. You'll be dead before the week is out, and my mother will be arrested. She'll make sure of that. As much as I hate to do this, I have to give her notice so that she can get to Malcolm. She either has something on him that she can use to shut him up, or she will have him killed."

I felt a pit in my stomach. I had no love for Malcolm, of course. He was a killer, and he apparently did it for greed. The world would be a better place without people like him in it. Yet, I still felt a pang. He was a human being, after all, with a family that loved him. And, before all of this went down, I did have genuine affection for him. As much as he was a bad man, I didn't necessarily feel that he needed to be killed. Yet, I could see that was going to happen. It was inevitable.

"I think that you need to tell me what happened with your mother. You danced around it before, but I think that it's time for it to be all out in the open."

Slade paced around the living room, and shook his head. "I swore myself to secrecy about this, but you're right. You're going to find out, sooner or later, what happened, so I might as well tell you everything." At that, he told me the whole story – about his mother and the murder of Hugh, and how Charlotte knew everything because she was there. I then knew just how desperate things were for him, and why he was always trying to do whatever he could to keep her secret.

Now that I knew what Charlotte had over Slade, I wondered how she was going to deal with Malcolm.

"Which way do you think she's going to go? Blackmail or murder?"

"I would say she'll have him rubbed out. Cut the brakes on his car or something of the sort to make it seem like an accident. Her family specializes in such things, after all."

I took a deep breath. "Are you sure that's what will happen?"

"Yes. I don't know that she has something over him that would cause him to completely fall on his sword and not roll on her. I really don't see that she'll have any other choice in the matter."

He put his arms around me, and I put my head on his chest. I felt strangely calm, yet, at the same time, it felt like it was all a bad dream. I put something in motion that would end with the death of somebody who I thought I liked.

"Hey," he said, putting his finger under my chin. He saw that there were tears forming in my eyes. "I know how you're feeling. Malcolm brutally murdered somebody, though. It's not entirely a loss for this world."

I nodded my head. "I just want all of this to be over."

"Of course you do." Then he kissed me. "It'll all be over soon."

I sighed and put my head on his chest. I couldn't believe that he wasn't angry with me, and it seemed to be the best possible outcome. Nothing was certain yet, but no matter - I was with Slade, he didn't hate me, and it seemed that he wanted to make love. I knew that I craved that as well.

"Vanilla," I said to him. "I can't handle more than that right now."

"Of course. I was thinking the same thing."

I unbuttoned his shirt and put my hands on his hard pecs. He reared back his head as I lightly sucked and licked on his nipples and bit his neck. He picked me up and carried me into the bedroom and lay me down on the bed.

He slowly but surely undressed me, and I did the same to him. I sighed as we lay there together, side by side, both of us naked. He was perfectly erect, and he entered me from behind. I felt the familiar sense of him filling me up, and I realized that I feared that I would never feel that sensation again. It was time to release all the anxiety that had built up in me during my trip to New York. He kissed me passionately as he slowly stroked in an out of me, again and again. I came to orgasm after orgasm before he did the same.

We were alone in the dark and the silence, and I wanted to drink it all in. For now, we were okay. What was going to happen tomorrow, I didn't know, but I have to savor that moment with him.

He held me close throughout the night, and I knew that nothing had ever felt like that.

I prayed that we could continue to be like we were forevermore.

Chapter Thirty-One

Slade - Present Day

The next day, I went to see Charlotte. It was a necessary evil, but it had to be done. As I told Serena, if she was blindsided, she would be much more dangerous.

After driving up the Five, and interchanging on many different highways, I arrived at her house. She was waiting for me outside the door of her house. "This better be good," she said.

"We need to talk," I told her. "And you're not going to like this."

We went into her house and both of us sat down. "Would you like a drink?" she asked.

"No, but I need one," I told her. "But I'm not taking one from you." I was afraid that she would drug it, to be honest.

"Well, then, out with it. Whatever you're about to say, out with it."

"Charlotte, I'm not pleading guilty to Jordan's murder.

Serena found the video that showed that Malcolm is the one, and she has already turned it over to the prosecutor."

She stared at me, and I already knew what she was thinking. "You would do that. You would put your girlfriend and your mother into jeopardy." She shook her head. "I thought that you were a better man than that. Okay then. You know what happens next. My family doesn't mess around. When I tell them I want a hit, they do it, and they do it quickly."

"Not so fast. I know what you did when you were a kid, and I have proof. What's more, I have a media contact. If you want your career to end before it has even started, I suggest you back the fuck off."

She crossed her arms and looked at me. I had her dead to right, and I think that she knew it. "I'm calling bullshit," she finally said. "I was stupid enough to fall for that once before, when you claimed that you had my abortion records. It didn't occur to me until recently that you were probably full of shit then. I think that you're full of shit now. Those records are sealed. That means that nobody can get them."

"Nobody but a professional hacker. How else do you think that I know about you murdering your teacher with the help of some of your girlfriends, and your diagnoses of borderline personality disorder and antisocial personality disorder? Listen, directors know about those disorders, too, because they come across actors and actresses who have them, all the time. They're not going to want to work with you when they know what you're capable of. You've managed to fool them this far, but if this gets out, you're finished in this town."

She raised an eyebrow. "A professional hacker? Oh, you've done it now, buddy. I'll have you and your girlfriend in prison so fast..."

"Oh, come on. You framed me for murder. Do you really think I'm worried about going to prison for some hacking? And leave Serena out of this. She had nothing to do with it. I got that hacker myself."

"I don't think so. You're covering for her."

"I'm not covering for her," I lied. "Leave her out of this."

She swiveled in her chair nervously. "I don't believe you."

At that, I brought out the thick file that I brought along with me. It had printouts of her juvenile records that included records about the murder, along with psychiatric diagnoses that she received at that time. "Believe me, because this time I have proof. And don't be stupid enough to think that if you destroy these records, I don't have them on my hard drive and various flash drives. Not to mention the fact that I have physical copies which are stored in various safety deposit boxes."

She took the file, and, with shaking hands, read what was on there. As she read, she shook her head. "I haven't even seen these records," she said, her face turning various shades of purple. "I haven't even seen them. How dare this mother-fucking doctor say these things about me? I don't have empathy or impulse control, and I have violent tenden- cies." She kept reading. "I have no concern for others, psychotic tendencies, and I can't regulate emotions or thoughts. I have a distorted sense of self, changeable moods, paranoia and am prone to lose touch with reality." She shook her head rapidly.

"Yes. It also says that you tend to idealize people. I guess that's where I come in."

She swallowed hard. "I can't believe this. This can't get out. This is personal information. Nobody will touch it."

I leaned forward in my chair. "Charlotte, you're the 'It' girl right now. There's buzz about you in this new film. Oscar buzz, from what I've been hearing from those in the know. I have no doubt that you're great in this movie. But, believe me, tabloids love to bring people down when they're on the way up. If you don't think that this murder and these diagnoses will be the talk of the town…" I shook my head. "I can't believe that you would be that naïve."

She rapidly shook her head. "You can have one. Take your pick, your girlfriend or your mother."

"What's that supposed to mean?"

"It means that I still want my pound of flesh. You might have this to hold over my head, but this is the only thing that you have right now. Malcolm will be taken care of. I don't want him to roll on me. That goes without saying. I can never, and I mean ever, be tied to Jordan's murder. And, if something happens, and I am implicated in his murder, then your girlfriend is dead and your mother is in prison. I'm sure that, considering that will be the consequences, you're going to be on board with my taking care of Malcolm. So, you only have this over me," she said, pointing to the papers in front of her. "I won't give you both."

I stood up. "You will give me both, or this report becomes public today. I already have a woman who has some fantastic media contacts, all of whom will be salivating to make all of this public."

She sat there, just looking at me. "Nope," she said. "You know what will happen if you do that. Again, if you go public with this, I'll have nothing to lose, and both your mother and your girlfriend will be in jeopardy. Now, I will ask you again. I will agree to either not have your girlfriend killed or not turn your mother in for the murder of Hugh all those years ago. That's what's on the table. You can't have both. You pick one, or you get neither."

Oh, she was good. Very good. And I had no doubt that, if I made good on my threat to go to the media with this report, she would do exactly as she said. She would put a hit on Serena and would turn my mother in for Hugh's homicide. I shook my head. Playing with her was complicated.

"Are you going to blink?" she asked me. "If this report becomes public, I have nothing to lose. Remember that."

I hung my head. She had me. I took a deep breath and looked up at the ceiling. I could give her one thing to placate her, and that would mean that I would either have to sacrifice my mother or Serena. That would be her "pound of flesh," and that would put our Mexican standoff back into place. It was smart on her part – if she wouldn't deal at all, I would be the one with nothing to lose by putting this report out into the world. I wasn't going down for Jordan's murder – Serena made sure of that. So, this report was all the ammunition I had.

If she wouldn't deal at all, I would have no choice. That report would be public, and my mother and Serena would be in jeopardy. But she was giving me something, and I had to choose. "My mother," I said quietly. I shook my head. This was an impossible choice, yet it was almost easy. There was no way that I would put Serena's life in jeopardy. I had the money for the best lawyer for my mother…yet she was sick. Who knew if she would get proper treatment in jail? Yet…I would get her out on bail immediately, and I would hire the best attorney money could buy to defend her. She would have a chance. Serena wouldn't. If I offered up Serena, she would be dead before the week would be out. I could try to protect her, but one man can't go up against an entire mafia syndicate.

She crossed her arms. "Really? You would throw your mother under the bus to protect your girlfriend?"

"You give me no choice," I said, feeling my heart break when I said that. After all she went through to protect me, and after the life she has had in general – I was going to make things worse for her. Yet, I had to do it. It was her or Serena. It was an impossible "Sophie's Choice," which was a story about a woman in Nazi Germany who had to choose which twin would be killed and which would be allowed to live. I felt almost as torn. I loved both women, but I couldn't bear to see Serena in jeopardy.

You'll help your mother beat this. The evidence against her will be extremely negligible. I drew my breath though, as I realized that I would be held to account for my role, too. Worse than that, I was going to have to testify against my mother, if it ever came to trial. I was going to have to lie, of course. I was the only witness, besides Charlotte. Charlotte's records might have to be a part of the trial, in order to impeach her, if mom's attorney could get his hands on the official records. That would be difficult to do – to get those records authenticated, so they could be used in court.

Then again, once my mother became a suspect, it would be fairly easy to tie her to Hugh. People saw them out that night – bartenders, waitresses, other patrons. If they have a good memory for people, they would be able to identify my mother as the person who was out with him. And, even though we cleaned up her old apartment, where Hugh was killed, it's difficult to truly clean up blood. The police would be able to use infrared to see that there was blood on the floor of her old place. It might be that my mother will have to resort to a self-defense claim if she ever hoped to beat this murder, and that would be difficult to prove. I had to admit to myself that there was a possibility that, since I was "giving" Charlotte my mother, there was a chance that my mother would spend the rest of her life in prison.

Charlotte swiveled in her chair. "Okay. Well then, you better warn your mother that she will be arrested for Hugh's murder. She'll probably be arrested today. Serena will be safe. There's that for consolation. And Slade, I want a stipulation on our agreement. I want Serena's firm to represent your mother." She narrowed her eyes. "That's an important piece of this puzzle. I can't tell you why, but that's what I want."

I was mystified as to why she would be so adamant about that, but I didn't feel in a position to bargain with her. Serena was safe, and besides, I really wanted her to work on my mother's case anyhow. I felt that she would go above and beyond the call of duty to make sure my mother had the best chance of beating a murder conviction. "Okay."

"Serena's firm, not just Serena. As in, the firm that will no longer be headed by Malcolm. The firm that is known as Brown, Walker and Groom." Those were the three names of the majority partners, including that of Malcolm, whose last name was "Groom."

It was my turn to narrow my eyes. She was up to something, that much was clear. Whatever it was, I was going to have to face it with Serena. Or help Serena face whatever it was that this goddamned spider had up her sleeve. "And if I refuse?"

She shrugged her shoulders. "The deal is off. Yes, the entire world will think that I'm a psychopath. But at least your stupid whore will be wiped off the face of this planet. Don't push me, Slade. Now, do we have a deal, or don't we?"

"Yes. We have a deal. I'll make sure that my mom is represented by Brown, Walker and Groom. Okay?"

She nodded her head and smiled. "Okay."

All at once, I was angry with Serena. I told her not to meddle in this. I told her, and she didn't listen. Now my mother was in jeopardy. I never wanted for that to happen – I always wanted it to be me who would be in jeopardy, not either one of them. My mother might be in prison for the rest of her life, all because of Serena.

I shook my head. No. It's not because of Serena. It was because of this psychotic bitch, Charlotte. Charlotte, and Charlotte alone, was the reason why all of this was happening. Well, Charlotte's psychotic machinations, combined with my stupidity in having Charlotte come with me to see my mother all those years ago. That simple act was the one that haunted me, and had haunted me, all these years.

She raised a single eyebrow. "I'm not entirely finished. There's going to be a big surprise awaiting your girlfriend. One that she will find pretty unpleasant, to say the least. If I can't kill her, or have her killed, then I at least need to torment her just a little."

"What's that supposed to mean?" I wasn't liking the sound of this. Not in the slightest.

"You'll see. Or, rather, she'll soon see." She swiveled in her chair. "I wonder how much she likes living in that cute little house by the beach. I guess we'll soon be finding out, won't we? And I wonder how much she enjoys working where she's working. I would imagine that her law firm will soon have a new, very important, client – one Margot Facinelli. Serena's going to want to work on that case, I would imagine. But maybe she won't. Maybe, when she sees who the new associate at her firm is, she'll want out of that firm."

"You're not making a lick of sense," I said to her.

"I'm not now, but I will be soon. At any rate, you have to leave. I have a very important phone call to make."

My heart started to pound. I was going to have to warn my mother about what was about to happen. I also had to wonder what it was Charlotte had up her sleeve for Serena. She was so cryptic – all that talk about how much Serena enjoyed her new home, and whether or not she liked working for her firm. What was that all about? I was going to find out soon, and I didn't know, at all, if I was going to like what I learned.

I called Serena from the car. "Hey," I said to her when she picked up. "I think everything's in the clear. You're in the clear, at least. And so am I. My mother will be arrested for Hugh's murder, though."

"What? Oh my god, no! No! Slade, I'm so sorry…"

"It's fine. It's what has to happen. It was either her life or yours." I shook my head. I was trying to sound nonchalant about it, for Serena's sake, because I didn't want Serena to feel too guilty about it. But the reality was much, much different. It was tearing me up inside. Charlotte gave me no choice, of course, but that didn't make things any easier. Would my mother survive? Did she have a way out of the murder charge? I had no idea. None. Zero. I wish that I did, but I knew that I didn't. Charlotte was diabolical, much more diabolical than I had given her credit for. She knew just where the tender parts were and just how to twist the knife into them. I had to give her credit where credit was due.

"Slade, you can't be that laid-back about this. Tell me what you're really feeling."

"I feel like crap, obviously. I need to talk to my mom about this, though. And Malcolm…well he's about to have a tragic accident. I need to leave it at that. Look for that to happen within the next day or so. Charlotte will get to Malcolm before the prosecutor will."

Serena was quiet. "We didn't really win, did we? An innocent life is still in the balance. And Malcolm…he wasn't innocent, not by any stretch of the imagination, but he's still a human being. He has children, for Christ sakes. A wife. His parents are still alive, and he has brothers and sisters. What he did was wrong, but I have definite mixed emotions about his impending murder."

"There's nothing that can be done about that. As I told you earlier, the worst-case scenario for you and my mother is that Charlotte gets caught up in her own web. If Malcolm rolls on her, and she's arrested, then all bets will be off. She'll have the hit put on you within the week, and my mother will be going down for Hugh's death. It's best that the suspicion isn't on her, because I can at least save you. She knows that if she touches a hair on your head, that report about her craziness and her past homicide will find its way to the media and she'll be finished. I have her, but only halfway."

"Well, can you please come over. I need to see you."

"I can't. Not right now, at least. I need to go and see my mother and explain everything to her." I felt my insides start to crush while I thought about that. I had spent all these years making sure that my mother was protected. And now, well…there wasn't a thing that I could do. I could only hope that perhaps, just perhaps, the jury would see her as merely defending herself in her own home. But it did look bad that the body was disposed of. That was my idea, of course. Maybe the jury would understand that move as well, though. My mother was scared, and she had just gotten out of prison for another murder.

"Come over as soon as you can," she said. "I'm feeling out of sorts. I hate all of this."

"I will."

We got off the phone, and I turned on the radio. I wanted to try to forget, just for a second, what was about to happen. I hoped that my mother could beat this charge, and I hoped that she would one day forgive me. I had screwed everything up when I made the hasty decision to dump Hugh's body, instead of going to the authorities and letting the chips fall where they may.

Was that a fateful decision? I was soon going to find out.

I hoped that I didn't find out the hard way.

Chapter Thirty-Two

Serena - Present Day

The next day, I went to see Charlotte. It was a necessary evil, but it had to be done. As I told Serena, if she was blindsided, she would be much more dangerous.

After driving up the Five, and interchanging on many different highways, I arrived at her house. She was waiting for me outside the door of her house. "This better be good," she said.

"We need to talk," I told her. "And you're not going to like this."

We went into her house and both of us sat down. "Would you like a drink?" she asked.

"No, but I need one," I told her. "But I'm not taking one from you." I was afraid that she would drug it, to be honest.

"Well, then, out with it. Whatever you're about to say, out with it."

"Charlotte, I'm not pleading guilty to Jordan's murder.

Serena found the video that showed that Malcolm is the one, and she has already turned it over to the prosecutor."

She stared at me, and I already knew what she was thinking. "You would do that. You would put your girlfriend and your mother into jeopardy." She shook her head. "I thought that you were a better man than that. Okay then. You know what happens next. My family doesn't mess around. When I tell them I want a hit, they do it, and they do it quickly."

"Not so fast. I know what you did when you were a kid, and I have proof. What's more, I have a media contact. If you want your career to end before it has even started, I suggest you back the fuck off."

She crossed her arms and looked at me. I had her dead to right, and I think that she knew it. "I'm calling bullshit," she finally said. "I was stupid enough to fall for that once before, when you claimed that you had my abortion records. It didn't occur to me until recently that you were probably full of shit then. I think that you're full of shit now. Those records are sealed. That means that nobody can get them."

"Nobody but a professional hacker. How else do you think that I know about you murdering your teacher with the help of some of your girlfriends, and your diagnoses of borderline personality disorder and antisocial personality disorder? Listen, directors know about those disorders, too, because they come across actors and actresses who have them, all the time. They're not going to want to work with you when they know what you're capable of. You've managed to fool them this far, but if this gets out, you're finished in this town."

She raised an eyebrow. "A professional hacker? Oh, you've done it now, buddy. I'll have you and your girlfriend in prison so fast…"

"Oh, come on. You framed me for murder. Do you really think I'm worried about going to prison for some hacking? And leave Serena out of this. She had nothing to do with it. I got that hacker myself."

"I don't think so. You're covering for her."

"I'm not covering for her," I lied. "Leave her out of this."

She swiveled in her chair nervously. "I don't believe you."

At that, I brought out the thick file that I brought along with me. It had printouts of her juvenile records that included records about the murder, along with psychiatric diagnoses that she received at that time. "Believe me, because this time I have proof. And don't be stupid enough to think that if you destroy these records, I don't have them on my hard drive and various flash drives. Not to mention the fact that I have physical copies which are stored in various safety deposit boxes."

She took the file, and, with shaking hands, read what was on there. As she read, she shook her head. "I haven't even seen these records," she said, her face turning various shades of purple. "I haven't even seen them. How dare this mother-fucking doctor say these things about me? I don't have empathy or impulse control, and I have violent tendencies." She kept reading. "I have no concern for others, psychotic tendencies, and I can't regulate emotions or thoughts. I have a distorted sense of self, changeable moods, paranoia and am prone to lose touch with reality." She shook her head rapidly.

"Yes. It also says that you tend to idealize people. I guess that's where I come in."

She swallowed hard. "I can't believe this. This can't get out. This is personal information. Nobody will touch it."

I leaned forward in my chair. "Charlotte, you're the 'It' girl right now. There's buzz about you in this new film. Oscar buzz, from what I've been hearing from those in the know. I have no doubt that you're great in this movie. But, believe me, tabloids love to bring people down when they're on the way up. If you don't think that this murder and these diagnoses will be the talk of the town…" I shook my head. "I can't believe that you would be that naïve."

She rapidly shook her head. "You can have one. Take your pick, your girlfriend or your mother."

"What's that supposed to mean?"

"It means that I still want my pound of flesh. You might have this to hold over my head, but this is the only thing that you have right now. Malcolm will be taken care of. I don't want him to roll on me. That goes without saying. I can never, and I mean ever, be tied to Jordan's murder. And, if something happens, and I am implicated in his murder, then your girlfriend is dead and your mother is in prison. I'm sure that, considering that will be the consequences, you're going to be on board with my taking care of Malcolm. So, you only have this over me," she said, pointing to the papers in front of her. "I won't give you both."

I stood up. "You will give me both, or this report becomes public today. I already have a woman who has some fantastic media contacts, all of whom will be salivating to make all of this public."

She sat there, just looking at me. "Nope," she said. "You know what will happen if you do that. Again, if you go public with this, I'll have nothing to lose, and both your mother and your girlfriend will be in jeopardy. Now, I will ask you again. I will agree to either not have your girlfriend killed or not turn your mother in for the murder of Hugh all those years ago. That's what's on the table. You can't have both. You pick one, or you get neither."

Oh, she was good. Very good. And I had no doubt that, if I made good on my threat to go to the media with this report, she would do exactly as she said. She would put a hit on Serena and would turn my mother in for Hugh's homicide. I shook my head. Playing with her was complicated.

"Are you going to blink?" she asked me. "If this report becomes public, I have nothing to lose. Remember that."

I hung my head. She had me. I took a deep breath and looked up at the ceiling. I could give her one thing to placate her, and that would mean that I would either have to sacrifice my mother or Serena. That would be her "pound of flesh," and that would put our Mexican standoff back into place. It was smart on her part – if she wouldn't deal at all, I would be the one with nothing to lose by putting this report out into the world. I wasn't going down for Jordan's murder – Serena made sure of that. So, this report was all the ammunition I had.

If she wouldn't deal at all, I would have no choice. That report would be public, and my mother and Serena would be in jeopardy. But she was giving me something, and I had to choose. "My mother," I said quietly. I shook my head. This was an impossible choice, yet it was almost easy. There was no way that I would put Serena's life in jeopardy. I had the money for the best lawyer for my mother...yet she was sick. Who knew if she would get proper treatment in jail? Yet...I would get her out on bail immediately, and I would hire the best attorney money could buy to defend her. She would have a chance. Serena wouldn't. If I offered up Serena, she would be dead before the week would be out. I could try to protect her, but one man can't go up against an entire mafia syndicate.

She crossed her arms. "Really? You would throw your mother under the bus to protect your girlfriend?"

"You give me no choice," I said, feeling my heart break when I said that. After all she went through to protect me, and after the life she has had in general − I was going to make things worse for her. Yet, I had to do it. It was her or Serena. It was an impossible "Sophie's Choice," which was a story about a woman in Nazi Germany who had to choose which twin would be killed and which would be allowed to live. I felt almost as torn. I loved both women, but I couldn't bear to see Serena in jeopardy.

You'll help your mother beat this. The evidence against her will be extremely negligible. I drew my breath though, as I realized that I would be held to account for my role, too. Worse than that, I was going to have to testify against my mother, if it ever came to trial. I was going to have to lie, of course. I was the only witness, besides Charlotte. Charlotte's records might have to be a part of the trial, in order to impeach her, if mom's attorney could get his hands on the official records. That would be difficult to do − to get those records authenticated, so they could be used in court.

Then again, once my mother became a suspect, it would be fairly easy to tie her to Hugh. People saw them out that night − bartenders, waitresses, other patrons. If they have a good memory for people, they would be able to identify my mother as the person who was out with him. And, even though we cleaned up her old apartment, where Hugh was killed, it's difficult to truly clean up blood. The police would be able to use infrared to see that there was blood on the floor of her old place. It might be that my mother will have to resort to a self-defense claim if she ever hoped to beat this murder, and that would be difficult to prove. I had to admit to myself that there was a possibility that, since I was "giving" Charlotte my mother, there was a chance that my mother would spend the rest of her life in prison.

Charlotte swiveled in her chair. "Okay. Well then, you better warn your mother that she will be arrested for Hugh's murder. She'll probably be arrested today. Serena will be safe. There's that for consolation. And Slade, I want a stipulation on our agreement. I want Serena's firm to represent your mother." She narrowed her eyes. "That's an important piece of this puzzle. I can't tell you why, but that's what I want."

I was mystified as to why she would be so adamant about that, but I didn't feel in a position to bargain with her. Serena was safe, and besides, I really wanted her to work on my mother's case anyhow. I felt that she would go above and beyond the call of duty to make sure my mother had the best chance of beating a murder conviction. "Okay."

"Serena's firm, not just Serena. As in, the firm that will no longer be headed by Malcolm. The firm that is known as Brown, Walker and Groom." Those were the three names of the majority partners, including that of Malcolm, whose last name was "Groom."

It was my turn to narrow my eyes. She was up to something, that much was clear. Whatever it was, I was going to have to face it with Serena. Or help Serena face whatever it was that this goddamned spider had up her sleeve. "And if I refuse?"

She shrugged her shoulders. "The deal is off. Yes, the entire world will think that I'm a psychopath. But at least your stupid whore will be wiped off the face of this planet. Don't push me, Slade. Now, do we have a deal, or don't we?"

"Yes. We have a deal. I'll make sure that my mom is represented by Brown, Walker and Groom. Okay?"

She nodded her head and smiled. "Okay."

All at once, I was angry with Serena. I told her not to meddle in this. I told her, and she didn't listen. Now my mother was in jeopardy. I never wanted for that to happen – I always wanted it to be me who would be in jeopardy, not either one of them. My mother might be in prison for the rest of her life, all because of Serena.

I shook my head. No. It's not because of Serena. It was because of this psychotic bitch, Charlotte. Charlotte, and Charlotte alone, was the reason why all of this was happening. Well, Charlotte's psychotic machinations, combined with my stupidity in having Charlotte come with me to see my mother all those years ago. That simple act was the one that haunted me, and had haunted me, all these years.

She raised a single eyebrow. "I'm not entirely finished. There's going to be a big surprise awaiting your girlfriend. One that she will find pretty unpleasant, to say the least. If I can't kill her, or have her killed, then I at least need to torment her just a little."

"What's that supposed to mean?" I wasn't liking the sound of this. Not in the slightest.

"You'll see. Or, rather, she'll soon see." She swiveled in her chair. "I wonder how much she likes living in that cute little house by the beach. I guess we'll soon be finding out, won't we? And I wonder how much she enjoys working where she's working. I would imagine that her law firm will soon have a new, very important, client – one Margot Facinelli. Serena's going to want to work on that case, I would imagine. But maybe she won't. Maybe, when she sees who the new associate at her firm is, she'll want out of that firm."

"You're not making a lick of sense," I said to her.

"I'm not now, but I will be soon. At any rate, you have to leave. I have a very important phone call to make."

My heart started to pound. I was going to have to warn my mother about what was about to happen. I also had to wonder what it was Charlotte had up her sleeve for Serena. She was so cryptic – all that talk about how much Serena enjoyed her new home, and whether or not she liked working for her firm. What was that all about? I was going to find out soon, and I didn't know, at all, if I was going to like what I learned.

I called Serena from the car. "Hey," I said to her when she picked up. "I think everything's in the clear. You're in the clear, at least. And so am I. My mother will be arrested for Hugh's murder, though."

"What? Oh my god, no! No! Slade, I'm so sorry..."

"It's fine. It's what has to happen. It was either her life or yours." I shook my head. I was trying to sound non-chalant about it, for Serena's sake, because I didn't want Serena to feel too guilty about it. But the reality was much, much different. It was tearing me up inside. Charlotte gave me no choice, of course, but that didn't make things any easier. Would my mother survive? Did she have a way out of the murder charge? I had no idea. None. Zero. I wish that I did, but I knew that I didn't. Charlotte was diabolical, much more diabolical than I had given her credit for. She knew just where the tender parts were and just how to twist the knife into them. I had to give her credit where credit was due.

"Slade, you can't be that laid-back about this. Tell me what you're really feeling."

"I feel like crap, obviously. I need to talk to my mom about this, though. And Malcolm...well he's about to have a tragic accident. I need to leave it at that. Look for that to happen within the next day or so. Charlotte will get to Malcolm before the prosecutor will."

Serena was quiet. "We didn't really win, did we? An innocent life is still in the balance. And Malcolm…he wasn't innocent, not by any stretch of the imagination, but he's still a human being. He has children, for Christ sakes. A wife. His parents are still alive, and he has brothers and sisters. What he did was wrong, but I have definite mixed emotions about his impending murder."

"There's nothing that can be done about that. As I told you earlier, the worst-case scenario for you and my mother is that Charlotte gets caught up in her own web. If Malcolm rolls on her, and she's arrested, then all bets will be off. She'll have the hit put on you within the week, and my mother will be going down for Hugh's death. It's best that the suspicion isn't on her, because I can at least save you. She knows that if she touches a hair on your head, that report about her craziness and her past homicide will find its way to the media and she'll be finished. I have her, but only halfway."

"Well, can you please come over. I need to see you."

"I can't. Not right now, at least. I need to go and see my mother and explain everything to her." I felt my insides start to crush while I thought about that. I had spent all these years making sure that my mother was protected. And now, well…there wasn't a thing that I could do. I could only hope that perhaps, just perhaps, the jury would see her as merely defending herself in her own home. But it did look bad that the body was disposed of. That was my idea, of course. Maybe the jury would understand that move as well, though. My mother was scared, and she had just gotten out of prison for another murder.

"Come over as soon as you can," she said. "I'm feeling out of sorts. I hate all of this."

"I will."

We got off the phone, and I turned on the radio. I wanted to try to forget, just for a second, what was about to happen. I hoped that my mother could beat this charge, and I hoped that she would one day forgive me. I had screwed everything up when I made the hasty decision to dump Hugh's body, instead of going to the authorities and letting the chips fall where they may.

Was that a fateful decision? I was soon going to find out.

I hoped that I didn't find out the hard way.

Next in The Temptations Series

vinci-books.com/dark-temptations

Caught between passion and peril, Serena and Slade must outwit their enemies to survive.

Serena and Slade are on a mission to take down the ruthless Charlotte. Battling her own demons, Serena must navigate living next to her tormentor, Derek, while fighting to keep Margot out of prison. The tensions rise and alliances are tested.

Turn the page for a free preview…

Dark Temptations: Chapter One

SERENA

I continued to look out the window, watching for Slade. I had to get out of here, but Derek was sitting on his porch, looking over at my house. I didn't know if he was doing that to intimidate me, but if that was the reason, he was succeeding.

Come on, Serena. You're braver than this. He's only a man. A man who managed to ruin my life, to be sure, but still only a man. What was he going to do? What could he do to me that he hadn't already done?

He was still violent, though. I knew that from meeting his girlfriend. Maggie was covering up as best she could, but I knew her secret. Since I knew that Derek was still violent, I really needed to make sure that I avoided him as much as I could.

Slade finally arrived, and came straight into the house. I wrapped my arms around him and held him ever so tightly. I wanted to just feel him, and know that with his arms around me, I felt truly safe. He would take care of that jackass next door if I needed him to. I knew this.

"What's going on Serena?" he asked me finally, after I had held onto him for what seemed like an eternity.

"My new next door neighbor. It's him. Derek. The man who has haunted me my entire life. He's living right next door."

He looked at me with understanding, and I could tell that he had suspected that this was going to happen. "I'm not surprised. Charlotte is getting her revenge. She can't kill you, but she can certainly make your life a living hell."

"I think that I need to leave for awhile. Can I stay with you?"

"Of course, I was hoping you would say that." He hesitated. "But Serena, I have a feeling that you're not going be able to totally get away from him."

"What does that mean?"

He took a deep breath. "Charlotte and I have some understandings, and it's very delicate right now. I don't know if I can trust her. I have these blackmail documents, so she's restrained somewhat. But one false move and you could very well find yourself in grave danger."

I didn't like the way he was talking, but I had to let him finish. "Okay. Go ahead and tell me what's going on."

"One of the stipulations that Charlotte made was that your firm would have to be the one to represent my mother in her murder trial, assuming that there is a murder trial, of course."

I narrowed my eyes. "Okay. That doesn't seem so bad so far."

Then it hit me. Maggie told me that Derek had a very lucrative offer with a law firm in town. I suddenly knew exactly which firm he was going to work for.

Slade confirmed my suspicions. "I have a feeling that Derek is going to be working at your firm."

I felt my heart drop to my knees. "Okay. Well then, I'll just have to find another job." I hated that I still felt that I couldn't be around him. I felt like a total coward, just cutting and running, but I couldn't have him around. My psyche felt fragile all of a sudden, as what had happened to me in those woods so long ago came flooding back. I felt like it was yesterday in a lot of ways. It was certainly still haunting me as if it were yesterday.

He nodded his head. "Yes, you will have to find another job. But my mother has to be represented by your firm."

"Well, that's impossible. I want to represent her. I need to represent her. I can do an awesome job on her case. I've tried cases like hers before, and I can be very persuasive with a jury."

"I know all that. But Charlotte's stipulation for agreeing not to harm you is that only your firm can represent mom. As I said, I think that she's full of crap, but I would prefer not to find that out for sure, if you know what I mean."

I was faced with another decision. I could cut and run and let Margot be represented by another attorney on the firm. Any other attorney wasn't going to be as passionate as I was about giving Margot excellent representation. Her case was going to be precarious anyhow. If I let another attorney try her case, there was a very good chance that he or she would lose. And Slade's mother would spend the rest of her life in prison.

Or, I could stick around the firm. I would have to see Derek every single day, assuming that Slade was correct in saying that Charlotte made sure that Derek had a job at my firm.

"You've put me in an untenable position," I said, stating the brutally obvious. Then I shook my head. "Sorry, that was uncalled for. Charlotte is the one who has put me in an untenable position." I tried not to think about the possibility that my first statement was correct – that Slade had put me in this position. He was the one who brought the poison known as Charlotte into my world. His actions were the ones that gave her so much power to begin with, starting with that night when he decided to cover up what his mother did.

Slade said nothing, but just wrapped his arms around me tightly. I tried to feel comforted by his touch and his scent, but I couldn't. All I could think about was the fact that I was going to be subjected to Derek. Even if I cut and run and moved in with Slade permanently – that wasn't quite on the table, although I had no doubt he would ask me to do so if that was what I wanted – I could never get away from Derek at all. He would be at my workplace every single day, and I couldn't just quit and leave Margot high and dry like that.

I suddenly felt sick. "Well, what's done is done. I need to leave this house." I had packed a bag of things, and my work clothes were in hanger bags. Bella and Gigi were in their traveling kennels. I was ready to go. "Let's get out of here."

As we left, we noticed that Derek was sitting on his porch swing, drinking a beer. He leered at me as Slade and I left, his beer to his lips, which were curled in a derisive smile.

Slade packed my things in the car, and asked me to wait for him in the front seat. I then looked out the window and saw him standing on Derek's porch, his hands on his hips. He seemed to be intently speaking with, who was looking angrier and angrier. At one point, Derek stood from his seat on the swing, and Slade pushed him back down. Derek immediately got back up, his fists balled up tight. He swung at Slade, who ducked and landed an uppercut fist right in Derek's stomach. Derek doubled over in pain, but rapidly got back up and punched Slade's face.

It was soon full on, as the two men scuffled on the porch for what seemed to be an eternity. I was almost in awe of Slade's cat-like grace that showed itself when he fought. He was in amazing shape, and he rapidly danced around Derek like a prize-fighter. He wasn't just a street pugilist, randomly throwing punches and hoping that they landed. He was more strategic than that, and showed a great deal of finesse. The upshot was that he landed many more punches on Derek than Derek did on him, and finally, he stood victorious over Derek, who was crumpled up on the porch.

Slade finally came to the car, after it looked like he had thoroughly lectured a crumpled Derek. "Let's go," he said.

"What was that all about?"

"Nothing."

I got quiet. I didn't like Slade not talking to me about the scuffle on the porch. At the same time, I knew that Slade was infuriated, and he just needed to calm down a little bit. He would talk to me when he was good and ready.

I watched him as his tense hands gripped the wheel. He stared straight ahead at the road, not saying a single word. His jaw was clenched tightly, and he kept shaking his head. "Bastard," he mumbled under his breath a few times.

I put my hand on his leg. "I hate to tell you this, but you're doing 90," I told him as he raced down the highway. He was passing everyone on the road, which was saying something, considering drivers routinely went 80 MPH or above on this highway.

He still said nothing as he weaved in and out of cars.

I sighed, looking out the window as the world passed by me at a faster-than-usual rate. I had no idea what to expect when I got to his house. I knew that Margot was there, but I didn't think that she was aware of what fate awaited her.

"I hate that bastard, and I hate that he wants to intimidate you," Slade finally said. "I told him that he was going to leave you alone at the workplace."

I nodded my head. "I can fight my own battles," I said weakly. Ordinarily, that was completely true. I had always been independent and a fighter. But with this situation…I didn't know if I could fight this battle. Derek had taken so much from me at such a young age. What he had done shaped me, and not necessarily for the better.

Slade put his arm around my neck as he continued to steer the car on the highway. "Serena, you can't handle this on your own. I know that you want to, but trust me, you need somebody in your corner on this. I know how to handle slimy assholes like Derek."

I tried to tamp down a little smile that was threatening. Truth be told, I liked to see this part of him. This protective instinct that he had for me was something that was almost intoxicating. "How do you handle him, other than giving him a beat-down? And, by the way, you're still technically out on bail. I anticipate that the prosecutors are going to drop the charges against you as soon as that video is authenticated, but that's still not a 100% guarantee. I would suggest you keeping your temper in check for the time being."

He sighed. "You find your opponent's weakness and exploit it. That's the only way to handle difficult people. With Charlotte, I blackmail her. With this guy, I threaten. He's a typical bully-coward, which means that he's easily intimidated. He'll never admit to being intimidated, because he's all about surface bluster. But, deep down, he can be intimidated by somebody who actually stands up to him. Or should I say he can be intimidated by a man who stands up to him. He'll still run over any woman, because he sees them as being weaker than he is. He won't run over me. Trust me on this."

"What did you threaten him with?"

He shrugged. "I just told him that I knew who he was and what he did, and he needed to watch his ass. If I heard anything from you about him treating you disrespectfully, I would expose him for who he is. I saw fear in his eyes when I was saying those things to him."

"Why don't you expose him? Or, for that matter, I can expose him."

Slade gave me the side-eye. "Two reasons. One, you don't have proof of anything. Two, him working with you was one of Charlotte's stipulations for not harming you. I have to work through what's going on with her. I need to test her a little, see how much she's bluffing and how dead serious she is about putting you in danger at her whim. I can't just do things willy-nilly that are going to piss her off, at least not until I figure out her game just a little better."

"She has her pound of flesh with your mother and with you for that matter. I would imagine that you're also going to be in quite a lot of trouble once the prosecutor finds out that you helped your mother dump that body. And you do know that I cannot represent both of you, because that would be a conflict of interest." It was always difficult to represent co-conspirators, as there was always the chance that one would be offered a deal to roll on the other. I didn't necessarily think that would be the case here, but if there was that possibility, I couldn't represent them both.

Slade shrugged his shoulders. "I have a very high-powered attorney on retainer in LA. I'm not concerned for myself." He took a deep breath. "Are you up to this? Defending my mother? She wants to speak with you tonight about her options. I want you to give it to her clearly and without bullshit. She needs to know what she's up against."

Out of the frying pan, into the fire. "I think that you know what she's up against. Hugh's blood is at her old apartment, and, with Charlotte's tip, I have no doubt your mother will be charged in his murder. She was out on parole for another murder at the time she killed Hugh. It's going to be an uphill battle for sure. I can get an expert witness who specializes in post-traumatic stress disorder to testify that your mother was reasonable in feeling threatened by Hugh at the time that she killed him. If the jury can buy that she was reasonable in feeling that Hugh was going to rape her, we can win a self-defense argument. If the jury isn't persuaded that her actions were reasonable, she'll go to prison for murder. It's all going to hinge on what I can convince the jury to believe about how threatened she felt, and whether or not a reasonable person in her shoes would feel the same."

Slade nodded. "I actually do know all of that, but I wanted her to hear all that from you. She has to have the confidence that you can represent her zealously, and you won't let a single stone go unturned. I'm counting on you."

Suddenly, I felt pressured. More pressured than I had ever felt at any time in my life. "Slade," I said, feeling nauseated. "You have to understand that the odds are against us here. Even under the best readings of the facts, your mother shouldn't have done what she did. I don't blame her for getting a gun and wanting to defend herself but she probably should have just told him to leave. I would imagine he would have just left, as it was a choice between getting out of there alive or getting shot. She shot him, no questions asked. It's not going to be easy to get her off of this."

Slade was staring straight ahead. We had arrived at his home, and he was just staring out the windshield of his car. I wasn't sure if he had heard me when I was talking to him, so I touched him on the shoulder. He jumped a little when my hand landed on his body. He shook his head. "I know that the odds are against my mother," he finally said after a long pause. "Believe me, I understand that. I'm relying on you to beat the odds."

"I'm hoping I can, too. But Slade, I don't want it to come between us if something happens. I feel that you're going to always blame me."

All at once, Slade looked angry. Really angry. "What are you saying? Are you telling me that you don't want to represent my mother? If that's what you're saying, then just say it. I'll find another attorney at your firm to represent her. I'm sure that there are plenty of lawyers at your firm that will jump at the chance to seize my healthy retainer for mom's representation."

"Slade. No. Calm down. I'm just expressing my concern that things between you and I might change if I lose this case. That's all."

He narrowed his eyes. "Then don't lose."

At that, he got out of the car and walked towards the house. I reluctantly followed him, feeling as if I was a prisoner who was being led to the death chamber. I walked slowly and deliberately, trying to slow down the process. I didn't want to face Margot and tell her the truth. I didn't want to see those eyes. She was going to look at me with hope, and, by the time I got through telling her what I needed to tell her about her chances, she was going to be in tears. The hope would be drained from her eyes. I had seen that particular transformation too many times in my position.

The last thing I wanted was to see that transformation happen in Margot's eyes.

Even so, I knew I was about to see just that.

Dark Temptations: Chapter Two

I continued to look out the window, watching for Slade. I had to get out of here, but Derek was sitting on his porch, looking over at my house. I didn't know if he was doing that to intimidate me, but if that was the reason, he was succeeding.

Come on, Serena. You're braver than this. He's only a man. A man who managed to ruin my life, to be sure, but still only a man. What was he going to do? What could he do to me that he hadn't already done?

He was still violent, though. I knew that from meeting his girlfriend. Maggie was covering up as best she could, but I knew her secret. Since I knew that Derek was still violent, I really needed to make sure that I avoided him as much as I could.

Slade finally arrived, and came straight into the house. I wrapped my arms around him and held him ever so tightly. I wanted to just feel him, and know that with his arms around me, I felt truly safe. He would take care of that jackass next door if I needed him to. I knew this.

"What's going on Serena?" he asked me finally, after I had held onto him for what seemed like an eternity.

"My new next door neighbor. It's him. Derek. The man who has haunted me my entire life. He's living right next door."

He looked at me with understanding, and I could tell that he had suspected that this was going to happen. "I'm not surprised. Charlotte is getting her revenge. She can't kill you, but she can certainly make your life a living hell."

"I think that I need to leave for awhile. Can I stay with you?"

"Of course, I was hoping you would say that." He hesitated. "But Serena, I have a feeling that you're not going be able to totally get away from him."

"What does that mean?"

He took a deep breath. "Charlotte and I have some understandings, and it's very delicate right now. I don't know if I can trust her. I have these blackmail documents, so she's restrained somewhat. But one false move and you could very well find yourself in grave danger."

I didn't like the way he was talking, but I had to let him finish. "Okay. Go ahead and tell me what's going on."

"One of the stipulations that Charlotte made was that your firm would have to be the one to represent my mother in her murder trial, assuming that there is a murder trial, of course."

I narrowed my eyes. "Okay. That doesn't seem so bad so far."

Then it hit me. Maggie told me that Derek had a very lucrative offer with a law firm in town. I suddenly knew exactly which firm he was going to work for.

Slade confirmed my suspicions. "I have a feeling that Derek is going to be working at your firm."

I felt my heart drop to my knees. "Okay. Well then, I'll just have to find another job." I hated that I still felt that I couldn't be around him. I felt like a total coward, just cutting and running, but I couldn't have him around. My psyche felt fragile all of a sudden, as what had happened to me in those woods so long ago came flooding back. I felt like it was yesterday in a lot of ways. It was certainly still haunting me as if it were yesterday.

He nodded his head. "Yes, you will have to find another job. But my mother has to be represented by your firm."

"Well, that's impossible. I want to represent her. I need to represent her. I can do an awesome job on her case. I've tried cases like hers before, and I can be very persuasive with a jury."

"I know all that. But Charlotte's stipulation for agreeing not to harm you is that only your firm can represent mom. As I said, I think that she's full of crap, but I would prefer not to find that out for sure, if you know what I mean."

I was faced with another decision. I could cut and run and let Margot be represented by another attorney on the firm. Any other attorney wasn't going to be as passionate as I was about giving Margot excellent representation. Her case was going to be precarious anyhow. If I let another attorney try her case, there was a very good chance that he or she would lose. And Slade's mother would spend the rest of her life in prison.

Or, I could stick around the firm. I would have to see Derek every single day, assuming that Slade was correct in saying that Charlotte made sure that Derek had a job at my firm.

"You've put me in an untenable position," I said, stating the brutally obvious. Then I shook my head. "Sorry, that was uncalled for. Charlotte is the one who has put me in an untenable position." I tried not to think about the possibility that my first statement was correct – that Slade had put me in this position. He was the one who brought the poison known as Charlotte into my world. His actions were the ones that gave her so much power to begin with, starting with that night when he decided to cover up what his mother did.

Slade said nothing, but just wrapped his arms around me tightly. I tried to feel comforted by his touch and his scent, but I couldn't. All I could think about was the fact that I was going to be subjected to Derek. Even if I cut and run and moved in with Slade permanently – that wasn't quite on the table, although I had no doubt he would ask me to do so if that was what I wanted – I could never get away from Derek at all. He would be at my workplace every single day, and I couldn't just quit and leave Margot high and dry like that.

I suddenly felt sick. "Well, what's done is done. I need to leave this house." I had packed a bag of things, and my work clothes were in hanger bags. Bella and Gigi were in their traveling kennels. I was ready to go. "Let's get out of here."

As we left, we noticed that Derek was sitting on his porch swing, drinking a beer. He leered at me as Slade and I left, his beer to his lips, which were curled in a derisive smile.

Slade packed my things in the car, and asked me to wait for him in the front seat. I then looked out the window and saw him standing on Derek's porch, his hands on his hips. He seemed to be intently speaking with, who was looking angrier and angrier. At one point, Derek stood from his seat on the swing, and Slade pushed him back down. Derek immediately got back up, his fists balled up tight. He swung at Slade, who ducked and landed an uppercut fist right in Derek's stomach. Derek doubled over in pain, but rapidly got back up and punched Slade's face.

It was soon full on, as the two men scuffled on the porch for what seemed to be an eternity. I was almost in awe of Slade's cat-like grace that showed itself when he fought. He was in amazing shape, and he rapidly danced around Derek like a prize-fighter. He wasn't just a street pugilist, randomly throwing punches and hoping that they landed. He was more strategic than that, and showed a great deal of finesse. The upshot was that he landed many more punches on Derek than Derek did on him, and finally, he stood victorious over Derek, who was crumpled up on the porch.

Slade finally came to the car, after it looked like he had thoroughly lectured a crumpled Derek. "Let's go," he said.

"What was that all about?"

"Nothing."

I got quiet. I didn't like Slade not talking to me about the scuffle on the porch. At the same time, I knew that Slade was infuriated, and he just needed to calm down a little bit. He would talk to me when he was good and ready.

I watched him as his tense hands gripped the wheel. He stared straight ahead at the road, not saying a single word. His jaw was clenched tightly, and he kept shaking his head. "Bastard," he mumbled under his breath a few times.

I put my hand on his leg. "I hate to tell you this, but you're doing 90," I told him as he raced down the highway. He was passing everyone on the road, which was saying something, considering drivers routinely went 80 MPH or above on this highway.

He still said nothing as he weaved in and out of cars.

I sighed, looking out the window as the world passed by me at a faster-than-usual rate. I had no idea what to expect when I got to his house. I knew that Margot was there, but I didn't think that she was aware of what fate awaited her.

"I hate that bastard, and I hate that he wants to intimidate you," Slade finally said. "I told him that he was going to leave you alone at the workplace."

I nodded my head. "I can fight my own battles," I said weakly. Ordinarily, that was completely true. I had always been independent and a fighter. But with this situation...I didn't know if I could fight this battle. Derek had taken so much from me at such a young age. What he had done shaped me, and not necessarily for the better.

Slade put his arm around my neck as he continued to steer the car on the highway. "Serena, you can't handle this on your own. I know that you want to, but trust me, you need somebody in your corner on this. I know how to handle slimy assholes like Derek."

I tried to tamp down a little smile that was threatening. Truth be told, I liked to see this part of him. This protective instinct that he had for me was something that was almost intoxicating. "How do you handle him, other than giving him a beat-down? And, by the way, you're still technically out on bail. I anticipate that the prosecutors are going to drop the charges against you as soon as that video is authenticated, but that's still not a 100% guarantee. I would suggest you keeping your temper in check for the time being."

He sighed. "You find your opponent's weakness and exploit it. That's the only way to handle difficult people. With Charlotte, I blackmail her. With this guy, I threaten. He's a typical bully-coward, which means that he's easily intimidated. He'll never admit to being intimidated, because he's all about surface bluster. But, deep down, he can be intimidated by somebody who actually stands up to him. Or should I say he can be intimidated by a man who stands up to him. He'll still run over any woman, because he sees them as being weaker than he is. He won't run over me. Trust me on this."

"What did you threaten him with?"

He shrugged. "I just told him that I knew who he was and what he did, and he needed to watch his ass. If I heard anything from you about him treating you disrespectfully, I would expose him for who he is. I saw fear in his eyes when I was saying those things to him."

"Why don't you expose him? Or, for that matter, I can expose him."

Slade gave me the side-eye. "Two reasons. One, you don't have proof of anything. Two, him working with you was one of Charlotte's stipulations for not harming you. I have to work through what's going on with her. I need to test her a little, see how much she's bluffing and how dead serious she is about putting you in danger at her whim. I can't just do things willy-nilly that are going to piss her off, at least not until I figure out her game just a little better."

"She has her pound of flesh with your mother and with you for that matter. I would imagine that you're also going to be in quite a lot of trouble once the prosecutor finds out that you helped your mother dump that body. And you do know that I cannot represent both of you, because that would be a conflict of interest." It was always difficult to represent co-conspirators, as there was always the chance that one would be offered a deal to roll on the other. I didn't necessarily think that would be the case here, but if there was that possibility, I couldn't represent them both.

Grab your copy…
vinci-books.com/dark-temptations

About the Author

Annie currently lives in San Diego with her two fur-babies, Bella and Toby, and her significant other, Joey. When she's not writing, she's busy reading, cycling all over town, watching cooking shows or classic old movies on TCM (Cary Grant is her favorite) and occasionally watching trashy television shows.